WELCOME TO AUMBRY VALLEY

THE B.I.T.N. BUREAU ASSIGNMENTS
BOOK ONE

KATHERINE DEMPSTER

ISBN: 978-1-7782049-0-6

Dedicated to anyone who has found themselves on a
road to nowhere.

CHAPTER ONE

 Nora slammed an empty copy paper box onto her coffee-stained desk. She knew what was coming when she put her lucky bamboo plant inside as gently as her trembling hands would let her. The browned leaves that scattered to the floor spoke to the luck that she had received from it. All of the plants that lined the paint-chipped windowsill in her runty, little studio apartment were in varying degrees of near death. When she arrived home that day, this one would be their newest neighbor. Another wilting trophy of failure. Now five in total, each one was from a job she had been fired from in the short three months since she had settled in Aumbry Valley. The edge in Dirtbag Derek's bellowing voice told her it would be wise to pre-emptively pack up the few things that she had accumulated in the two weeks she had spent mindlessly trying to sell people magazines over the phone. As if anyone had a

hard time finding such rare enigmas as magazines, they needed strangers to bother them to make a purchase.

Nora's skills for office work were as honed as her green thumb and her places of employment rarely kept her long. She knew that the temp agency who had taken her on would let her go as soon as they heard she had been fired yet again. It had been the same over and over since she had moved to the small town on the edge of nowhere to start her life on her own two feet.

Soon enough, her supervisor would be saying the same things she had heard from all the others:

"Nora, you need to work on your attitude!" As if it was easy to have a positive attitude when you hated every minute of every day when you were trapped in a monotonously pointless job.

"Nora, you can't have fire engine red hair and be taken seriously in an office environment!" Because what she looked like mattered to a job that was simply entering clusters of meaningless numbers into a computer log for eight hours a day?

"Nora, wake up!" Okay, that one was on her.

There was the warning she gave herself every day since she started working for Dirtbag Derek, who considered eye contact to be looking down her top, and she screamed it in her thoughts again: *"Nora, you can't punch your boss!"*

He was a squat sleaze of a man with slicked hair and too-tight pants. When she entered his office, he prattled on to her breasts about how she just was not working out. Her sales were low, there were complaints about her bad attitude, and he wished there was another way to work the situation out. Nora silently stood and headed for the door. Looking away from her chest just long enough to give her a consolatory pat on the ass as she turned to leave was too much for Nora. Dirtbag Derek sure looked her in the eyes when she swung. Her knuckles were throbbing by the time she returned to her desk to grab her meager possessions. The ache in her molar that had been torturing her for the past month joined in. So much for staying long enough for the dental plan to kick in. Setting her purse in the box alongside her plant, she grabbed a worn pen with Call Direct Sales printed along the side. Another one for her collection. Nora frowned when she realized it would probably be the last one that she would swipe as a temp. Looking around at everyone who had gathered when Derek started screaming for security, she grabbed the bright blue tape dispenser from her desk, tossing it in the box. She squared her shoulders and smiled. The little wins can get you through the day, and this sticky restitution would be hers.

The proud strut and steely smile she hid behind had worn off by the time she reached the elevator. The reality of her situation flooded her mind making the nearly empty box in her shaking hands feel like it was filled with burdensome boulders; each one a worry that flooded her mind. The fact that she would turn twenty-five in a few months and be once again unemployed. That she was drowning in a strange town that she had only been in for a few months. That she didn't have the money for her rent - again - and could barely feed her cat. It all exploded as a flashing neon sign, with a few blown bulbs, across her list of worries. The only things she had were her cramped apartment and that cat, Silas. He was a stray ball of dirty, matted fur that followed her for four blocks on the day she moved into her new place. He had since become her best friend and constant critic. He would have a few nasty meows when she came home with another half-dead plant and not his favorite kibble treats.

She pressed the elevator's down button rapidly, struggling to balance the cumbersome box, and needing to get out of there before security came. That humiliation was one that she would not wait around for. There was little worry that the jerk would call the police on her because he was well known to them already. The little packets of party powder he always had on hand in the top drawer of his desk were enough for him to keep himself from involving the authorities.

"You better get that sweet ass out of here before security drags it out!" Dirtbag Derek screamed down the hall as the elevator dinged and the door slid open.

"Go ahead, Derek! Mention my ass one more time! I would love to sue this piece of shit company for sexual harassment!" Nora barely held on to her belongings while flipping him off and stomping into the elevator. It was an empty threat, of course. She had no money for a lawyer, and it was easy to see that Call Direct Sales was destined for bankruptcy at any moment with no cash to give, but it felt good to yell back at that sleaze. Looking at her watch, it was ten-fifteen. If she timed it right, she would be able to get into her apartment while her landlady, Jenny, was out at Mommy and Me gym class with her daughter.

Jenny was only a few years older than Nora and the sweetest woman she had ever met, generously cutting her slack with the rent that she did not deserve. The building, a boxy old former Italianate mansion that was now broken up into apartments, had been inherited by Jenny's husband before he passed away. Nora had tried to find polite ways to ask how he had died – as polite as that subject could be broached – and Jenny always skirted the inquiries with quick answers of an illness.

Never attempting to fill in any details and the sadness in her eyes was enough to get Nora to stop pressing. Her daughter, Olivia was only two when he was killed the year before but was now the happiest and brightest three-year-old. She adored the little girl, who for some reason called her Norma and always smiled when she heard her running up and down the small hallway that connected their first-floor apartments, dragging her dolls along the old, peeling wallpaper.

A century or so before, the four floored building would have been a grand mansion for some well-to-do business owner or the like when the town was flush and prosperous. An engraved marble sign above the front door declared it to be Dunhope Manor. Since then, having been turned into six apartments, including Jenny's, and Nora's own little space on the main floor, it was better suited to be called No-Hope Manor. The second and third floors had three separate residences with the fourth floor permanently blocked off. There were only two other occupants in the building: an elderly woman named Gail, and her myriad of songbirds on the second floor, and a man in his forties, Norman, whose intense shyness and agoraphobia kept him mostly barricaded in his third-floor apartment. It didn't make for a lot of money coming in for Jenny to cover bills, especially with how quickly the building had been deteriorating.

Coming up short for the month's rent was not going to make things any better. Hopefully, she would be able to trade off some babysitting time for a break one more time.

Looking at the elevator's floor buttons, she saw that the lobby had already been pressed and was startled to find a man leaning on the opposite wall, watching her. He was older than she was by at least three decades but ridiculously handsome in the way of a golden age of Hollywood actor. His suit was perfectly tailored and clearly expensive, and he was grinning broadly down at her with dazzlingly perfect teeth.

"Bad day?" he asked when the doors closed in Dirtbag Derek's fuming face. Any other day, Nora would have been more than happy to engage such an attractive salt-and-peppered dish of a man on the ride down to the lobby, but today was not any other day.

"Yeah, getting fired will do that," Nora replied with her eyes on her unlucky bamboo plant.

"What happened?" the stranger asked, obviously not reading the leave-me-alone vibe she was actively projecting. Nora looked up at him, wondering why he would be so curious to start up a conversation on such a short elevator ride, and found him still staring down at her with the same charming smile.

"I punched my boss," she muttered. The box in her arms started to feel heavier.

His eyes widened with humor, and he straightened his suit jacket, "Oh, my. That's never a good idea."

"Yeah, well it's not a good idea to try to look down my top every chance he got, either. I guess we both learned something today." There was something about his light-hearted laugh in response to her answer that made Nora feel comfortable and she was surprised to find herself letting out a snort of a laugh with him. The elevator stopped in the lobby and Nora gave him a nod as she walked out.

"You're spunky, aren't you?" he asked, following her out. Nora cringed at the word. Spunky was so belittling. As if she were a pre-teen cheerleader bursting at the seams with raw-raw-raws. She noticed that he had a soft-brimmed fedora in his hands as if he came straight from Madison Avenue in nineteen fifty-five. Maybe he was even older than he looked. The only wrinkles on his face were the crinkles beside his eyes when he smiled at her. Even if he was genetically gifted at aging, he couldn't have been older than fifty. She looked blankly at him for a moment before walking away from the elevator. The sooner she got home and into the bath with the last of her box of wine, the better. It may be the last chance she had to enjoy the old, cracked clawfoot tub - the best part of her apartment - before she and Silas were out on their asses. Jenny could only put kindness over her own pile of bills for so long.

"I may have a job for you," the man called out to her, "if you're interested."

Nora stopped with the door pushed open on her hip, "Listen, fella, I don't know what you want from me, but I've already had a day from hell, and it isn't even lunchtime yet." He may be attractive, but she was not to the point of giving *jobs'* as a job yet.

"I'm just offering you a position that I think you were born for," he spoke as he closed the space between them, "That's what my job is. Finding people that are fit for very specific assignments." He held up a business card when he reached her. He held open the door for her as she took it.

Narrowing her eyes, she read the intricate black lettering on the thick, velvety white card. The only words printed were 'Elijah Beasley" and below, 'The Firm'.

"So, you're offering me a *position* at someplace called The *Firm*." Nora moved him out of the way with a shove of the cardboard box. "Listen, perv, I appreciate the offer, but I'm not much of a dancer, let alone in heels on a pole." She moved quickly through the door and onto the sidewalk.

Elijah was still chuckling with amusement when he caught up with her, putting the card on top of her purse that was wedged in the box. "I assure you this is not a gentleman's club or anything of the sort. It's a job that is best discussed at my office. The address is on the back." Elijah tapped the card and smiled widely, an impressive air of self-confidence cascading from him. "I assure you that this is nothing untoward. I hope to see you at nine am tomorrow if you have any interest in what we can offer you. No strings attached." Nora's frown showed her lack of eagerness. "What do you have to lose?" He nodded politely and flashed his movie star smile once more before making his way down the quiet street and out of sight.

Nora set the box down on the bench in front of the building and picked up the card. *1365 Beech Avenue, 9 am*, was written gracefully in blue ink on the back.

"What kind of company handwrites their address on fancy business cards?" She looked down the street to see if she could still spot him, but he was gone as quickly as he had appeared. She flipped it over again to read his name. "The Firm? Yeah, that doesn't sound made up at all." She started to toss it in the garbage and found she couldn't. Was she really in a place to turn down a job offer?

Aumbry Valley was not a bustling town of employment and opportunity. The desert roads that led into the small town were dotted with palm trees that grew thicker as you traveled down into the valley. The summer sun was hot and dry, which made the lush, green oasis of trees that filled the surrounding mountains seem impossible. The valley they created protected the little town from the dust and tumbleweeds that made up the area above. It was as pretty as a postcard and for good reason, it was a summer destination for the wealthy who owned the enormous summer homes sprinkled within the trees on the hills surrounding the valley. When her aunt had first mentioned the town to her, Nora couldn't even find a website for the tiny town, and it was only a blip on a few maps if you zoomed in close.

The actual townsfolk existed within the small jobs of shops, a tavern, a handful of restaurants, and the general labor they could find in service of the wealthy who seemed to call all of the shots. The only way to find any jobs seemed to be through an employment group that made placements. Help wanted signs were not something that she had found in the short time she had been trying to make a go of it there. A posh nightclub, Mystique, at the far end of the main street, had seemed like a fun place to work when she first arrived, but she couldn't even get a foot in the door for an interview. The day that she knocked on the locked front door, a woman glared down her nose at her, advising that the exclusive club was not looking for any level of additional staff, and swiftly closed the darkened door. Jenny had been the one who had explained the strange employment placement system in Aumbry Valley. Rich people loved to control the working classes.

With job opportunities deeply lacking, she was looking down the barrel of losing everything and having to turn up on her parents' porch back east, hat in hand. Nora knew that they would never let her live it down and she couldn't live with the smug smiles they would have plastered on their cold faces. The Goodman's, Adam and Gwen, did not live up to their name and could not be less interested in their daughter's happiness.

She crumpled the business card and shoved it back into the box. If anything, it may be good to give to the police if a sketch of Elijah Beasley should appear on the six o'clock news as a suspected serial killer. Her day looked up a bit when Cherry Bomb, her ancient but loyal K car, started up without a fight. It was the only thing she had left of her Aunt Quinn, who had gifted it to Nora two years before. Quinn, her father's much younger sister, was only ten years older than Nora and never one to stay in one place for long. She was nothing like Adam Goodman's intensely chilly demeanor. She was everything that her brother was not. A free spirit, she was warm and engaging, and exciting. Always looking for her next adventure, which was easily funded by a trust she had been dipping into since her twenty-fifth birthday, she would disappear into the world of her newest life experience. It would be weeks, sometimes months before Nora would lay eyes on her, keeping up with her whereabouts through letters dotted with stamps from around the globe. Even with her exciting life, Quinn would always touch base and make time to stop for a spell to visit with her only niece, who she affectionately called Squirt. Whenever she was in the city, she would let Nora tag along to wherever she was going. Concerts, museums, upstate for hikes in the trees of the dense forests or through the flowers of the countryside. She had been Nora's hero from day one.

Heartbreaking to Nora, Quinn's last exit for adventure seemed to be for good. Something changed in Quinn when her father - Nora's grandfather - passed away. They had both been exceptionally close to Noah Goodman, a kind man, who as a renowned field archeologist, shared a lust for life and a wit matched only by his intelligence. A spark in Quinn died instantly when he passed. The most important anchor to home that she truly had was gone and announced that she was heading west and never coming back. She was sure that her aging tin can of a car, that she kept in her father's garage, would make it clear across the country, so she gifted it to Nora, wishing her adventures of her own. Nora didn't hear from her for five months, the longest she had even been out of touch by far, and when she did, the brief letter was postmarked Aumbry Valley. Phone calls and texts were unanswered, but that was on par for a woman who loved to go off the grid. Searching online, she had found very little about the town. Finding that Aumbry was the name for a cupboard that held sacred items in churches, Nora worried that she may have stumbled into a religious cult of sorts. That didn't stop her from packing that car up with her few important things and heading out to find her.

Making the trip across the country proved Quinn's belief in the car lacking, and Nora couldn't wait for her to see what she and Cherry Bomb were able to accomplish. Unfortunately, Quinn was nowhere to be found when Nora rolled into town, and she couldn't even find a trace of her ever being there. Her cellphone had been disconnected. The address she had for her was a vacant lot. It was the final blow to Nora's faith in her family. With this last disappearing act, Quinn had made it clear that she was serious about cutting herself off from the family, including Nora. At that moment she told herself, no matter what, she would never go back east, and she would not dare to step foot in the family home again. She had her faithful jalopy, for which Nora's crayon-red colored hair had been dyed to match the night before she left home, and her cat. Other than Cherry Bomb, Silas, the cat was Nora's closest confidant since Quinn had left. The decision was made that they were the only two things that would matter to her over all others. She would start over on her terms, and Aumbry Valley was as good a place as any. At least the coldest of nights were still warmer than the winters back east.

Her mood was dry and bleak when she pulled up to her apartment building to once again find all of the closest street parking full. A crack of thunder opened the skies as she pulled into a free spot two blocks away. Perfect. At least her bamboo plant would have a nice drink on the way home. The façade of the building still had the impressive presence of the former home it once was and hid the rundown interior that was now home. She stepped through the heavily ornamented door and into the building's narrow foyer, as she wrung out her soaked ponytail.

"I'm guessing that box isn't holding your rent check, is it?" Nora froze when she heard Jenny call out from her doorway down the hall.

Busted.

"Shit. I'm really sorry. I know I'm late again. I'm going to get it to you soon," Nora said, desperation in her voice. She hadn't been able to sneak into her apartment unnoticed as she had hoped. It was just as well. It would be cowardly to avoid someone who had treated her so kindly.

Jenny crossed her arms and frowned, leaning against the open-door frame to her own small apartment, "That's what you always say, Nora." Her expression wasn't anger; it was disappointment. That somehow always cut deeper. Nora felt ashamed to take advantage of someone who was becoming as close to a friend as she had.

She gave the patient woman gave a pleading look, "I know, and I always do get it to you,' she said with an uncomfortable grin when Jenny smirked and raised an eyebrow. *Eventually*, I always do."

Jenny's lips twitched, holding in a smile at Nora's tragic, soaked appearance. "Nora....," she sighed.

"Why don't I watch Olivia for you? As interest on what I owe you." Nora didn't have much left to barter with. Spending time with that crazy little person was something she was always up for, anyways. Whether she was paid or not.

"I'll keep that in mind for when I need it. But for now, I'd rather you spend your time finding another job. I'm assuming that's needed by the looks of that sad-looking box?" Jenny nodded her head towards the now sopping wet mess in her tenant's arms.

"It is. But it wasn't my fault." Jenny started to retort, but Nora cut her off, "I know I always say that, but this time it really wasn't my fault. Dirtbag Derek had the gall to grab my ass! Right in front of everyone!"

Jenny stood up straight, anger flashing in her eyes, "What? Nora, that's awful. He seriously laid his hands on you? What are you going to do?"

"Nothing, I'm just glad to be out of that place. And I will look for another job first thing tomorrow. I just need to have a bath, wash that place and that man off me, and start fresh in the morning." She remembered the business card in her pocket and balanced the ripping box under her arm as she pulled it out. "I already have a lead on one."

When Jenny walked over to read it, Nora turned it to the handwritten time and place before tossing it back in the box. The fewer questions the better, seeing as how she did not currently have any answers to give about who Elijah Beasley was and what exactly The Firm did.

"See? I have an interview with them tomorrow. Nine AM sharp!" Nora smiled broadly, trying to look sure of herself. "I'm sure I'll get it and you'll be the first one I see when I get my first paycheck. I promise you, that."

Fumbling her key into the door, she made a quick exit from the uncomfortable conversation. "Wish me luck!" She could feel Jenny's frustration radiating through the wall.

A blur of grey fur circled her legs as Silas greeted her, nearly making her trip as she set the box down in her kitchen nook. Catching herself on one of the two stools in front of the breakfast bar that separated the kitchen from her living room/bedroom, she watched as the plate she had left out toppled to the floor, surprisingly not breaking. Silas strolled over and licked at the crumbs that were still left from her morning toast as Nora glowered at him. "I don't need a broken neck to be the icing on the shit-cake that today has been, mister." Snatching the plate from him, she put it back up on the small bar that served as her dining room table, desk, vanity, and the only light source in her minuscule galley kitchen.

The studio, which Nora generously called claustrophobic, did not have room for much. Visitors weren't something of a regular occurrence to Nora's place, just as she liked it, so most nights were spent reading blogs, watching animal videos, and planning trips that she would never be able to afford. Making up the entirety of her living space, was a well-worn loveseat that she sat in front of a crooked end table which held her laptop in place of a television. Having WIFI, no matter how slow, included in her rent was a huge bonus, and Nora took advantage of it every night. Her bed pushed against the back of her couch and a dresser pushed against the wall made up her bedroom. When she had left college to follow her aunt, she had only brought her clothes, her laptop, a few books, and a handful of trinkets that were special to her. The only splurge that she had sprung for since moving in was a plush grey cat bed that matched Silas' fur perfectly. She blew a good chunk of her first paycheck on it as a celebration of her taking him in and their new life together in Aumbry Valley.

He chose to sleep in the box it was delivered in.

Everything else she had found in the two well-stocked thrift stores, or her favorite, on the side of the road. One of her favorite perks to the small town with a high concentration of migrant wealthy remodeling their mini-mansions was that there was always an abundance of second-hand finds. Their trash became every treasure she owned. The looks on people's faces when they saw her driving down the main street of Aumbry Valley with a dresser strapped haphazardly to the roof of little Cherry Bomb would always be one of Nora's best memories of moving into town. It was even better when she found it was a gorgeous teak and chrome Art Deco piece that was hiding under several sloppy layers of paint. Looking at the dresser, guilt felt heavy in her chest. As beautiful as it was, every time she would look at it there was a reminder of who she was, or more so, what she had made herself become out of stubbornness. The poor little rich girl.

Nora was no stranger to the trappings of wealth. The bedroom she grew up in was more than twice the size of her apartment and Jenny's whole building could fit inside her parents' opulent five-story brownstone. As owners of an antiquities shop back east, Adam and Gwen Goodman were either traveling the continents to stock up on dusty old relics or attending snooty fundraisers and galas to make connections with the breathtakingly dull wealthy elite who were quick to part with their money for a vase or chair that would make the other rich and boring people jealous of their acquisitions. The gloomy rooms of the rambling row house were stuffed floor to ceiling with priceless pieces that Nora was strictly forbidden from touching and an endless number of staff that avoided the curious child. The nannies and tutors and assorted hired help that were expected, by Nora's parents, to do the brunt of the child-rearing found little interest in the awkward young girl. They had no problem treating her as an unwanted bother, just as her mother and father did. She was sent to elite private schools the second she was old enough to be shipped off but, the slightest glee she felt from escaping the harsh darkness of her family home was short-lived when she found that even in the vast halls of the exclusive schools, she still could not find her footing. The social hierarchies were vicious and repellent to her. When Nora grew into her teens and began to voice her opinions and lash out, she was deemed nothing more than a spoiled brat with no real-world intelligence. Her mother and father had an uncanny knack to make her seem as if she was just too much and not nearly enough with just a spit of a few words. Every moment of her life was scheduled and planned out for as far as she could see.

The most freeing moment in Nora's life was realizing that her parents didn't hate her. They simply didn't want her. They had a child only because they believed that is what people did. Marry, get rich, have a child to create continuity, get richer, and eventually die with the legacy of wealth forever passed on through the family name. Nora came to understand that it didn't matter who the child they would create was. They would resent them as a necessary burden, no matter what.

The only space she had to find her voice was with her grandfather and Quinn. Even though he was well into retirement by the time Nora came along, Noah Goodman loved to include her and his daughter Quinn in his passion for history and adventure. He was known to say, on more than one occasion, that there was a nefarious feeling to a space that someone called their own yet never used or cared for. She knew he was coyly referencing the vast collection of rooms in her parents' home, but she hoped that he was referring to her as well. He and his son never saw eye to eye, and it bothered him to no end to see how the only attention Adam gave Nora was to occasionally smother her with his need to keep up the appearances of perceived perfection. When her grandfather heard that Nora was interested in studying anthropology in college, after spending nearly three years working in her parents' shop after high school. he was so proud of her for stepping out of her shell. He made a point to encourage her to find a path that was hers alone in order to make a life that gave her joy and fulfillment of self. That positive push had buzzed in her ear ever since. It buzzed each of the three years that she studied Art History after caving to her parents' insistence. It buzzed when she thought of a world that would be forever cold and small if she stayed under her parents' thumb and it roared when, three credits shy of graduating, her grandfather died, and her Aunt Quinn left town for good. Her world was then beyond cold and small, and just like what had happened to Quinn, it felt empty. In his will, he included a letter to Nora. It was tucked in a small silver casket box that had sat on his desk for decades and was all he left to her. It was all that she needed.

'Nora-bird,

Always keep digging. Never live solely on the surface, my sweet girl. All of the best and most important things tend to find themselves buried. It's important to work as hard as you can to find them, to free them. So, I ask you to always be searching for what you can not see. Along the way, you will be surprised to find yourself and your way in this vast world. Don't let them bury your spirit, my dear Nora-bird. Always, always, always keep digging.

Love for you always - Grandpa.'

Every dollar he owned was divided up amongst charities that were close to his heart and that made Nora proud of how vast her grandfather's heart was. She didn't need his money; she knew what great wealth could turn people into. She just needed to know that such a great man cared for her and believed in her right up until his last breath. That was all she needed to pack up her life and start again. She knew she could go home in her heart - if you could call that emotionless museum a home. Nora also knew that it would be the end of any free will that she had found in the small amount of time that she had been on her own. She would be buried.

It wouldn't be a step forward by any means, but it would be better than taking advantage of Jenny's goodwill. Nora's face fell at how she had selfishly relied on the kindness of her only friend simply to escape from a life that was cruel, but comfortable. Looking down at the water-drenched box, the business card caught her eye and she plucked it up.

The Firm.

Silas stood up on his hinds and sniffed at the crumpled card.

"There is this option, buddy, but I may never come home to you if this is as creepy as it seemed." Silas rubbed his head across the card before strolling over to his empty bowl. Even Silas could tell times were getting dire. Looking through her cupboards for lunch options, she was glad to see she had some instant ramen that was still on the safe side of its expiry date. When the smell of soup drifted from the microwave, Silas turned his nose up at the kitty kibble she had poured into the dish and climbed up on the stool beside the breakfast bar.

"Fat chance, Diva. This feast is all mine," Nora snapped, shooing the cranky cat down. He landed beside the damp cardboard box with a thud, slinking over to inspect the contents. A judgemental mew and a side-eyed glare were his response to seeing the plant set inside as if he knew what that meant.

"I know, I know. I got fired again."

After savoring the last few broken noodles in the bottom of the cup, each bite carefully chewed on the opposite side of her toothache, she tossed it in the sink with the spoon. Picking up the plant from the box, she placed it on the crowded windowsill with the other sad-looking attempts at greenery. The only one that was perennially perfect was a solar-powered plastic flower with a sunshiny happy face that bobbed in the light. A gift for her twelfth birthday from Quinn. Nora frowned at it and slid it behind a browned ivy. Setting the rest of the contents on the counter, she retrieved the pen to add to the large mug that held the rest of her previous employment souvenirs. 'In my defense, I was left unsupervised' was ironically printed in bold red letters on one side of the cup. Looking at the bottom of the box she found the bright blue tape dispenser and held it out to her cat.

"We have this now! Maybe I could become crafty and open a store, becoming disgustingly wealthy with a reality show?" She pulled a strip of tape off and stuck it to the edge of the box. "What do you think this could be?" She pressed the business card to the other end of the tape. "Business card organizer? This could be my million-dollar idea, Silas!" Silas walked away to curl up in his favorite box. "Okay, maybe not."

Nora pulled off the card and tape and stuck it to the wall, tossing the remnants of the cardboard into the corner. Silas looked up with interest. He would be all over that filthy, ripped mess as soon as it was dry. Picking up his completely neglected, fluffy cat bed, Nora tossed it on the loveseat before laying back against it as a plush pillow. Pulling up an internet search, she tried as many variations of The Firm as she could think of without finding anything that looked like it could be linked to the mysterious Elijah Beasley. Her phone buzzed and let out a chirp when *Aumbry Job Placement* flashed on the screen. Her heart sunk into her stomach as she answered knowing what was coming.

The sweet older woman who ran the job agency told her that she was officially off the list of applicants and would no longer be contacted for jobs. She was sympathetic to what had happened to Nora with Dirtbag Derek, but there had been too many other incidents in the past to continue as a temp with her. Nora muttered apologies and thanks for the wishes for the future before she flung herself back onto the couch, tossing her phone to the floor.

Pulling the elastic from her ponytail, she twisted her bright red locks up into a pile on top of her head and plopped her laptop onto her stomach. The tab was still open to Quinn's Insta photos, hundreds of little square memories staring back at her. Still the same ones from over a month ago; no signs of her new adventure.

Nora couldn't dwell on her worry and anger that twisted together for her aunt. It was time to start yet another job hunt and look after herself. A pad of paper that she had written OPTIONS on sat beside her and remained otherwise blank after over an hour of searching. There had to be somewhere that hired outside of the temp agency. The elites in their mini-mansions couldn't have that much control. Could they? Giving her pen a nibble, lost in thought, the blazing pain of her toothache shot across her cheek and exploded in her head.

She launched the pen across the room. "Goddammit!" The pen hit Elijah Beasley's card, knocking it off the wall to the floor. Nora stared at it where it landed. It couldn't be that easy. When things seem too good to be true, they most definitely were. A handsome stranger that appears in the elevator moments after she is fired, when her rent is later than it had ever been and only ten dollars to her name had to fall into the category of too good to be true. There had to be a catch. The fact that she had no idea what the actual job entailed was certainly one, and why could he hire outside of the employment group?

The low battery alert pinged on her laptop. Plugging it in, she bent over to pick up the card. 1365 Beech Avenue, 9 am. Worst case scenario, Elijah is some crazy rich guy that ties her up in his secret dungeon lair. Not ideal and would not help with rent. In the best-case scenario, it's another mind-numbing desk job that gives her money for cat food and the roof over their heads. Silas mewed from his box, extending his leg for a stretch. Her tooth ached. Nora decided that the best-case scenario would be a dental plan, be it a dungeon or a desk job.

Be it dungeon or desk.

CHAPTER TWO

Nora's resolve to attend the interview had not lessened after a good night's sleep. Her dry cereal, without milk due to the lack of milk in the fridge, was encouraging enough if she needed another push out the door. Her coffee stock was at an all-time low, putting the public at large in grave danger if she ran out. She portioned just enough to wake up and make herself presentable. Sprinkling in a pinch of salt, just as her grandfather had made it, Nora filled her nose with the warm, life-bringing steam of hot go-go juice. Sipping away the morning rage, she looked to the clock – seven am – and then to her wardrobe. It was sparse, thanks to the limited space in Cherry Bomb when she hit the road from her college life. Anything that she had picked up since had been basic office clothes or sweats from the thrift shops in town. Not having any idea what the job entailed made it difficult to know what to choose. The lack of choices didn't leave a lot of options to pick from. Living under her family's umbrella of wealth had provided her with an endless supply of dazzling fashion options that, she hated to admit, she did miss. She wondered if they still sat in her closet in her childhood bedroom, or if they had been cleared out to make room for something else.

Her closet in her current home was a clothes rack, held together on one end with duct tape. She pushed each hanger to one side and then back. A black cotton blazer with black cigarette pants seemed the most professional choice. A white V-neck t-shirt from her laundry pile finished the look after she gave it a sniff and double-checked for stains. It seemed to be the most business-like ensemble that she could come up with. There was something about Elijah Beasley that made her feel like she needed to dress a little more black tie than office mole. Her only shoes: a pair of spiked, bejeweled heels from her senior formal, her well-worn leather ballet flats, or her go-to grey Chucks sat in front of her while she finished her coffee. The heels were a no-go, that much she knew. If this guy was crazy and she had to run, she didn't want to be that damn damsel in distress that falls and twists her ankle Also out were the ballet flats. They were slippery as oil on shiny floors. The sneakers were the best choice and she thought they looked cute with the pants. Silas lovingly rubbed against her dark pants, leaving a streak of grey fur in his path.

"Thanks, buddy. Just what my outfit needed." Nora brushed it away and pulled on her sneakers. "I'm over here worried about what shoes to wear in case this guy is a crazed psycho, just so I can keep your bowl full. The least you can do is leave me uncovered with your hair for one morning."

Running a brush through her half-dried hair, she noticed how much the red dye was fading from her locks. The vibrant red was turning to watery pink faster than she liked. The jar of dye that she preferred had been scraped clean with her last treatment and even if she could afford more, which she couldn't, there was little chance of finding it in the small shops along the main street of Aumbry Valley. Looking at the clock again – eight-fifteen - there was no time to dry it. A neatly set bun would have to do. Less hair to grab that way, just in case.

Nora was aware of how casually she tossed about possible threats. She could hear Quinn laughing at Nora even considering those scenarios. Her imagination had always leaned towards the darker, worst-case mind-set, giving her free-spirited aunt no end to teasing her. Whether it was truly to cope with a real threat or if her life had become so bland that she was inventing adventurous drama, she was still not talking herself out of going to the interview. The time she spent as a kid wandering around the great expanse of the city, and its vast forest-covered park had made her hyper-aware of her surroundings thanks to the ever-present big city predators. Her reaction to danger had evolved from fight or flight to see what happens. Her grandfather had said she had the curious mind of an adventurer, which Nora always found pride in. Aunty Quinn said it was a death wish. Nora liked to believe her grandfather was right. It was most likely, at least in part, the root of her lifelong obsession with true crime stories. Slinging her patched-together messenger bag across her chest, she grabbed her keys.

"Wish me luck, Silas." He responded with a leg over his shoulder and the beginning of a grooming session. "Classy, bud," Nora grinned as she shut the door behind her.

Cherry Bomb started up with a purr on the first try for the second day in a row. Nora tried not to jinx herself by thinking things were turning around for her. Giving the dashboard instruments a double-take, she noticed that the fuel gauge was showing full. It was showing less than a quarter tank when she had parked it the night before. Either something strange was happening with cosmic intervention or Cherry Bomb's fuel gauge was now broken.

"Are your switchy switches on the fritz, girl?" Nora flicked at the dial, but it remained at full.

Hopefully, there was enough gas to get her to the interview. Pulling on her seatbelt, she realized that her feet were not touching the pedals when she sat back in the seat. Pulling the handle and sliding the driver's seat forward, it clicked three times. A creeping sensation set in and quivered up her spine. Nora had not moved that handle since she was gifted Cherry Bomb. Quickly turning to the back seat, she was thankful to find it empty; everything else looked as it always did. Pulling out into the lane, Nora tried to calm her mind, making every excuse she could think of as to why her seat was moved. If the gauges are wearing out, maybe the seat was as well. Maybe she was trying to find anything to distract herself from her nerves. Any job interview was intimidating. This one was doubly so. Not only was she running out of options to stay in Aumbry Valley, but she also had no idea what she was walking into. This job could be anything if it was a job at all. Picturing Elijah Beasley's kind smile, she tried to be optimistic. He had a friendly face and a gentle way about him. This could be just the opportunity that she's been waiting for.

Beech Avenue was only a short drive from her apartment and before she could talk herself out of it, she was parking out front of a nondescript, run-of-the-mill, four-story beige-bricked office building. Squaring her shoulders and smoothing a loose hair behind her ear, she marched to the front door with purpose. Checking the mounted board in the dark lobby, she found The Firm listed on the second floor. So far, so good. Her sneakers squeaked against the dull cream-colored tile across the lobby to the elevator. No security guards or balaclava-covered-would-be kidnappers were lurking about when she pressed the elevator up button. That didn't stop the uncomfortable feeling of being watched and it had her looking over her shoulder more than once while she waited. No one was behind the elevator's doors when it dinged open to reveal even more washed-out beige décor. When it lifted her to the second floor, the beat of her heart picked up along with the nerves that swirled in her stomach making it lurch. She took deep, slow breaths to keep her coffee and cereal down.

There was no turning back now.

When the doors slid open again, Nora stepped out into a dingy hallway that flickered with fluorescent lights that led the way down to a chipped grey metal door. It was not the clean, bland space of the lobby. It was shabby and menacing. Nora turned back around to the elevator just as it slid closed in her face. She swallowed her fear and turned back to the grey door at the end of the hall. The Firm was etched across it in bold, black lettering. One foot in front of the other, she walked the worn, carpeted gauntlet to the office.

Nora took the door handle in her sweating hand, "Here goes nothing."

Her voice was small, as she pushed her back straight, lifting her chin. The room she entered was not the dungeon she was imagining but a dungeon of another sort. The water-stained ceiling tiles matched the dirt-stained carpets that ran wall to wall in the tiny office. An elderly woman, with faintly purple hair done up in short curls, sat at an aluminum desk opposite the door. She clicked away swiftly on a computer's keyboard with one hand and flicked a cigarette into an over-filled ashtray with the other. This was worse than a crazy man who holds people captive in his lair.

This was another call center job that would slowly suck her soul from her body.

Nora shook off the self-pity and stepped forward to the desk. A job is a job, and she should be thankful for the chance to pay her bills. Thankful to have one last chance to stay in the little town she had decided was her new life. She stood at the desk, waiting to be noticed.

When she softly cleared her throat, the woman looked up, startled. The nameplate in front of her said only 'Pearl'.

"Can I help you with something, dear?" Her smile was genuine and put Nora a little more at ease.

"I was told to be here for an interview. For nine am," Nora replied in the politest voice she could muster. Looking up at the clock behind the desk, she saw it was only eight-forty. Being early was never her strong suit and she gave herself a mental high five for it. She handed Pearl the business card she had been given.

"Oh, you were, were you? Are you Miss Goodman?" The woman hacked a cough and squashed her cigarette out in the ashtray before shuffling through some papers. Nora's eyes narrowed and she took half a step back. She realized she had not given Elijah her name. Or had she? Pearl sat motionless, looking up at her, waiting for her to answer.

"My name is Nora Goodman, but I don't know if..."

"You're all set," Pearl said with a smile much younger than the rest of her face. She set aside a file folder on her desk. Nora could see her name printed across the cover. "Have a seat and Mr. Beasley will be out for you soon."

Nora backed away from her and peeked out of the tiny window – the only window – to the alleyway and dumpsters below. The view of a crappy office job. She tried to replay the details of the brief conversation she had with Elijah Beasley. There was nothing she could recall that gave her insight into what the job could be.

"Excuse me," Nora said to Pearl, "what exactly does The Firm do?"

Pearl gave her a wry smile, obviously amused. "A little of everything I suppose."

Nora frowned at the non-answer, but nodded politely, "Huh, okay."

"There's nothing to be worried about, my dear. Mr. Beasley is a wonderful man and an even better boss. I've worked with him for...oh, my...centuries if a day," Pearl smiled brightly.

Nora's eyes were drawn to Pearl's cheeks and then to the rest of her face. The skin seemed to have a shimmer, almost translucent like water. Not just her skin - her whole body did except for her dusty pink skirt suit. Nora rubbed her eyes and looked again. Pearl had lit another cigarette and was taking a long pull from it. Her skin was pale but perfectly normal. Nora blinked a few times and stepped over to the waiting area chairs. Her nerves were getting the better of her.

Interviews were something that she could usually nail. The friendly smile with enthusiastic head nods was something that she had mastered to get through her parents' stuffy events. Nora knew this time it was more than any old interview; she was in dire straits for steady employment and had to be her best gleaming version of herself. She pulled out her phone and smiled at the screen saver of Silas sleeping happily in his box.

I'll get this job for us, Buddy. Don't worry.

Nora focused on staying calm. She focused on the sound of Pearl's nails clicking away on her keyboard and tried not to turn green from the thick cigarette smoke that drifted around her. The creaking door to the hallway opened, just a crack, and then swung shut again. A second wider swing was held by a metal crutch that clanged against the chipped metal door. Nora jumped up to help the man who was struggling to make his way in. His leg was wrapped in a brace from ankle to hip and it was making the navigation of the heavy door impossible.

"Thanks," he said after Nora helped him untangle himself from the doorway.

"No problem," Nora said, as he slumped down in one of the worn office chairs along the wall, "That looks like a nasty break."

"It was a lot worse a month ago, but it's still a pain in the ass." The man glared at the brace.

"Would you be Ezra?" Pearl peered at them over her computer monitor, the friendly expression still settled across her face.

"I am, yes ma'am," he replied with a nod. He had a crooked grin that lit up a boyishly handsome face. The idea of competition for the job made Nora suddenly more nervous. She hadn't even considered that she would be competing against anyone or anything aside from her own ineptitude. The employment agency in Aumbry had just assigned the jobs as they came, and she had gotten used to it. Although, it was nice to have someone else there with her for the mysterious interview.

"You try to make yourself comfortable and Mr. Beasley will be with you shortly," Pearl said, going back to furiously typing and exhaling smoke.

Nora looked over the brace that was strapped to his leg with wide swatches of Velcro. If anything did go down with Elijah, at least she could outrun this guy. She didn't smother her giggle in time.

"Leg injuries give you a laugh, do they?" Ezra asked, with a hint of humor in his voice. He looked to be around the same age as Nora, but a babyface like his could be hiding years in either direction. His ashy-blonde hair curled along his hairline above friendly chestnut-colored eyes.

Nora sat slowly beside him, minding his leg, "No, not at all. Sorry, my mind is somewhere else." Smiling sympathetically, she nodded towards his leg, "That looks pretty uncomfortable."

"You've got a good eye," Ezra laughed at her observation. Nora liked how deep it was. It sounded like it erupted from the pit of his stomach, shaking his shoulders.

"What happened?" Nora asked and noticed him blushing. She immediately wished she hadn't pried, "If it's okay to ask."

"No worries, it's okay. It was pure stupidity," Ezra rolled his eyes at the thought. "I am the type of person that can trip over my own two feet going up a flight of stairs and I thought I could take on a job in construction." He looked to the ceiling with a shake of his fist, as if cursing the universe for not stopping him. "I fell from the scaffolding on the very first day. The first hour actually," he shook his head, "A fear of heights and roofing do not agree with each other."

Nora gave him a tight smile, "That's awful. I'm sorry to hear," she paused before offering her hand, "I'm Nora Goodman."

"Ezra Davis. Nice to meet you." His hand was warm but rough.

"So, you're here for the job interview too?" Nora asked him, looking up at Pearl. The small woman took a long haul from her cigarette, consumed by whatever she was typing.

"I am. You too, huh?" Ezra queried, his eyes following Nora's to Pearl.

Nora was sure that her eyes were playing tricks on her again at the sight of her seemingly limpid skin.

"I am," she answered, not looking away from the receptionist. They watched as Pearl had a coughing fit into a tissue. She stamped out the butt of one cigarette before lighting another. It had to be all of the smoke, that filled the room, playing tricks with her mind. Out of the corner of her eye, she noticed Ezra lean forward, just for a slight second, and looked curiously at Pearl. Maybe she wasn't the only one noticing that something seemed off.

"Do you have any idea what this job is?" Ezra asked, slowly looking back to Nora.

"Not at all. You?"

Ezra shook his head, "No idea. When I was leaving the clinic for a check-up yesterday, some guy started talking to me and said I was due for some good luck. He offered me an interview for today on the spot. There doesn't seem to be a lot of options in this town for work being offered. Well, at least not that I see being posted. I even had to go through a temp agency for the roofing job. I figure a job is a job when I have bills to pay."

"The same thing happened to me," Nora looked around the drab room again and lowered her voice. "I was getting a real rich-people hunting me for sport kind of vibe from him, but from the looks of this room it's giving me a worse feeling."

Ezra's smile returned with a quizzical tilt of his head, "What could be worse than being hunted for sport?"

"Another dead-end office job," Nora announced, with a grimace.

Ezra's brow crumpled and he scoffed, looking at her as if she suddenly had two heads, "That would be worse than being hunted for sport?"

"I'm guessing you haven't had a lot of office jobs." Nora kept her voice low, to keep her words from reaching Pearl. The tiny woman had a momentary giggle and gave a sly side-eye to the pair to her surprise. Nora felt the heat wash over her face. Another job that she would lose before it even started. She gave Pearl her best attempt at a charming smile and then looked at Ezra, her face rumpled with embarrassment.

"I think an office job would suit me just fine," Ezra nodded to his crutches, "I've mainly done handyman jobs in the past. When I can keep my feet on the ground, I'm pretty good with tools," he said with a proud grin. "Once I left my sister's restaurant...well, my father's restaurant. It's hers now. Once I left, I took odd jobs to make some cash to get out of town." His eyes darkened, and he shifted uncomfortably in his seat, saying nothing more.

Nora sat in silence for only a moment. "So, you're not from Aumbry Valley?"

There had to be a connection between them that would explain why they were both given such a strange opportunity. A family restaurant and handyman work didn't quite pair up with a former rich girl turned college dropout and office flunky.

"No, I came here for a clean start," Ezra said with a tinge of anger in his voice that let Nora know that he wasn't open to discussing it any further.

Nora clamped her lips. One of the reasons that she preferred her own company was that she tended to ask too many questions to those around her. It had been the cause for more than argument with uppity private school teachers and more than one firing in her temp jobs. She looked around the room, scanning the nicotine scanned walls, shifting in her seat.

"I have a fixer-upper on the northside of town that I was hoping to flip for some extra cash, but it's starting to grow on me the more I work on it," Ezra added as if he could sense Nora's discomfort. "That's why I took on the construction job, hoping to blend the two. But roofing was not for me," he said with a light pat on his leg brace.

A whoosh of air behind Pearl grabbed their attention. Where there was once a paint-worn wall, a large hidden door had slid open to reveal Elijah Beasley standing in another costly-looking suit. He clasped his hands in happiness at the sight of them.

"You have both chosen to take me up on my offer! I am truly delighted." He extended his hand into the room behind him, gesturing for them to enter. Nora helped Ezra to his feet before following Elijah into the massive space behind the wall. The rounded, windowless walls reached up twice as high as the small office they had just left, most likely to the roof, and were covered in a silky, deep blue wallpaper. The brass sconces that circle the room, shone on the charcoal grey floors and sparkled the thin veins of gold that trailed through what had to be over four thousand square feet.

"Oh, shit Ezra. They are most definitely *hunt-people for sport* people," Nora said under her breath, but it echoed across the vast space. Elijah Beasley gave an amused laugh, smoothing his tie as he sat behind an impressive mahogany desk in the center of the room. The detailed carvings were certainly handmade and old, Nora noted. Probably Victorian, maybe older, but in pristine condition. They may hunt people for sport, but they had good taste in furniture. Her parents would be frothing at the mouth to get their hands on it and the intricate Tiffany lamp that sat on its corner.

"Miss. Goodman, I have assured you that you are in no way in danger by attending this interview, and I will assure you once again," Elijah lowered his gaze to hers, "I have no intentions of harming you or behaving in any way that could be construed as untoward," he motioned to the plush, burgundy wing back chairs that were sat in front of the desk, "Please. Simply sit and listen to what I have to say."

Nora's feet were not keen on moving much further into the room. "How do you know my name?"

"I know a lot about you, Nora Goodman. And just as much about you, Ezra Davis," Elijah said, sitting back in his high-backed leather seat, "That is part of my job. Now, please, sit and let me explain," he gestured again to the chairs, "Mr. Davis, you really should rest that leg."

Nora looked around the room before deciding to take a step further, even as Ezra bravely wobbled over to the chair. Taking another step forward, she realized that people were standing along the wall behind her on either side of the sliding door, which quickly whooshed itself shut again. Her eyes popped and her jaw dropped looking from each one to the next. Around a dozen stood at attention between plush sofas that matched the burgundy fabric of the chairs, and they were the most gorgeous human beings that she had ever seen. Dressed in matching black, military-style uniforms, the men and women stood frozen, their eyes alert and on guard.

"What's with the Glamor Guards?" Nora asked, still taking each one in. She had never seen such a gathering of attractive-looking people. She unconsciously tugged at her t-shirt, pulling it smooth, and ran a palm across the hair that had slipped from her bun. They paid no attention to her gaping at them. "Ezra, are you seeing this?"

He didn't have to say a thing; his silly crooked grin was ear to ear as gawked at the woman standing closest to his left. He nearly missed the chair when he sat and steadied himself with a crutch before setting them both on the ground beside him.

"Please, Miss. Goodman. Let me explain," Elijah gestured towards the chair once more, his voice still as polite as ever. Nora moved towards him, while her eyes flickered to each side of the room and back, trying to take it all in. Other than the bizarre runway lineup along windowless walls, the only other strange thing she noticed was the strong scent of freshly baked, warm sugar cookies that filled the room. It was oddly soothing. She breathed in the sweet aroma as she sat beside Ezra, her apprehension lessening.

"Now, before we start, I need to have you each sign an NDA," Elijah snapped his fingers as he spoke, prompting one of the Supermodel Squad to hand him a paper-filled folder. The only sound in the room was the thud of her boots' footfalls on the polished marble.

"A what-now?" Ezra asked, peeking over the desk to see what he held.

"A non-disclosure agreement, Mr. Davis. Whether you accept the positions that I am offering you today, or not, you may never discuss what you are told within these walls." Elijah looked from one to the other

"What do you mean *accept* the position? Did I get the job? I mean…we got the jobs?" Nora asked, excitement in her voice. It can't be that easy! Although, she still had no idea of what she was being offered.

"You are being offered positions here, yes. Regardless of your acceptance or decline of these positions, you must first sign these NDA's." Elijah answered, his eyes on the stack of stapled papers in his hands. Nora bumped her elbow on Ezra's chair to get his attention that had drifted back to the guard who had made her way back to her post along the wall. He didn't seem as excited by the prospect of work as she was.

"Oh, sorry. What's this now?" Ezra shuffled himself up in the chair, leaning into the conversation.

"The NDA, Mr. Davis. I require you both to sign one before we carry on with our business," Elijah looked up from the papers and smiled tightly.

The mention of the legal document again captured Ezra's attention, "What exactly do you do here, sir?"

"We can talk about that as soon as you look these over and grant your signature on the last page, at the bottom," Elijah said, setting the folders on the edge of his desk in front of them.

Nora had never had to deal with legal papers of any sort other than signing her acceptance papers to college and her apartment lease. Her three years of Art History certainly didn't get around to discussing NDA's and the sort. Sliding the papers from the desk, she scanned the legal speak that filled four pages. The top of the first page had a large decorative B in gothic swirls with BUREAU printed in a tight, fine print underneath. "B Bureau? Is that you? Beasley's Bureau? Bureau of what" Nora flipped the page picking out words such as confidentiality, legally binding, and governing. Her eyes stopped when she read 'threat of lawsuit or further action'. A lawsuit would be a joke, as she had nothing to take, but further action? What could that even mean?

"Mr. Beasley, if we don't sign these, can we just leave?" Ezra asked and started to set the papers on his desk.

"Of course, Mr. Davis. No harm, no foul. But let me assure you that it seems more nefarious than it is. Such is the way of lawyers," Elijah replied, delighted in his joke.

"This does seem like something a lawyer should look over," Nora added, without looking up from the paperwork.

"I understand your concern, and there is some room on some subjects. However, if we are to continue with our discussion, I need you to sign these now," Elijah still sat relaxed in his seat, but his voice now held a tinge of impatience, "Unfortunately, until those are signed, there is nothing more I can tell you of what we have to offer you here," he leaned forward to point to the papers, "If you bring your attention to Section E, Sub-section thirteen, you will see that by signing and moving on to the next phase in the disclosure process, you will be financially compensated for the NDA signing alone."

Nora flipped quickly to the last page of Section E and scanned the lines until she found thirteen.

"Holy shit," Nora exclaimed in a quick exhale of breath.

By signing said Confidentiality Agreement at the time of the first presentation, the potential Employee will immediately receive a cash disbursement of One (1) Thousand Dollars.

A grand? That would cover her rent, a full fridge, and a takeout feast for herself *and* Silas. Nora's hands started to shake. It couldn't be that easy. Could it? She was due some good luck after so long. Could this be it? "I just have to sign this, and you hand over a thousand bucks to me?"

"Yes, my dear. Simply sign, accept the courtesy payment, and we can move on to discussing the ins and outs of this Bureau's dealings," Elijah advised and took the lids from two heavy-looking fountain pens. He set one in front of each of them.

Picking it up she noted that it was as heavy as it looked and had swirls of gold and silver from tip to tip. It probably cost more than her rent for a year. Another piece that her parents would die to get their claws on. It didn't have a company name printed on the side, so Nora saw no need to try to pocket it for her collection. She placed the papers against her leg and scribbled her signature on the line without another thought.

"Wait! Whoa, hang on here. Nora, maybe we should think about this some more," Ezra said leaning forward to grab at her NDA. Nora pulled it from his reach and set it on the table in front of Elijah.

"You can wait if you want, but I'm in," Nora said with a beaming smile, even though regret was already washing over her. "Come on, Ezra. Let's hear what he has to say. It's a grand just to listen to him!"

Ezra pressed a tight, frustrated breath through his lips, "I don't think this is a good idea."

"You can go, then. I'm sticking around to see what he has to say," Nora jumped in her seat when one of the Glamor Guards appeared at her side and presented her with a white sealed envelope. She didn't know if it was her happiness at her windfall or not, but the smell of fresh cookies wafted even thicker in the air. Opening the envelope, she found ten, crisp hundred-dollar bills. Jackpot!

Ezra looked from Elijah to Nora, to the circled group of guards, and back again. With another frustrated sigh, he picked up the pen and quickly signed. Tossing the paper and pen onto the desk he muttered to Nora, "Well, I'm not letting you go into this alone."

"Wonderful! I assure you that you have both made the right decision," Elijah exclaimed and handed the signed documents to one guard while another handed Ezra his stipend. He shoved it in his jacket's pocket without opening it. "Well, we should get started. There is a lot to tell you. What this Bureau does, and The Firm as a whole, does is not only essential to the world with the services that it provides, but it will also give you limitless opportunities of excitement and even more money." Elijah's eyes flashed wide as he spoke the last enticing word.

Ezra gave Nora a sideways glance and slid down in his chair. He was looking less than enthused by the situation that they found themselves in. Nora tried to ignore him. It was his choice to stay. She shouldn't have to feel guilty about a perfect stranger's irritation.

"What do we have to do?" Nora asked, ignoring the discontented grunts coming from Ezra.

Before Elijah could answer, another hidden door across the room slid open. A tall man, with wispy, silvery hair that was well past being called thinning strolled into the room with a bright white smile. The jaunt in his step did not pair well with his aged appearance. He moved as if he were half of his age, at most when he sashayed into the room wearing a dressing gown over pajamas, all made of indigo silk, with matching slippers. The metallic threads of the rococo patterns that swirled across the fabric shimmered in the soft light of the room. He was both bafflingly casual and dressed to the nines all at once. It certainly was not what you would expect for job interview attire.

"Ah, Elijah! Are these our new recruits?" His eyes were ablaze with interest as he took them in.

"That they are, Mr. Lester. Allow me to introduce Mr. Ezra Davis and Ms. Nora Goodman."

"Please, call me Gabriel," Mr. Lester said as he gave them each a nod. He turned his jovial face from Nora and Ezra to give a scan of the guards, who remained as still as statues. His expression changed instantly, giving them a very unwelcoming glare. His nose twitched with repulsion before turning his bright grin back to Elijah. "Are we all signed off? May I speak freely?"

"The ink is still drying, Mr. Lester. I think it would be wise to give them some details of what to expect before you speak...freely," Elijah gave Gabriel a knowing wink. Nora didn't know what that was to mean, but it did take a little bit of the sparkle from her excitement.

"Fair enough. I do think that my method is far more straightforward, but it is your office and your recruits," Gabriel answered with a slight whine in his voice. Nora could tell that this man must be a handful. Energy radiated from him like a hummingbird; he never stayed completely still. He was the opposite of Elijah's graceful calm.

"Thank you. So, as I was saying...," Elijah Beasley's words were cut short when Gabriel popped onto the table in front of him, settling on the edge with one long leg tossed over the other. Nora and Ezra shot straight up in their seats, startled by the speed at which he moved. He certainly was spry for his age.

"You are going to love it here! I dare say there is never a dull moment," Gabriel squealed, excitedly. Elijah leaned sideways in his chair to look around him with annoyance as Gabriel carried on, "There has been quite the vetting process to take you two on. It's been ages since we've had fresh blood around here!"

"Gabriel!" Elijah stood from the chair, a hand on his shoulder, "Enough of that, please!"

Gabriel gave a theatrical frown, slinking down from the desk, "Fine then. Your office, your recruits," he repeated. Moping, he walked around the desk to stand behind Elijah. Nora sat rigidly in her chair now, unsure of what to make of the strange man.

"As I was saying, the positions that we are offering you will bring a lot into your lives being that this is a very unique place of employment," Elijah said, sitting back down and calm once more.

"Yeah, we've got all of that. Excitement, important stuff, lots of money. But what is the job? What are we supposed to do?" Ezra's voice was getting as hostile as the tension in his expression. He looked from Elijah to Gabriel and back, wanting answers.

Nora tried to keep herself calm, the envelope in her hands stuffed with cash, acting as a security blanket. If nothing else, she could pay Jenny in full. A thousand dollars was more than a week's pay at any of her temp jobs. Temp jobs that she no longer had access to. She wanted to know what the job pertained to, what would be required of her, and a million other things, just as Ezra did. She found that the strange situation she was in seemed to cause the constant barrage of questions that she was known for to stick in her throat, and she could just smile like a lunatic. For once she was speechless. She was glad to have Ezra beside her, even if he was a complete stranger. It had been quite some time since she had been thankful to not be on her own.

"Fair enough, Mr. Davis. I will lay the cards on the table," Elijah leaned forward towards them, while Gabriel bounced on his heels like an impatient child. "We are a security agency of sorts. We...," he paused, gathering his thoughts, "we are a group of Agents that provide a layer of protection to a community that knows nothing of our very existence. The society that you are currently a member of. We also provide a service to the members of our community."

"You expect me to believe that the best recruit you could come up with is a guy with a busted leg?" Ezra started to struggle to his feet. "I don't know what you guys are into, but this is all too weird. I'm out."

"Please, just hear me out," Elijah said with his hands up as a gesture of peace. Ezra's jaw clenched, but he remained seated as he was asked to. "Most of what I am going to tell you is going to sound quite unreal, insane even, but I promise you that it is the truth," Elijah announced, turning an ugly eye to Gabriel when he snorted.

Nora's worry started to get the best of her, the hairs on her neck responding by standing on end. The reality of her uncertainty returned. Looking around the room, the scent of sugar cookies swarmed thicker around her. She looked for vents where it may be pumping through. She found nothing but the sconces and opulent wallpaper along the wall. Could they be using the most delicious kind of gas ever made to poison them, or manipulate their minds? Other than her up and down feelings of unease, she felt completely normal and in control of her senses. It certainly didn't seem like a dangerous place, at least the room didn't. It also didn't look like any room she had ever seen with her own two eyes, either. The overwhelming situation made it hard to focus on what Elijah was saying. When she turned to Ezra, she found him staring back at her.

"Are you okay with this so far?" Ezra bobbed his head towards the two at the desk.

"I don't know, but we're here. We may as well hear them out," Nora said, tucking the envelope into her bag that she clutched on her lap. Elijah was waxing soft with them, she could tell, and the other shoe was going to drop at any moment. She straightened up in her chair, forcing her mind to be calm and pay attention.

"You're quite right, Ms. Goodman," Elijah said. Looking at Ezra, he continued, "Alright then, I suppose I will begin by letting you know that, although you are just meeting us, we are well aware of you and who you both are," he held up a hand when Ezra began to speak again. "Let me give you some information that will answer many of the questions you have, and when I'm done you may ask whatever you like." Ezra's mouth clamped with a frown. "Mr. Lester is correct when he says that we have not hired in some time. This Agency is older than you could imagine, older than Mr. Lester, even."

Gabriel swatted Elijah's shoulder, "Easy now," he scolded with a giggle.

Elijah repaid with a small grin before he cleared his throat and returned to his stuffy business demeanor, "All joking aside, what we do require of our employees is a certain personality. With a mind that is accepting of what others may scoff at. I assure you that when we were scouting you, we became certain that you are the perfect additions to our team," It was Nora's turn to shift in her seat with frustration. Elijah was speaking in circles and not saying anything that brought clarity to why they were there, "We exist in the darkness because those who we protect, and who protect others from, live there. In the dark shadows that are rarely noticed. Beings who are not as you are. Beings that are a threat to humanity's very existence," Elijah spoke evenly, pointedly.

"So, you catch terrorists and such? I can promise you I'm not qualified to…," Nora stopped when Elijah's eyes turned to her with a stern, raised brow.

"The world itself contains much more than what meets the eye. There are many beings that you are not aware of, yet you have lived side by side with them. They are just as we know humans to be. Some are good, some are not. What we do is protect all the good from the few that are bad. We protect them from monsters. True monsters, just as you've read about in storybooks. In this division of The Firm, we protect, and protect others from, vampires."

Elijah spoke the word as if it was the most normal conversation to be had. He leaned back in his seat pleased, with his hands clasped in his lap, waiting for their response. Nora and Ezra sat in silence, waiting for him to go on. When he didn't, they erupted in laughter. Elijah looked to Gabriel with amusement at their reaction.

"I should have known better than to believe that this was a serious job offer," Nora said looking around for cameras, or to see the Glamor Guards crack a smile. They stood frozen in place.

"Vampires? You expect me to believe that you are vampire hunters?" Ezra pressed a hand to his stomach against another explosion of laughter. "You can't be serious?"

Nora pulled the envelope of bills from her bag, "Is this even real money?" Flipping through the hundreds, they certainly looked real. If it was, she hoped she would be able to keep it when the prank was over and done with.

She shot back against her chair, her legs pulled up protectively when Gabriel again launched onto the desk, this time landing on his feet. Standing above them, he hissed before opening his mouth wide to expose long, razor-sharp canine teeth. "Is this real enough for you?"

CHAPTER THREE

Ezra shrieked, tumbling from his chair beside Nora; braced leg tangled on the armrest and locked him in place. Nora, froze in place, eyes wide and holding her bag tight to her chest. They both stared at the tall man before them who was brandishing a frighteningly sharp pair of fangs.

"How the hell did you do that?" Nora's voice was trembling and breathless.

"Do what? This?" Gabriel flicked his fangs in and out of his mischievous smile, looking quite pleased with their reaction to his reveal.

"What the hell?" Nora pressed herself against the back of the chair and looked down at Ezra. Seeing him struggling to right himself, she leaned over to slip his leg free of the chair and helped to pull him up. He kept one hand on her arm when he sat again, horror blanching his face.

"Are you telling me that you are vampires?" Nora's voice still shook, "This cannot be real."

It had to be a trick. But what was the point of it, if it was? Whether or not it was – Nora could suddenly feel the heavy vibration of danger in every inch of the room. The Glamor Guards moved forward a step, in unison, when Gabriel jumped to the floor and landed at Nora's feet.

Gabriel retracted his fangs once more, "Well, I am a vampire. This guy only wishes he was," he laughed, pointing at Elijah who still sat in his chair, now with irritation burning in his eyes towards Gabriel.

The vampire took two steps back from Nora and gave a sneering glare to the guards who responded by stepping back to their places against the wall without a word. Nora started to wonder who exactly they were there to protect.

"Very helpful, Gabriel," Elijah said flatly, a frustrated look locked firmly on him. "Can you ever contain yourself?"

"I'd forgotten how long you dance around the facts during these meetings. It's info about a *job*, not a poetry reading. Need to know and move on. They're humans. Let's not pretend we're chatting with gods," he snickered and leaned on the heavy desk, "It has been quite a while since I've been a part of this nonsense for good reason, and I still think this is beneath me. I've simply sped up the process," Gabriel grumbled. His mood swings were not easy to follow.

"You've sped up the process? You have nearly killed them with fright!" Elijah shook his head and sighed, annoyed. "Sit over there and let me finish up." He pointed to a sofa against the far wall.

"Only if you make those smelly beasts move," Gabriel pouted at the guards standing on either side of the sofa.

Nora's heart pounded against her chest as she looked around for the beasts that he spoke of. She followed his look of disgust to the gorgeous men and women that made up the circle of guards. How he could be disgusted by such yummy-looking humans, she had no idea. Nora's nose crinkled at thought of why a vampire could find them yummy; as she could be, as well. Her stomach turned. The hidden doors all remained shut, not even a trace of where they appeared from could be seen. She needed to get out of there.

"Fine," Elijah sighed, giving a nod to the guards on either side of the sofa. Without a word, they stepped away, moving to the other side of the windowless room.

"Thank you," Gabriel replied coolly, and moved in a flash, too quick to see, to the couch to recline with his feet up. "Carry on, then."

Watching his speed, Nora knew that she wasn't a part of a prank. Nothing human could move like that. "You're not a very good vampire hunter if you have one lounging around your office," Nora said, trying to keep her voice light while frozen to her seat. Talking her way out of that room was going to be her only option.

"As I said, vampires, as with all other beings, can be good and they can be bad. Not all vampires are out to feast on humans," Elijah ignored the giggle and snort that came from Gabriel and continued, "Some are living lives, just as you and I are, and are merely a product of their situation. Some would say, the more spiritual of the lot, that they are a result of fate. Their destiny, if you will. So, no, we are not here to *hunt* vampires. We are here to deal with the troublemakers. The nefarious beings who take advantage of everyone around them. The ones that see themselves about the rules of their nature."

Nora turned to Ezra when he slowly leaned over, his face tight, eyes narrowed, and locked on her. "Are you buying any of this?" he asked, his voice stronger than expected.

She turned to the man lounging across the sofa, his slippered feet propped up on the armrest, "I mean...the man has retractable fangs and can move faster than a zipper in a brothel, so..." Nora stopped when Gabriel roared with laughter.

"Oh, Elijah! I like this one. Cute and crass — my favorite." Gabriel sat up on the couch, clapping playfully. "Forget what I said about not wanting to be involved with all of this. I want to be the one to give her the serum."

"Gabriel...," Elijah said with warning.

"I call dibs, Elijah. This one is mine," Gabriel crossed his arms, "It is demeaning enough for you to think someone of my stature needs to be a part of what? A basic Familiar's Ascension?" he rolled his eyes at Elijah's glare, "Whatever you want me to say, I should at least get to pick which pet is mine."

Ezra sat at attention, "What the fuck are you all talking about? What serum? And I am no one's pet!" He held a crutch out, ready to weaponize it if he had to.

Nora could hear the fear that shook in Ezra's voice. She was unable to look away from the gleeful vampire that blazed a toothy smile at her as he bounced on the sofa when he called them *pets*. The words 'serum' and 'mine' spun on repeat in her head. There were certain elements of the supernatural world that she had always believed in. Ghosts, curses, witches, and the lot. They were always something that seemed improbable, yet possible. Not like the fear of monsters under her bed that she had outgrown when she was a kid. That being said, she did still make sure to keep her feet under the covers at night.

"What is he talking about? What is a familiar ascension? You aren't going to try and make us...like him, are you?" Nora asked, looking to Gabriel, desperate to stay calm and get out of that room alive.

"Dream on, little lady!" Gabriel roared with laughter, "You watch too many movies, sweetie. No one just *gets* to be a vampire. Agree, take the money, and let's get on with it. You don't need to be looking a gift horse in the face. Your little human mind wouldn't understand the big truths of the real world, anyways."

Nora was sure everyone in the room could hear the pounding of her heart. Especially the overly amused vampire. Ezra was scanning every inch of the walls around them. Nora hoped he could come up with an idea, any idea, to help them. "That's it? You aren't going to tell us more than you're a vampire and we will work for you? What is the serum you're talking about?" she asked, hoping for anything that didn't sound as insane as the last few minutes.

"You're not joining our ranks, missy. You're being offered a position as a Familiar and nothing more. Stop asking so many questions and be grateful for the job," Gabriel barked from across the room, giving Elijah a sharp glare that was impossible to miss. "What? I told you we should have just been straight from the start. You always make things more complicated than they are. We have more important things to deal with and I'm tired Elijah," he pouted and let out a dramatic yawn that made Nora think of Silas.

"Gabriel, that is enough!" Elijah Beasley's voice roared and rippled against the cold marble room, "I will not tell you again." They stared each other down until Elijah broke the knowing look and turned his attention back to Nora. The tension in the room became a physical, hot pressure that radiated from Elijah and pushed against every inch of them, threateningly.

"Please...please don't hurt us..." Nora whimpered, feeling Ezra's trembling hand tightening on her arm. The dim room pulsated with heat and rage in a way that they had never experienced; the bulbs of the sconces flickered, and the lamp on Elijah's desk grew too bright for their eyes.

In the space of half of a heartbeat, Elijah returned to his cordial manner, an affable smile set in place, "Look at the state you have left them in, Gabriel. What a mess," Elijah spoke as he rose from his chair and moved grace-fully in front of his desk. He leaned nonchalantly against it while he ran a manicured hand along his dark, satin tie to smooth it once more. There was something calming about his slow motions and the way he leveled his gaze softly, first to Nora and then to Ezra. The heated, electric energy in the room slipped away, leaving her lungs to drag in slow, concentrated breaths.

Gabriel stood from the sofa, disappointment shading his eyes, unaffected by the chaos the room had erupted into. He flashed a sardonic grin to the guards, who stood stone-faced in place, as he passed, putting a face of bravado to hide the embarrassment of being scolded. Pushing a bare space on the wall, it slid up to reveal a small bar area, filled with crystal decanters and glasses. He picked up what looked like an embellished glass thermos and poured himself a highball glass of a thick crimson liquid. Nora swallowed deeply to keep her stomach contents where they were. Ezra's hand relaxed on Nora's arm until it slipped off and back onto his chair.

"Good. That's better, yes?" Elijah clasped his hands together swiftly and pulled the two from their dazed, contented minds. "I shall just cut to the chase, then. We are B.I.T.N," he said, pronouncing the acronym as bitten.

"Bitten?" Ezra asked and cleared his throat. "As in vampire bites?"

"No, although for this division it does make for a bit of fun, doesn't it?" Elijah beamed and spoke the letters, "B, I, T, N stands for Bureau of Identification and Tracking of Non-mortals. In our division's case, it is specifically dealing with vampires."

"You're not called The Firm?" Nora asked, thinking of the very plain business card she was given.

"We are. That would be the umbrella term for all of the bureaus and their specific divisions as a whole. The actual name is impossible for mortals to pronounce, so we found the simple use of The Firm to be more effective," Elijah said, crossing his arms casually.

"And what do expect from us?" Ezra asked, his voice sounding stronger and surer again. He shot a quick glare at Gabriel, who gave a snorted into his blood-filled glass, obviously not as frightened by the sarcastic predator as Nora was. She wished she could summon more courage at the moment.

"We are responsible for seeing to the assignments that are handed down from our superiors," Elijah answered, making a point to ignore Gabriel. "At times, mortal humans can be of great use to us," Gabriel scoffed again as Elijah continued, "We would like you to become our newest Familiars. You would shadow the ones we have tasked to do the, shall we say, heavy lifting. The more experienced agents who track and eliminate our problems. Your responsibilities to them would be that of helpers. A sort of assistant to deal with their menial needs."

"You're going to pay us this kind of money," Nora patted her bag, "and all you expect us to do is run errands for you guys?" *There was no way that's all they expected of them.* "I don't have to be a human blood bag or sex slave or anything."

Gabriel clucked a laugh and clapped his hands together, "I mean it, Elijah, I have dibs on that one. She is just too much!" He beamed at her, the crimson residue still on his teeth.

Elijah held up his hand to silence Gabriel, who returned one particular finger in response.

"She's right, there's no way you're going to pay us big bucks just to be your lackeys," Ezra added.

Too good to be true was too good to be true. Nora knew that as gospel.

"You will find that money is not an object for The Firm and its Bureaus," Elijah said, raising his arm to gesture to the opulent room around them, "Generosity to the humans that serve us is something we take great pride in."

The money was a strong selling point. The supernatural beings calling the shots were not.

"Are you...are you a vampire, too?" Nora asked Elijah, nervous for his answer. She didn't even know if it was okay to go around and ask folks if they had fangs.

"I am not," Elijah said simply.

"So, you're like one of us? A human?" Ezra asked, shifting uncomfortably in his seat.

"I am not and what I am is of no concern to you at this moment," Elijah replied curtly, pulling out two new documents from a folder. He sat one in front of Nora and then Ezra. It seemed to be more legal-speak, except for an iridescent seal that shimmered impossibly bright. Nora started to reach for it when Elijah held up what appeared to be a long gold pin, about a foot long and sharp as a razor. "If you agree to what I've told you, we just need one little prick of the finger and one little fingerprint, just here," he pointed to the blank line at the bottom of the page, "and we can begin your Ascension with the serum Mr. Lester has mentioned."

"Yum, yum," Gabriel quipped with disgust as if whatever they called the serum was nothing more than sewage.

"Who would like to go first?" Elijah stepped forward expectantly, a folder in each hand.

Purposefully making herself bleed in the presence of a vampire had to be a bad decision. Nora held her hands in fists as if protecting her fingertips from the golden pin. Ezra pushed himself to his feet with his crutches and tossed the envelope of money on the desk with a thud.

"I'm not sure what you guys are playing at, but I've heard just about enough. Thanks for the entertainment, but I'm going to be on my way," he said, turning to Nora, "Are you coming?"

Nora sat frozen in her seat. This was the strangest moment that she had ever found herself in. She wanted to stand and leave with him, not that there was an open door that they could leave from, but it couldn't be that easy. The choice that she had been given at the beginning of the meeting didn't seem to be on the table any longer. It was complete insanity, with the idea of monsters and vampires and yet, there appeared to be just that lounging across the room on a sofa. Ezra stood resolutely beside her as she tried to sort out all that she had witnessed in such a short amount of time.

Elijah gave a slight side glance to Gabriel and moved silently around to the other side of his desk. Lifting the petite lid atop an elaborately engraved gold box, he revealed a well-worn, black button that was built into the tabletop. "If you would like to leave, that is not a problem. It is displeasing, but not a problem."

Pushing the button twice, two sections of the smooth marble wall behind him slid open to reveal small rooms opposite the door that they had originally entered. That door, the one that led to the dingy office, that led to the outside world, and their escape, remained closed. Nora's eyes widened and her jaw went slack when she took in what the newly revealed spaces held: a sturdy-looking metal recliner, like a medieval dentist's chair, with heavy-looking, worn leather straps on the arm and footrests. The ambiance and decor matched the carpet-worn front office much more than the luxe space where she was currently rooted in place.

"You are certainly free to leave, Mr. Davis, as you were told and with your thousand dollars. However, the information you have been privy to does require an Exiting process," Elijah held his hands up protectively when Ezra tensed, and his jaw locked stiffly in defiance. "Now, now, nothing painful, but we can't have you leaving here with the full knowledge of The Firm. I'm sure you understand."

"You're sure I *understand*? Are you kidding me?" Ezra turned towards the wall that hid the door to freedom, limping along on his crutches. He stopped when the guards started to close their circle around him. "Come on, this is crazy!"

"It seems as if we have come to the end of the conversation." Elijah's voice was resigned with disappointment, but his words sounded ominous. He snapped his fingers and Nora found herself lifted to her feet by the hands of two Glamor Guards. They picked her up like she was nothing more than a rag doll. Her pleas for release were drowned out by Ezra's screams to the guards who had moved in on him. There was no way to break free of the strongest grip she had ever felt.

"Let go of me!" Nora screeched, struggling against the iron grips, "Get your goddamn hands off of me!"

In seconds she was moved to the frightening side room to the left, tears blurring her eyes. There was no way out, no one to help her, and she cursed herself for stupidly getting into such a dire situation. There was almost no need for the heavy leather straps that were locked onto her wrists and ankles. She was immobilized by terror and could barely pull in a breath, let alone fight back. She hadn't even decided to say no. She hadn't even stood to leave as Ezra had. Whatever happened next, she hoped it would be quick.

Chapter Four

Gabriel slipped into the room just as the door slid shut in the face of a towering, red-headed, female Glamor Guard. He leaned casually against a tall, metal cabinet and gave her a broad, fanged grin. His eyes scanned her, taking in the sight of her sitting petrified and strapped to the chair. The walls of the room felt too close. Nora's eyes darted back and forth from the vampire to every inch of the mostly empty space, trying to find a way out. The fear that she would become his next meal helped her focus on keeping a rational mind, kicking her into survival mode. As rational as one could be with a vampire standing before you. She started to find the strength returning to her body as she struggled against the thick leather straps that had been placed around her wrists and ankles, although she knew she wasn't strong enough to break them. Her skin burned as she tugged. In a flash of movement that was too swift for her eyes to follow, Gabriel moved to her side. He leaned in close to her trembling face.

"Now, now, Ms. Goodman, no need to be frightened. You are not in danger," his voice was as cool and smooth as ice. His fangs retracted quickly when he saw her staring. "I guess those *would* be a reason to be frightened," he laughed, "but I assure you, I have no intention of harming you. If you want, I could even use my influence to make you feel perfectly at ease."

"Your influence? What the hell does that mean? And if I'm supposed to be at ease, what is the point of this?" Nora flailed her hands within the restraints. Being tied up was not an interview process she had experienced before. It was not doing anything to set her at ease in the closed room with a deadly vampire eyeing her up. "Please don't bite me." Her voice was small, and she couldn't stop herself from cowering; her inner strength retreating once again. There weren't, unfortunately, a lot of other options at the moment.

"Bite you? I'm not going to bite you, Ms. Goodman. I don't eat my *friends* and I hope we can become very good friends," Gabriel tilted his head to the side and giggled, "I suppose that's not true. I have been known to nibble on some special friends, but rest assured you are not my type."

Nora did not feel better with his revelation. There was no way to physically overpower her situation, so she was going to do what she did best: talk. "So, what is all of this, then?" She tried to keep her voice even. "Why are you holding me strapped to a chair? You're an all-powerful vampire, Mr. Lester. I doubt you need to go to this sort of lengths to get humans to do what you want."

"Gabriel is fine. Mr. Lester is so stuffy; and let me say, flattery will get you everywhere with me," he beamed. He did seem as though he would be a fun guy if there wasn't a chance of him turning you into a snack.

"This all just seems like overkill," Nora grimaced at her own choice of wording, "I mean, what do you want from us? There has to be an easier way to get people to work for you. I didn't even say no out there," she swallowed trying to keep her mouth wet enough to keep talking, "I just want to get out of here alive, Gabriel."

"That depends entirely on you, pretty girl," he said, pulling an old, paint-chipped aluminum chair up to her side and sitting. He crossed one long leg over the other, "Mr. Davis was being clear that he wanted nothing to do with us, and unless they can convince him otherwise, his memory of being here and all of us will be stripped from his mind and he'll find himself elsewhere with a surprise envelope of cash in his pocket. That is also your option number one. If you're dumb enough to choose it."

"They're going to do that influence thing you were talking about?" Nora wondered what Ezra was going through at the moment and hoped he wouldn't be harmed. She couldn't hear a thing through the room's concrete walls, which help her imagination run wild with all of the most terrifying images from horror movies that she had ever watched. The aesthetic of this current room was a sharp contrast to the elegant simplicity of the grand office she was just in and the perfect setting for her fear to get creative. Whatever this influence thing was, there would be no one to hear her scream.

"No, not that. He does not have the pleasure of a vampire in charge of his Ascension. His will be...different," Gabriel said, contempt dripping from his voice. Nora did not like the sound of that.

"What is that? You keep saying that word. Ascension?"

"That is option number two, darling," Gabriel's face brightened, "Your Ascension is the beginning of your life with us. Not something a vampire normally takes part in, but we're short on time, short on staff, and honestly, it's a gift I don't think humans are generally worthy of. But I like you, so I won't complain. You should just say thank you, sit back, and feel as lucky as you are."

Lucky was not how Nora would define her current situation. "But what is it? What happens?" Calling it an Ascension did not sound as simple as more paperwork.

To think, she jokingly thought the worst-case scenario would be rich folks that hunted people for sport. She was not that far off. At least she would have had a running start from those nut jobs.

"Like I said, it's a gift. That's all I'm going to say about it." He straightened the lapels of his dressing gown and shifted the silk belt until it lay smooth, "Say yes and I will open your mind with my influence, a vampire's way of *tooting* around in your head, and then I will inject you with the serum that will set in motion the changes in your mind and body. It will help you with your *tasks*," he tossed out the word as if it were draped in air quotes.

If there was an option to let them go with a wiped memory, there did not seem to be a need for restraints. She didn't think there was an option to say no. "What's in the serum?" Nora worked to steady her voice.

"I can't tell you that," Gabriel sighed, his boredom growing.

Nora pressed her lips tightly, trying to think of anything she could say to get out of that chair, out of that building, unscathed, "Well, what will it do to me exactly?"

"I can't tell you that," he picked at a loose thread on his sleeve.

Talking was getting her nowhere, "I'd like to just leave if that's an option. I'm guessing it's not," she leveled her eyes on him, summoning all the inner power she could muster, "So, just tell me what's next or let me go."

He stood, sizing her up, and moved to the cabinet. He slowly opened a drawer with a metal-on-metal screech.

"Ms. Goodman, I can let you go right now if you'd like. You're not being held against your will. Humans just have a way of overreacting that ends up hurting them more than we could ever do. This setup is for *your* protection," Gabriel said calmly, taking a tiny gold vial and a very long syringe from the tall, rusty cabinet, "You should know, though, leaving now would be a very stupid move on your part." Nora stared at the intimidating needle he balanced on his palm. The vampire smiled with humor at her wide-eyed reaction, "It's not as bad as it looks. This gift is a once-in-a-lifetime sort of thing, sweetie." Nora's body stiffened as he walked closer. "Vampires have a way of getting inside your mind and moving things around. I'm sure you've heard of that in one of those silly books or movies. They've almost gotten that part right," Gabriel rolled his dark eyes at the thought, stuck the syringe into the polished gold vial, and pulled back the plunger. His nose twitched with revolt when he set the vial aside. Not a good sign of what it might be. "If you agree to be one of ours, I will use my influence over your mind to open it up to the serum and we'll have you on your way. The other option is that I use my influence to wipe your mind of us and this place, just as it seems it will be happening to Mr. Davis. Although, he is being taken care of by a sloppier bunch of folks that will no doubt make a big to-do about it. I like things cleaner, simpler."

"Is there another vampire that will do the mind trick on him?" Nora worried about what was happening to Ezra. Hopefully, his mind had been wiped and he was on his way. The way Gabriel held the needle expectantly told Nora she was right that option one was not an option at all.

"No, I'm the only vampire that got roped into this nonsense," Gabriel snorted.

"What will happen to me if you wipe my brain of all of this and let me go? Will you all leave me alone?" Packing Silas into Cherry Bomb and driving until they were out of gas, Aumbry Valley disappearing in the rear-view mirror, seemed like heaven on earth.

"I can't tell you that. I'm sure you can make assumptions. You're a smart girl," Gabriel stared at her flatly, balancing the syringe between two fingers.

"For making a damn life-altering decision, you certainly can't tell me much!" Nora's irritation with Gabriel was turning her fear into rage.

Gabriel laughed broadly, "Life-altering decision? Good grief, you humans are so dramatic. Look, we haven't pulled you, or Mr. Hop-along in the next room, out of our asses, Ms. Goodman. Nora...may I call you Nora?" She replied with a glare. "No? Too soon? Suit yourself," he winked and moved to her side, holding the syringe up to the overhead fluorescent light. It was clear as water and shimmered a rainbow of colors like a prism. "We know a great deal about you, your past, your abilities, your limitations, and your...," he raised his brow with a smirk, "current financial situation." Nora didn't like how much information they had on her and knew it was time to shut up and listen. Gabriel tilted his head curiously when she looked to have physically relaxed a touch. "The only way that your life has changed is that you are now aware of us, and we're giving you a golden opportunity to earn some cold, hard, moolah," he rubbed his fingers together indicating cash, "If you're dumb enough to not take advantage of that, that will be on you. Your small life will remain your small life and you can go running home to your vapidly self-centered parents with your tail between your legs."

He knew more about her than she was comfortable with. She looked down at her strapped wrists. "So, no matter what, I'm not getting out of here without you poking around in my brain, right?"

"Oh, I wouldn't dream of missing out on that pleasure," he smiled pleasantly, fangs and all, "But what you seem to be missing, darling is that I'm a fucking vampire and you're merely a human. Your life changed the moment *we* set eyes on *you* and there is nothing you can do about it. I can erase your memory and set you on your way to living your sad, basic life and you'll have no idea of any of this," he spoke with a bored exasperation of the option, "However, what you seem to disregard is that we will still know about you. You will still live in a world where predators live amongst you, and you will have no idea of the danger that you are in," he flicked the syringe will a long, bony finger, "Or, you can join us, accept this gift, and put your life to good use."

"Wait, if you can just wipe all of this from my mind, why the NDA? Why all of the paperwork?" It seemed pointless for all-powerful supernatural beings to need to threaten legal action. It's not as if they'd stroll into court and explain the situation. Taking her life would be more on brand and a lot easier than the court system, anyways.

Gabriel tossed his back, laughing at her question, "It is ridiculous, isn't it? It is pointless, meaningless! The truth is that Elijah has a silly obsession with humans, especial-ly the business practices," he laughed again, harder, "You have to have noticed the stacks of papers and folders all over his desk? He tries to play it off as if he just doing things differently to make the humans more comfortable adjusting to us all, but he's really just playing office by adding all of that in. Isn't he the cutest? I guess doing this job for as long as he has, he does what he can to make it fun. That being said, even his ideas of fun are the most boring things you can think of."

When she had woken up that morning, real and unreal had been a lot easier to differentiate. No matter what ridiculous situation she could have come up with, the reality of what she was currently sitting in would not have come close. Elijah was a demon who pretended to be human at work. Gabriel Lester was a vampire who would crack jokes from one side of his mouth and flash fangs from the other. He also seemed like the type to lose interest in a new toy, which happened to be her at the moment, quite quickly. She knew she had to say yes or no at that moment, while he was smiling, even if it meant Gabriel would do as he pleased anyway. It seemed prudent to stay on the right side of the pow-erfully undead. Walking away seemed like the best bet and the thousand dollars would help her out for a short while. That is, if they kept their word and that even happened. She knew Gabriel was right. What would stop them from coming after her again? Or any of the other supernatural things she didn't even know about that already lurked in the world? If they could wipe her mind of their existence, they could wipe her memory of the much-needed cash, as well, and she would end up where she started. Although now she would have made herself an enemy of literal monsters.

Nora looked up at the vampire. The real, in the flesh vampire. "I'm sorry. I know this is all just a day at the office for you, but for me? I didn't even know vampires were real when I woke up this morning."

"We are, sweetheart," Gabriel held his arms out in a flourished display, "Not all are as fabulous as this one, unfortunately."

"Vampires can be awake during the day, too?" Nora remembered the only window she had found was the tiny one beside Pearl that overlooked the alley. Maybe they could be up during the day as long as they weren't in the light. The idea of walking around with a twenty-four/seven threat of blood-suckers was a little too frightening.

"I can't tell you that."

"Of course, you can't," Nora said with frustration. Why would he give any insight into his life to his possible prey? There were so many different versions of vampires in books, movies, and tv. Which ones were more like the real ones? The real ones. The real, in the flesh vampires like the one that had his full focus on her at the moment. *How could vampires be real?*

She looked at Gabriel and, for the first time, really noticed his eyes. They had seemed black as the night before. Now she could see a shining layer that glowed in the light. They looked more like her cat's eyes than a human's. She found herself drawn into the glow and closed her eyes tightly to break the spell.

"You know, what? I like you. I really do. You have a fire inside of you that intrigues me," he said, gently placing the needle on a tray atop the cabinet, "and since I can wipe your brain at any moment, I'm going to be completely honest with you, okay? But you have to promise not to tell Elijah, not that you could. He's being so stiff about," he narrowed his eyes, pressing his lips tightly for a moment as if to stop himself from continuing. "Well, not that it matters. I'll just give you a little taste of our world and wipe away what I need to, right?" He watched Nora staring back at him, "Get ready to have your mind blown!" Nora pushed back against the chair that trapped her when Gabriel sat quickly beside her, his manic energy returned, "Why not? Let's dish! So, you already know I'm a vampire," he flashed his fanged smile, "but you don't know what Elijah is, do you?" he lifted his finger to his lips, "Shh, it has to be our little secret," he winked before continuing, "That tightly wound man out there is a *demon*! More specifically, a drude, I guess," his mouth popped open with excitement at the reveal, "He used to be all about nightmares and such. He's a night man, like me," Gabriel flirted up an eyebrow, "He's my rude drude with attitude!" Nora didn't realize she was holding her breath as more revelations poured from the gossipy vampire. "He's more into the business end of power, now though. He's a happy little paper pusher," Gabriel paused thinking of other secrets to divulge, "Oh! And that serum?" he pointed to the needle, "That's a concoction of fae blood. That's why it smells so bad. Just like those smelly fae out there guarding the building."

Nora's mouth opened and closed like a fish before she could form words, "Fae, as in fairies? It's blood?" Her mind tried to process the existence of demons and fairies even as he carried on with his confessions.

"You got it, lovely. I simply can't stand the disgusting odor that drips from them. No vampire can, really," Gabriel said, and mocked vomiting before turning his smile back on, "Oh, this is fun! I do love talking to humans. It's like talking to a pet. It makes you feel better, and you know they can never tell anyone your secrets." He stood from the chair before continuing, "Just like how you chat with your little pussy cat. Silas, is it?"

Nora squirmed at the details this man seemed to know of her.

"Although with humans I do have to erase your little minds to make sure that happens, don't I? If I choose to keep them alive that is," he sauntered over to the tray and picked up the syringe, tilting his head. His mirrored eyes were locked on her. Her head spun with his constant mood changes. "And as for how I'm awake in the daytime, that is purely your fault as I am still standing here waiting for your basic little human mind to make a very easy decision and allow me to retire for the day," he stretched his arms dramatically and yawned, before moving in a blink to be nose-to-nose with Nora, "My patience is running thin."

Nora's heart raced as tears silently burned down her cheeks, "Please, I just want to leave. I don't want to die." She pulled her arms tense against the restraints, knowing there was nothing she could do.

"Die? You're not going to die!" Gabriel laughed at the thought, "At least not at my hand. You need to calm yourself, girl. I swear humans are more dramatic than banshees." He stepped back and softly brushed his ice-cold hand down her cheek, dragging away the tears, "I just want you to know the reality of the world that you live in. It just so happens that before we met, you were ignorant to the fact that you are only alive because we allow it. Do you realize that now?" His words didn't make her situation seem any better, but there was a genuine affection in his voice that felt out of place with what he was saying, "Your eyes are just being opened to a different ebb and flow of what life is outside of your little bubble of a life. You're not going to die, but the world as you know it has come to an end, and that's not as bad as it sounds. Everything we love ends. Life, a good meal, an incredible orgasm. It's fine. We move on. But some things end and bring you new joy, like suffering, and storms, and your own ignorance. You can keep the end of your sad little life and begin again anew with a real purpose, or you can put your head back up your little human ass and never know when we're right around the corner."

"So now, I'm either with you or against you?" As she spoke the words, she knew they were two sides of the same coin and not choices. There was too much that she didn't know and there didn't seem to be any time left.

"All I'm saying is that we've always been there, and we always will be, sweetie. We hide in plain sight, the best and the worst of us, so it's not our fault if you were unaware of the dangers. I'm offering to help you see the world as it is. Every answer that I can provide you resides within this," Gabriel said and held up the syringe. It will also give you increased strength, and speed, and heighten your senses. It can be a lot of fun for you humans."

"Strength? Is it fairy steroids or something?"

Strength was something she could use at the moment.

"No," Gabe said with a roar of laughter, "But I do hope you'll take it. I'm not going to make you do anything you don't want to, but if you don't take this shot, I'm not responsible for what happens to you when you walk out that door. None of us will be. Don't be stupid, Nora. Honestly, you are just too much of a treat to not keep around."

Nora tried to force a smile in response to what he seemed to deem a compliment. She didn't like a crazy vampire calling her a treat. "If I do agree to take that stuff and work for you, then what?" She knew that there were miles of information that he wasn't telling her and even more that she wouldn't be able to comprehend.

"If you agree, and I truly hope you do," Gabe's face lit up with excitement, "then I shall look deep into your lovely brown eyes until you are under my influence and then I will infuse you with the essence in this serum."

"You wouldn't scramble my brain or anything, would you? I don't want anyone messing around in my head." The influence crap seemed to be the one thing that was going to happen, either way, so she wanted some reassurance.

"Stop being dramatic, I wouldn't be scrambling anything. I love your weird little brain just as it is. All I will do is open your mind to allow the serum to take effect."

Nora hated that she was intrigued, "And there's no way to just be a familiar without that stuff?"

"Nope." Gabe laughed his little giggle, "Admit it, you want this. All of this. The adventure, excitement, and mystery! I know you want the paycheck," he grinned rubbing his fingers together, again. "I think you have great promise in being an asset to us. To the agency. You also need to appreciate that you are being given a choice here, Ms. Goodman. So many are not," his voice flattened with the last statement.

Nora was uncomfortable being paid such a thick compliment from someone who should know nothing of who she was. She wondered how long they had been following her. Looking into her life. She wondered how much they knew and felt ill at the idea of being watched. Her life had been permanently altered. They would always be able to watch her.

Gabriel watched her struggle with the realization, rolling the syringe on his palm, "To be honest, I don't think you want to go back to things being as they were. Struggling to live a life that bored you to your core. Having no purpose, no friends, no ambition, no known future. How long did it take you to even get your ass in college? I think you want this opportunity. I think you are desperate for it. I know you miss the cushy life you had under your parents' golden roof. Wouldn't it be nice to never have to worry about going back and groveling to your cold, loveless mother and father again, Ms.

Goodman?" The mention of her parents again had her sitting up as straight as the restraints would allow. They knew about her parents, they knew about her cat, they knew about her lack of money; what didn't they know? Everyone she ever knew could be in danger because she showed up for a damn job interview.

Nora knew at that moment that she was going to go through with it.

He was going to mess around in her head, no matter what. Going along with his wishes seemed the safest choice for her and everyone she knew. There was no way that they would put that much effort into learning about her to just let her walk away. Whatever this all was, whatever their true intentions were wanted with her, she worried who all could be in danger if she didn't go along with what he wanted. Jenny and Olivia's innocent faces crept into her thoughts.

"Fuck it. Do it," Nora squeezed her eyes closed, leaning back against the back of the chair. There was barely a moment to regret her choice before Gabriel was looming, an inch from her face. She could feel his close presence as if a cool breeze was lingering in front of her, even though there was no breath from him. Her lungs held onto the air as if it was the last breath she would take.

"You have to open your eyes for this part, Ms. Good-man." Gabriel cooed.

Her eyes slowly opened to see Gabriel's broad, pointed grin, and dark, focused eyes right in front of her face. The glow started as a pinprick in the center of his pupil and slowly swirled into his iris. In an instant, comfortable darkness overtook and enveloped her. Her body felt as if it had fallen into a cozy slumber that had her floating down from a balmy sky. She couldn't remember why it was happening or where she was falling from or to where, but it didn't matter. It felt so good. So safe. So calm. Everything was going to be alright. Forever, just as she was. The emotions that had been taking her to the highest levels of fear and down to the lowest level of uncertainty were gone. A haze of contentment wrapped around her protectively. Going forward, she would be okay. She knew it in her core, although she didn't know why.

A cold shock through her veins had her snapping back to reality and in the chair. A deep aching pain throbbed in the side of her neck, and she reached up expecting to find blood.

"You son of a bitch! Did you fucking bite me?" She pulled her hand away, finding no spilled blood. Touching the site again, her fingers rubbed at a slight lump that was swollen on the side of her neck. She realized that the restraints were no longer on her wrists or ankles.

"I don't eat my co-workers, Ms. Goodman. I would not dare be that intimate with someone I work with!" Gabriel smiled slyly and winked from the chair he now sat on in the corner of the small room, "Gah, always the drama queen, it was just the serum. How are you feeling?"

The pain lessened to nothing more than a pinch as she took inventory of her body. Arms and legs could move, eyes could focus. Everything seemed just as before other than her neck and the freedom to move her arms and legs. She paused, curious, and ran her tongue over her ever-aching molar – that no longer ached! Reaching up, she ran a finger over it. No sensitivity at all.

"Did you fix my tooth?" Of all the impossible things of the day, this one was a win.

"Me? No. I may have a proclivity for seeing you humans squirm but I'm not a dentist," he humored and flashed his fangs, "If you were having issues with your tooth the serum would have corrected it. One of its many benefits," Gabriel replied, lazily crossing his legs. His frenetic energy from earlier seemed to have worn off. His pale face had greyed, and his red-rimmed eyes were heavy with exhaustion. Whatever had happened when she was out had taken a lot out of him. He looked as if he had been awake for days.

"I'm not a vampire or anything, now, am I?" Nora felt around her canine teeth which seemed to be the same as always.

"You are not a vampire, Ms. Goodman. I have not bitten you. I have not turned you. I will never do either to you," he said with bored frustration, "You seriously need to get past that." He yawned widely, fangs shimmering in the dim light of the room.

"So sorry," Nora snorted, "How silly of me to find any of this unusual." She slowly stood up, glad to find that her legs didn't shake. "What exactly just happened?"

"You were mesmerized by the influence of *moi* and infused with the serum. After an evening of rest, you'll be ready to start being of use tomorrow," Gabriel stood tall, a look of satisfaction washing over him.

The door behind Nora slid open. She noticed her bag tossed against the wall and picked it up before starting towards the door. A nervous feeling of uncertainty washed over her. Could it be that easy? "So, I can just go?"

Gabriel tilted his head, his eyes narrowed with a thought he didn't care to share flashing in his eyes. "Yes, dear. Off you go. I've barely had a nap today and looks this good requires a lot of beauty sleep," he fluffed at his thinning white hair, "Please speak to Pearl in reception for the information you require to begin this new chapter in your life. Welcome to the BITN Bureau, Ms. Goodman."

The relief of escape flooded her with excited adrenaline. "Don't you mean Agent Goodman?" she asked with an awkward chuckle, making her way quickly to the door that led back into Elijah's opulent office space. There was a lift in her voice and a bounce in her step; she felt invigorated. All of the paralyzing fear that had gripped her seemed to have magically evaporated.

"Agent? Let's not get ahead of ourselves, sweetie. Remember that you're merely a familiar." Gabriel wagged a finger at her.

"Oh sure, my bad. Baby steps into the secret paranormal world." She paused to reach into her thoughts to see if she found anything different, or information that seemed new. "I don't feel any different, by the way. I don't think your brain juice took."

As she finished the last word, Gabriel flashed his fangs and moved toward her at lightning speed. Her body reacted before she could calibrate what was happening. Lunging out of his path, she somersaulted twice and nimbly landed on her feet. Her body was crouched, ready for another attack.

"You sure about that, Ms. Goodman? Seems to be working quite well." Gabriel smiled like a proud papa and strolled out to Elijah's desk in the next room. "Although you stink like shit now, thanks to that swill," he crumpled his nose. Picking up a file, he turned to Nora who was still squatted in place, trying to understand what her body had just done. "I'm sure you are aware that you are not to speak to anyone about us and your new employment status, but if you are forced to speak of anything," in a blink he was crouched toe to toe with Nora, "...you will refer to us only as The Firm. Understood?"

Nora nodded as best as her neck would allow.

Gabriel stepped back, his expression brightening, "Ugh, seriously, I hope the smell is worn off by tomorrow or I'm taking a personal day." He shook his head as Nora gave herself a sniff. She couldn't smell anything different, "In any case, I'm quite looking forward to working with you, Ms. Good...," he stopped and looked at her with a cheeky grin, "...*Nora*. Elijah certainly was more than right about you. You're going to be a fun little kitten to play with."

One moment he was there and the next he was gone from the room in a blur. Yet another magically appearing door slid shut before she had even realized it had opened for him. The vast marble chamber that made up

Elijah Beasley's office was seemingly empty. No Glamor Guards, no Elijah, no Ezra. Nora cautiously stepped out of the side room. The second side room door remained closed, as was the one they had originally entered through.

"Hello?" Nora called out with an echo, "How do I get out of here?" She walked to the section of the wall that had revealed the door leading to the dingy reception room and could not find a handle to slide it open again. She knocked, "Hello?"

The side door to the second creepy chair room slid open behind her, making her jump. Elijah coolly strode out, gave her a polite nod, and left through the same door that Gabriel had. As soon as it shut, the door to the reception slid open. Nora started towards it until she heard footsteps behind her. Turning hastily, she found Ezra Davis walking out of the frightening side room, a look of awe across his pale face. He walked freely without the cumbersome brace on his leg.

He looked up to see Nora and gave her a baffled smile before he was able to speak, "What the hell was that?"

CHAPTER FIVE

Pearl looked up briefly from lighting another cigarette to hand Nora and Ezra each a file folder. She made herself clear that they were only to look at the contents when they were safely at home and alone. She repeated it twice and paused until they both nodded with acknowledgment. Telling them to report back to the office at nine PM the next day, she watched with amusement as the dazed pair wandered out of the office.

"That's PM, kids. As in nighttime," she called out to them.

They walked in stunned silence to the elevator and then out onto the street.

"This is all too surreal. I mean, did any of that just happen?" Nora stood frozen in front of the innocuous-looking building. "It would make more sense if it was a gas leak or maybe I had a stroke?" The slight ache that remained in her neck at the site of the injection told her otherwise.

"Can two people have the same stroke? Because if not, it has to be a gas leak," Ezra said, scrubbing a hand through his hair, his face twisted with disbelief. He looked down and leaned his weight on his now healed leg. "Seriously? How?"

Everything on the street looked as it always did. People in cars, on bicycles, and walking down the sidewalk as they made their way through their mundane daily routines; completely unaware of the monsters that were perched on the top floor of the building that rose beside them. The sun above shone down on them, well past the eastern sky where it sat when Nora had entered the office. Looking at her watch, she saw that the time was nearly five in the afternoon.

"We were up there for almost eight hours!" Nora exclaimed and watched Ezra check his wristwatch, "I could swear it was only an hour or two." A creeping feeling slithered over her at the thought of being unconscious for that long. Alone in a room with a vampire. She automatically ran her hands over her neck again, as if she may have missed bite marks earlier. She scanned Ezra's neck and found nothing unusual.

"What the hell have we gotten ourselves into? And they just let us walk out, knowing what we know?" Ezra stared back at the door they had just exited, "This is too much." He bounced his weight on his leg again.

"I thought you weren't going to go through with it." His eyes didn't look like he had been given a supernatural lobotomy. They were wide with the same shock and awe as Nora's. He had been given the same file, currently gripped tightly in his hand, just as she had, and was told to come back, just as she had. He must have agreed. Which did not seem to be how he was leaning when he was dragged into his restraint chair room.

Did they do the magic brain-scramble on him even though he said no?

The thought frightened Nora and solidified the fact that these beings really could do whatever they wanted to them. The friendly smiles and banter hid the truth: they were trapping humans to do their bidding. Although, they did somehow heal her broken tooth and Ezra's busted leg.

"It feels better than before I broke it," Ezra said, seeming to notice her staring down at his leg, "It's the strangest thing," he paused in thought, mindlessly rubbing his thigh, "I was one hundred percent against being a part of this," his eyes narrowed, trying to clear the fog that had settled over what he had just experienced.

"Did you change your mind or did they...," Nora did not want to think that they would make him do anything against his will, but she knew they could. In her heart was sure they would. The feeling of contentment that she felt under Gabriel's gaze washed over her memory. She could have agreed to anything at that moment. She worried that she may have.

Ezra shifted his eyes from Nora, "No. I was able to, I don't know. Calm down, I guess? And then Elijah must have explained things better. I don't know, I guess I'm all in just like you." He shrugged with a small, baffled smile, "Whatever all of that was, I feel so good! I feel strong, you know? So much damn energy!"

She was doubtful that a simple conversation could have made him do a complete one-eighty. He seemed content in the outcome, either way, and it was comforting to know that she was not going to be alone for whatever was to come. Ezra still did not meet her gaze, lost in the amazement of how he felt.

"How did they do it? I mean, did you have the needle and stuff?" Nora lowered her voice when a boy nonchalantly pedaled past on a bike.

Ezra snapped back into the moment when the bike whizzed by and he looked at his watch again, "It's almost five. I need a drink. Want to go somewhere we can talk, uh, about..." He waved his hands about as if to say *all of this insanity.*

"Like real-life fucking Vampires?" Nora asked in a whisper.

Ezra's eyes widened and he shook his head in disbelief. "And that creepy-ass chair! Were you strapped down with the leather straps on one of those chairs, too?" Ezra clamped his mouth shut when a woman passing by appeared scandalized by his words. She stomped past them with a huff. "I don't think we should be talking about this here. Do you have a car? I came by taxi."

Nora pointed to Cherry Bomb still parked in front of the building. They climbed in while Ezra told her how excited he was to be able to drive again, now that his leg was back to normal. He prattled on quickly, obviously overwhelmed. His voice was white noise when Nora took note of the fuel gauge still sitting at full. If they had been following them, learning about them, could the sudden appearance of a full tank of gas be from them? To make sure she made it to the interview? It would explain the seat being moved. If they had been messing with her car, what else had they done? They could have been in her apartment, and she would never know. It's not like Silas could let her know. She jumped when Ezra slapped his hands on his legs, excitedly.

"I can't remember ever feeling this hungry! Do you like Mexican food?" Ezra asked and gave quick directions when Nora nodded. She hadn't spoiled herself with restaurant food in months, not that there were a lot of options in the tiny town. Silas being her only friend, it was better to eat at home than alone in a restaurant. Basic groceries and rent took up enough of her limited funds, anyways. She didn't need to seek out places that would just tempt her. Reaching into her bag to feel the fat envelope of cash safely still stashed, there was a brief moment of relief that she let wash over her. She buckled up over her bag, not wanting to let go of the security that money brought to her. She pulled away from 1365 Beech Avenue and followed Ezra's brief directions to the restaurant.

The sun faded awning along the building proclaimed the restaurant to be The Dirty Cantina and had the worn exterior to match the name. It gave Nora a distinct vibe of incoming food poisoning. Skirting a nervous glance at Ezra, she found him looking thoroughly amused at her unease. "Are you used to fancier places?" he teased as they walked up to the entrance.

"Hardly," she scoffed, making the bell above the door jangle as she tugged it open. Her cheeks reddened at the thoughts of the extravagant restaurants and events she had been accustomed to as a child. That is when her parents bothered to drag her along. Her past was not something she was going to dredge up with Ezra, at the moment. Even with everything they had to process from the day, she was going to stick with the plan to rebuild her life far away from every aspect of her past. Either way, she was not going to be taken down by a dive bar after surviving a day with a vampire. "I just don't think contracting salmonella is a fun way to end an already insane day."

"It's a great restaurant, trust me," Ezra followed her in and guided her over to a corner booth. The interior was much more vibrant and cleaner than the exterior would have implied. Much like BITN's office building. Nora remembered Ezra had mentioned his family had owned a restaurant in his hometown so he must have some insight into good food.

"What kind of restaurant does your family own?" Nora asked, settling into the booth.

"It's a breakfast joint. Bacon and eggs and pancakes and the like. Meg's Eggs. It's named after my mom," he answered with a wistful smile before a memory darkened his eyes. His shoulders tightened, as he shifted in his seat, his healed leg bouncing in place, "With both of my parents gone, my sister and her wife run it now." He stared at the table, not offering more.

Nora was deciding if she should push further when a pretty brunette waitress with a friendly grin stopped at the table and greeted Ezra by name, setting a basket of fresh chips and salsa on the table, along with menus, "Start with the usual?"

Snapping from his thoughts, he nodded up to her, "Yeah, that would be great, Sarah," he turned to Nora with a smile that he was working hard to force brightly, "Did you want a drink? They have a small-batch craft beer here that's top-notch: Bitter Bruja."

"Sure, sounds good," Nora nodded to the waitress. When she turned to the bar, Nora gave her attention back to Ezra who was again staring at the table in silent thought. The manic adrenaline that had been flowing through them as they left The Firm was starting to wear away. They sat, staring blankly at the menus in front of them. Sitting in silence had always made Nora uncomfortable. She picked at the paper placemat in front of her, her tight, uneasy stomach not wanting anything the menu offered. Whatever memory of home he had gotten himself stuck in had switched Ezra's mood to a quiet brooding. Nora clucked her tongue, awkwardly looking around the room at the few other patrons. Her eyes landed on the bar, where Sarah the waitress was filling their glasses.

"Wait, did you say Bitter Bruja?" Nora asked Ezra with a laugh.

"Yeah," Ezra answered with a questioning curiosity.

"Doesn't Bruja mean witch in Spanish?" Nora's eyes widened, hoping he would see the humor in it.

Ezra's lip twitched into a crooked smile, "It does. I guess it's quite suitable for today, isn't it?"

"I couldn't think of something better if I had the energy to try," Nora started to laugh and had a hard time reining it in. The weight and chaos of the day poured out in a fit of laughter that shook her shoulders and burned every muscle in her stomach. It was even contagious to Ezra who couldn't help but feel lighter at the sight of Nora busting a gut.

Even the waitress was not immune when she returned with their drinks, "What's so funny?" she asked with a grin.

"Sarah, you wouldn't believe it if you heard it," Ezra answered and kicked off the second round of hysterics. Sarah gave them a quizzical look before leaving them to their outburst. When they finally caught their breath, Nora looked around to confirm that there wasn't anyone within earshot. The waitress had retreated to the kitchen and the closest customers were a couple that sat well across the room beside the front window. She wondered if anyone else in the restaurant had any idea of what was happening right under their noses. Could any of them be fully aware and just going about their lives among the creatures of the night that she now knew of? Could they be something other than human? On the surface, they all looked like regular people. What was real and what was not would be a difficult call moving forward with their new normal. *Normal.* Not what she would consider vampires, demons, and fairies, but here she was.

"How are we dealing with all of this so well? Shouldn't we be running home and hiding under our beds, or something? How are we sitting here sipping witch beer and chatting like it's simply a night out? After what we learned today? After what we saw today?" Nora looked around the restaurant, wondering if anyone else could know what was happening under everyone's nose in the tiny town. She wondered if the others were even people. There was a chance that they not only knew, but they could also be a part of the supernatural community that she was now aware of. The few other patrons to the cantina seemed to be plain old humans. Was there even a way to tell if they weren't? She took a long gulp of her beer. Ezra was right, it was one of the best she'd had, even though she preferred wine.

Taking a deep breath to compose himself, he looked Nora in the eyes, staring for a moment, astonished. "I don't know. I honestly don't know. I feel better being here than alone in my house with my thoughts, after today. I can tell you that much."

"Yeah," Nora agreed quietly. The idea of being alone at the moment, without witnesses, was frightening. The peaks and valleys of her emotions were starting to exhaust her.

"All that I know is as soon as I was in that chair my whole body just relaxed. I felt...I guess, accepting of it? It all just made a lot more sense. Even though I can't explain a moment of it. I was so...angry," he paused, his eyes moving back and forth in search of the foggy memory, "and then I wasn't."

Nora moved closer, keeping her voice as low as she could, "What did they do to you? Gabriel said it would be different not having a vampire do the thing...the Ascension," Nora asked and took another sip of her beer.

"I don't remember much until I came to," Ezra stared at the table, "Elijah and I spoke and then a few of those guards came in, and..." Ezra stilled as he dug into the lost moment, "I just don't know. Everything went super dark, and I felt like was falling asleep, but I could feel the chair and the straps," his hands flattened on the table, his body remembering the moment more than his mind, "The next thing I know, I felt like I was having the best..." his cheeks flushed, and he leaned closer to her, "you know...sex," his eyes were wide, and an embarrassed grin bent his lips. He paused to make sure they were still out of everyone's earshot, "It was like nothing I could imagine. No one was touching me, or even near me. Then it stopped as quickly as it started. When I did wake up, I felt like I had downed two pots of coffee and my heart was going to explode. I thought the straps on the chair were going to rip through me because I couldn't stop pulling against them," he took a long chug from his glass, "and then I just relaxed, and the room came into view again. Elijah was the only other person left in the room. He took off the straps and told me to come back tomorrow." He rubbed at his now healed leg and looked up when Nora didn't speak. "Isn't that what happened to you?"

"Not really. I guess Gabriel can do it differently. I just felt sort of stoned and calm, and then woke up to a pain in my neck from the shot," she said and touched the small dot that remained on her neck.

"Shot? What shot?" Ezra looked at the tiny puncture mark on her neck. He felt around on his neck and didn't find anything. Nora looked him over and didn't see a mark, either.

"You didn't get a shot? How did you get the serum?" Gabriel's confessions popped up and her eyes grew wide, "Was it the fairies? The Glamor Guards?" She played his words over in her mind and was surprised that she hadn't made her forget.

A mix of concern and confusion washed over Ezra's face, "I'm sorry, the *what*?"

"Gabriel told me they're fairies, those sugar-smelling guards that were there!" Nora looked around, as well, to make sure no one overheard the insane words that were coming out of her mouth and continued in an even more hushed voice, "The serum, he said it's fairy blood." Ezra stared back at her slack-jawed. "And Elijah Beasley? He's a bloody demon! He called it something else, too. Drudge, or dude...drude! Whatever the hell that is." Nora was still in disbelief that someone that looked so harmlessly charming could be a demon straight up from hell.

Ezra sat blank-faced and blinking, silently trying to process what she had just said. When he finally returned to the moment, he shook his head in resignation, "What the hell have we gotten ourselves into? How could all of this be secretly around us forever and we had no idea. How could we never have any idea or any encounter..." his eyes darkened with a step closer to remembering something that was hiding in the shadows of his mind, just out of reach. He shook his head, frustrated.

"What is it? There's something you're not telling me," Nora pushed. If they were to survive their new world together, keeping secrets was not a good place to start.

"I don't know. It's just...I don't know. I know it's something that Elijah said, but I can't..." he trailed off and avoided Nora's questioning eyes by flagging down Sarah as she came out of the kitchen. Even though she knew it was none of her business, Nora didn't like that he might be hiding something. Not if he was going to be her only ally among supernatural predators. It could be that they messed around in his brain too much, and that was the strange option he hoped for rather than not being able to trust him. From what she could tell, Elijah was not as forthcoming about things as Gabriel had been. What if they had forced him to join them and wiped it from his brain? The idea was so violating. Going against her nature, she forced herself to swallow the hundreds of follow-up questions she was desperate to ask. He either couldn't or wouldn't tell her what happened. It wasn't worth pressing him if he would only get upset. She chewed the inside of her cheek to keep her mouth shut.

When the waitress arrived at the table, Ezra handed her his menu. "I'm going to go with the chicken tacos with cilantro rice, today. Thanks. You know what, make that a double order," he requested and turned to Nora, "I'm starving. What are you gonna get? Everything here is good."

Nora could tell he was actively trying to make his voice even and casual. It was something that she knew they would have to do a lot in the future. The thousand dollars that sat happily in her purse softened the blow of that realization. Not that she didn't have a lot of experience with false smiles and pretending to be content. Her childhood prepared her for that. She wondered if that was one of the reasons The Firm had pulled her from her obscure life and shone their menacing spotlight on her.

She picked up the menu, looking over the options that she had been blankly staring at. For the first time since she was in college, she could order anything that she wanted. To her surprise, she found herself feeling the exact opposite of Ezra. She wasn't hungry in the least, even though everything looked delicious. Her stomach had no intention of accepting anything but the beer that she sipped. Handing the menu to Sarah, she decided on a cup of coffee. A second beer sounded good. After what she had been through a third and fourth beer sounded good, but not on an empty stomach. She still had to drive Ezra home and get herself safely locked in her apartment, so it was not the best time to get a strong buzz going.

"Are you sure? The food here really is excellent," Ezra asked, seeming surprised that she didn't seem as hungry as he was.

"I believe you. It smells amazing. I'm just not hungry at all. I'll just nibble some chips." Nora picked one up and cracked it in half. She wasn't even hungry for that.

"Okay, I guess just my tacos then, please," Ezra said to Sarah, and she turned on her heel to place his order.

They sat quietly for a moment before her need to break the silence overtook her, "How did you end up moving here? Aumbry Valley is kind of in the middle of nowhere," Nora asked, poking her chip around in the salsa. He could always refuse to answer her questions, but he may as well get used to her talkative nature. They were on the ground together in the strangeness of the new world that they found themselves in and Nora knew that they would have to lean on each other.

Ezra paused, thoughtfully taking a long draw from his beer. Luckily, he didn't appear to shut down and Nora was happy when he started to speak. "That's kind of a long and complicated story, best left for another day." He smiled when Nora sighed with frustrated curiosity and looked her over, "I'm thinking you aren't from here, either?"

"Why would you think that?" Nora asked, impressed that he would know that. Ezra took a lock of her fading fire-engine red hair that had slipped from her elastic and tugged at it.

"You don't exactly have the look of someone that's born and bred in a small town, and you don't seem like you're planning on leaving if you're willing to take a job with...," Ezra lowered his voice, *"vampires and demons. This seems like a town you have to choose to be in."*

Nora nodded. He seemed quite astute at reading people, "It seems to be a town that can trap you, as well," she added. They were the flies on the web now. Only time will tell what the spiders do with them.

He continued, "That's becoming clear, isn't it," he shook his head at all that had started to be revealed before pressing a grin into his lips, "Also, there is no way that you could have grown up here and not know about this restaurant," he gave a short laugh when Nora nodded in agreement, "So, I'm thinking you've come here to either escape from something or to find something. That's what towns like this are perfect for."

Nora risked him clamming up and pressed again him for more while he was being more open, remembering he had said he was looking for a fresh start, "What's your deal, then? Escaping or searching?"

"A little of both, I guess," Ezra replied, picking at the coaster under his beer.

That was all she was going to get. There was a sadness in his eyes that told Nora it wouldn't be kind to pull at whatever his reason was. "I came here hoping to find my Aunt Quinn. She moved out here and I was hoping to reconnect with her. She was like a big sister to me, growing up."

"Do you think she knows anything about the…uh…The Firm?" Ezra took another long gulp of his beer.

"I have no idea, but I hope not. I do know that she wouldn't know anything about my new role with them. Quinn has no idea about my life anymore. She wasn't even here when I got here a few months ago." Nora swallowed the angry pit that started to grow in her stomach. She had pushed Quinn out of her mind shortly after she had decided to settle in Aumbry Valley alone. There was a point when she had hoped her disappearing from her life was a lesson. That she was trying to teach Nora about striking out on her own and would appear at her door with a bottle of wine and a hug when she succeeded. It did not take long until she admitted that it was just flighty Quinn being flighty Quinn and that Nora cared a great deal more for her aunt than she did for her.

"Where did she go?" Ezra asked. He didn't seem to have an issue prying for details while holding his personal cards close to his chest. Instead of being bothered by that, Nora felt a slight kinship. She wasn't the only nosy one at the table. They may just have enough in common to make the best of their surreal new jobs.

"No idea," Nora gulped the last of the beer in her glass. She didn't want to think of Quinn anymore. Another silence settled over them, this time more comfortably. The frustrating feelings toward her aunt were swallowed by the incredible moments of the day that she shared with the stranger who sat beside her. Vampires, demons, fairies, the hours that she has no recollections of. "It happened, didn't it? Vampires are real, aren't they?" Nora thought of how quickly Gabriel could move, the flame that seemed to dance in his eyes when he was so close that their noses were almost touching. His fangs. His razor-sharp fangs.

"I feel like a fool to agree with you, but I've seen some crazy things before that I think there is nothing to do but believe them. Cautiously, at least." Ezra's attention remained on his empty glass until Nora spoke again.

"What do you mean you've seen crazy things? Crazier than today?" Nora could not begin to imagine anything stranger.

Ezra gave another uncomfortable pause, regret for his words clear on his face. His eyes went back to the table, another memory that he refused to share playing across his eyes. "You know how life is. There are things you can't explain, you know?"

"I don't think there is anything I've ever seen that was even close to as weird as what happened today," she leaned closer, "What have you seen?"

Ezra threw his head back, swallowing the few drops of beer that were left, and loudly clanged it on the coaster. He looked at Nora with a tight smile, "Nothing I want to talk about right now."

Nora sat back against the booth, mentally scolding herself for digging in with the same questions again. This guy locked himself up tighter than Fort Knox.

Regret at his tone immediately overtook him and he visibly softened, "No offense, it's just not something I talk about."

"No problem, I get it. We barely know each other. I'm generally a solitary chick, so I do get it. Trust needs to be built," Nora said gently, and Ezra nodded gratefully. "We do have to work on that if we're going to survive whatever it is we've gotten ourselves into." Thinking of the folders that Pearl had given them when they left and the strict instructions that came with them had Nora sitting at attention. Reaching into her bag beside her, she didn't find it. Before panic could set in, she remembered that she had put it on the backseat of Cherry Bomb before pulling away from the building. Remembering Pearl's warning, it seemed best to leave it out of reach and un-peekable until she was safely home. Having the unknown information sitting so far away from her started to seem dangerous. Looking around on the bench seats, she didn't see Ezra's either. "Did you leave your folder in my car?"

Ezra sat up straight at the mention of the documents, looking around, until he breathed a sigh of relief, "Yeah, I left it on the seat."

Nora could only see the bumper of her car, "Mine's there too. Do you think they're safe out there?"

Ezra thought for a moment and shrugged, "I have no idea what's in it. Seems better locked in a car than on a table in a public place." His eyes drifted to the window with worry creasing his face, "I mean, maybe we should keep them with us."

"I think we were kind of stupid to not go straight home with them. Pearl made it clear that they were for our eyes only." Nora wondered if she should go and retrieve them or throw down money for the drinks and book it home. With the shock of the day's revelations and the rush that came with it, a debriefing seemed perfectly logical at the moment. In the calm, poorly lit reality of the restaurant that she found herself in now, she felt foolish and more than a little uneasy. Not knowing what was inside of them, a public place may not be the best place to leave them unattended. Her car was locked, so they were secured, but supernatural beings may not be intimidated by a car's lock. "I'm going to grab them. I'd feel better having them with us," Nora said, standing from the table with her bag, just as Sarah had arrived with Ezra's huge platter of tacos and her cup of coffee.

"Are you leaving?" Ezra looked back and forth from his food and Nora, unsure of what to do.

"No, I'm just going to bring them in," Nora called over her shoulder as she pushed through the door. Scurrying out to Cherry Bomb, she found herself looking at every face that passed by and into every shadow that was starting to crawl out from the setting sun. The anxious feeling of being hyper-alert had her on guard for anything out of the ordinary. Grabbing the folders, she tucked them into her bag without even a peek inside. When she returned, she found Ezra digging into the huge platter of tacos. He looked up with his full cheeks bulging and nodded when Nora patted her bag.

"You sure you don't want one?" Ezra held out the plate of piping hot food.

"No, I'm good. I'm just not hungry right now," Nora said and shook a pinch of salt into the coffee. She wanted to chug it down to get them out of there and on the road home sooner rather than later, but she had to wait for Ezra to finish his feast. She took a sip and cradled the warm mug in her hands.

"You realize that's salt you just put in your coffee, right?" Ezra looked green at the idea.

"I know. It's how I've always had it. It's how my grandfather taught me to drink it. Believe it or not, it makes it sweeter," she held out the mug to him, "Want to try it?"

Ezra held his beer up, "No, I'll take your word for it," he said around another huge mouthful of rice, "I can't believe how hungry I am. So far, the only thing this job has brought me is a fixed leg and a bottomless stomach. Luckily it looks like they'll be paying me enough to keep the food coming," he downed half of a taco in one bite.

"I had something else happen when we were there," Nora said just above a whisper. "After I came to, Gabriel charged at me..."

"He what?" Ezra cut her off, his eyes wide with anger as he choked down his food.

"Not to attack me or anything." Nora paused to remember exactly how it had happened. She didn't think it was to attack her. "I don't think he would. He doesn't seem like the type."

"The type? The type that's a human munching vampire? He seems more like the friendly neighborhood undead-man to you, does he?" Ezra shifted in his seat, realizing he was a little too loud with his question.

Nora snorted, "Okay, I know. It seems dumb to say, but it just didn't feel like an attack."

Ezra blew a long breath from his nose, his eyebrows raised with skepticism, "It didn't feel like an attack when the vampire charged at you?"

"Will you let me finish?" Nora asked, flatly.

Ezra answered by stuffing another half of a taco in his mouth.

"Anyways, I was saying something like how I didn't think anything had changed except for my toothache…"

"You're toothache? You got a toothache from it?" Ezra asked, lifting the last taco halfway to his mouth.

"No, I'd had one for weeks, and it fixed it. Like how they fixed your leg." Nora stopped when Ezra looked from her to his leg and back, eyes narrowed. "Okay, so fixing a cracked tooth is not as impressive as healing your damn femur, but still." She stopped again when the waitress returned to ask if they wanted anything else.

Nora tapped her full mug, "I'm good."

"Yeah, I'm good, too. Thanks. Just the bill when you have a chance," Ezra smiled broadly at the young waitress as if he knew her well. She smiled back, a little longer than to be cordial. Nora wondered if she was another reason why he preferred this spot. He finished the last mouthful of rice and put his crumpled napkin and fork on top before she picked it up. His attention turned back to Nora when Sarah had retreated to the kitchen with his dishes. "So, what happened after the toothache?"

"I was saying that I didn't think anything changed, and Gabriel charged at me in that crazy flash way he can move, and I swear to you – I leaped out of the way, into somersaults, and landed on my feet as if I was going for gold in the Olympics! I don't know how I did it."

"Are you serious?" Ezra asked, staring stunned.

"I wouldn't say it's a day that needs tall tales added in, Ezra. Yes, I'm serious! It was crazy." Nora couldn't believe how quickly she had reacted. She wasn't a klutz like Ezra proclaimed to be, but she had been nothing that you would call an athlete, either.

He looked her over as if he was looking for a sign of change or super-power. "I just met you, but you look the same to me."

"I *feel* exactly the same. You know, except for my tooth. And you look the same, except for the whole...," Nora gestured to his healed leg. "Whatever is in that serum, fairy blood or not, is a miracle maker."

Ezra rubbed mindlessly on his thigh. He sat in thoughtful silence for a moment. "Fairy blood. Do you think we were *really* given blood? That's so gross, right? And why do you think they did that Ascension thing differently with us? And what exactly was it? Why did they have to do that to us?"

Nora shook her head with ambivalence to the surge of questions that poured from him. These weren't questions that a regular person should ask, let alone know the answers to, "I don't know where to draw the line on what is true or not, let alone why anything has happened anymore, without feeling like I've lost my mind." One day had completely turned her world upside down.

"Are we seriously considering going back there tomorrow?" The edge in Ezra's voice made it clear that he was not keen on the idea.

Nora looked out the window towards the street and the lamp posts that were starting to light up the dark sidewalk. The hairs on the back of her neck bristled. "If we don't, I have a feeling that they wouldn't just leave us be." Nora pictured the old vampire movies of the monsters creeping into the helpless woman's room and feasting on her. Human beings turned into beasts of the night. The undead viciously torturing helpless mortals for their twisted amusement. It did seem better to be on their side rather than their target. "We got through one day, we'll get through a second. After today, I have way too many questions that I need answers to. We may as well see this out."

"Why do you think they picked us? You'd think they would have vampire groupies or other, I don't know,"

Ezra shook his head with frustration, "vamps and the like to work for them?"

"I don't know. I don't know if I want to know. My brain is fried just trying to wrap my head around what they dropped on us already."

Ezra nodded solemnly. They didn't speak much after paying the bill and quickly made their way to her car. They made cordial small talk to make themselves more at ease until they pulled up in front of a cute, work in progress, Craftsman-style house that Ezra had directed her to. Small town or not, Nora hadn't spent much time exploring the garden-lined side streets of the sweet older homes that made up the neighborhoods of Aumbry Valley. It may now have revealed itself to be quite sinister but the houses that were fixed up were lovely. Nothing like the uber-rich homes in the hills, of course. These houses were quaint and cozy with character and history. Just what that history was, was a daunting thought now that she knew some of the secrets that the valley held.

Nora offered to pick him up the next evening, and Ezra pointed happily to a bright blue Jeep sitting in the driveway.

"Thanks, but with my leg back in working order, I think I want to get back behind the wheel again."

"What's its name?" Nora asked, looking over the open-topped two-door car.

"Who? My car?" Ezra looked at her as if she were crazy.

"Yeah! This is Cherry Bomb," she said lovingly and rubbed her dashboard, "Ezra, meet Cherry Bomb, Cherry Bomb meet Ezra."

"You named your car?" he laughed, "No, I don't have a name for mine."

"You have to name your car if you want it to be good to you," Nora said and tried to think of some suggestions, "How about Bluebell, or Blubert?"

"Blubert?" Ezra repeated, amused.

Nora could tell that he was not taking her seriously. That didn't mean that she was going to drop it. Naming your car, like a boat, was a superstition that she put weight into, "Is it a boy or a girl?"

"It's a car," Ezra laughed again.

Nora noticed his deep dimple again. It highlighted his babyface. "I'm telling you, you need to name your vehicles. It's good luck to name your car. You have to admit we could both use all the luck we can get!" Nora gave him a knowing stare and grinned until she remembered the folders in her bag. The naming of the car would have to wait. As much as she was enjoying Ezra's company, and the ease they seemed to have with each other, she wanted nothing more than to be safely locked in her apartment with Silas. Her expression turned serious as she handed his folder to him.

"I guess I'll go dig into this now," he stared at the closed paper folder, "What do you think is in here?"

"I wouldn't even attempt a guess after today." She wouldn't go against Pearl's instructions and open it up before she got home. It worried her that it contained things that were not to be seen by anyone else. She had never so much wanted to see something and never see something all at once.

"Fair enough," he said and picked up a pen from her center console. He scribbled his phone number on her folder and passed the pen and his folder to her. "Just in case," he said, ominously. She wrote down her own and handed it back as he stepped out of her car, "I'll see you tomorrow?"

"I guess so." she replied with trepidation, "I don't think we have a choice."

"I think you're right," he tucked the folder under his arm, "I'll see you at nine pm, sharp."

As she pulled away and made her way back home, she hoped that he meant it and she would not have to deal with the uncertain future alone.

The ride between his house and hers was only a few blocks. After a quick, paranoid stop at the supermarket, she soon found herself rushing through the hallway and locking her apartment door behind her. Silas tangled his way around her legs, mewing his hello when she sat the stuffed bags on the counter. The cheeky cat jumped up immediately to inspect the loot.

"I made it home alive, Sy, and with treasure!" Nora scratched his chin and pulled out a bag of his favorite treats. "Been a while since you've had these, huh?" She ripped open the package and set a few on the floor, laughing when he pounced down on them. Putting the groceries away, she paused and looked with relief and pride at the stocked fridge and cupboards. It was too hard to decide what to eat now that she finally had options. Even with the buffet before her, she found her stomach still didn't ask for food. She picked up the jar of fire-engine red hair dye, smiling. The exact brand she had favored back east and hadn't been able to find since she arrived in Aumbry Valley. It wasn't much of a stretch to wonder if it had been stocked just for her by the new supernatural beings she had just met. They seemed to be able to reach every inch of her life. It was exhilarating and terrifying all in one breath.

The folder couldn't be ignored any longer. Any answers she could get were waiting inside that unassuming beige file.

Pulling it from her bag, she opened it and sat cross-legged on her bed. Inside she found a copy of the

NDA she had signed, a description of what it would entail being a Familiar, and the duties that were expected of her. They all seemed to be pretty basic tasks that an assistant would normally be tasked with. The main fill of her time, it seemed, would be to be on call for errands and deliveries for the more involved agents. Exactly what she would be delivering wasn't noted and Nora tried not to let her mind drift to what vampires would need to be delivered. She didn't even know if the people that would be in charge of her would-be vampires or humans.

Or even something else.

More questions to add to the stack. Most of the documents were reiterating, in multiple legal ways, that she was to keep everything she sees, hears, or learns of the supernatural world completely to herself. That seemed easy enough. Even if she did tell anyone what had happened to her, they wouldn't believe her. They would more likely lock her up in a rubber room than go vampire hunting on her word. She scoured every document to try to find anything that would give insight into what had happened to her in that horror room but there was nothing. There didn't seem to be anything truly unusual in the papers until she got to some very specific details about vampires.

Under no circumstances will you willingly allow yourself to be fed on.

"Ew," Nora squirmed. That was an employee rule that she had yet to encounter. It seemed like something that should go without saying. From what she was reading, a Familiar was pretty much what they were portrayed as in books and the like.

She had signed on to be a vampires' bitch.

At least she wasn't a part of their meal plan, and she had that rule in writing. She pulled out the next stack of papers to find another contract, detailing that she would answer to Elijah Beasley and would need to be available at all hours of the day and night if the agents required her. She would be directly reporting to a demon. *A demon*! Her awe at that revelation screeched to a halt when she started reading the next page. Her jaw dropped. The salary they would be providing her would be seventy-five thousand dollars a year. To start! And with generous bonuses!

"Holy crap!" Nora went over the words to make sure she was reading it correctly, "Seventy-five grand?" Silas jumped up beside her, curious about the shouting, "For that kind of money: Nora Goodman, Vampire bitch reporting for duty!"

She picked up the grey floofball beside her and gave him a happy snuggle. "I'm going to keep you in treats and toys, that you'll probably ignore, for a long time with that kind of money Sy!" Her voice of reason tried to speak up, telling her that a salary that high couldn't possibly be for simple errands. There hadn't been much reason in anything in the past twenty-four hours, so it was easy for Nora to ignore the worry of what was to come. Even if just for a passing moment. Looking to the last page, where there would normally be a signature, Nora found a small fingerprint of blood under her name. Checking each of her fingertips twice, there was no sign of a prick to the skin, just as she had no memory of making the print herself.

If it seems too good to be true...

Nora continued to ignore the little voice. Tonight, she would let herself celebrate with some nice wine from a bottle, not a box, and sweetly scented bubbles in her bath. Whatever tomorrow brought was officially out of her hands.

Chapter Six

She sprung up from her overly warm pillow when Silas jumped on her chest, done with politely waiting to be fed. Nora grabbed the clock from her nightside table. Her hair was tangled in front of her eyes, and she had to wrangle it back to focus on the time. She didn't want to be late for work again. The neon red numbers told it was almost three. She laid back, relieved that it was still nighttime. There were a few more hours of sleep before dealing with Dirtbag Derek and the multitude of people hanging up the phone in her ear. Blinking, she noticed the sunlight creeping beams through her curtains. Worried that the alarm was on the fritz, she grabbed her phone and saw the time was correct – and it was PM.

"What the hell?" Nora jumped from her bed, the lingering cloud of sleep making her unsteady. The bed came up quickly behind her as she slumped back down. The chaos of the day before flooded over her, the shock of it all returning. She covered her eyes with her hands, steadying herself with deep gulps of air.

There would be no more early mornings rushing to sit behind a desk and be leered at by Dirtbag Derek. No more complaints of her tediously boring collection of jobs.

Vampires and demons and supernatural beings would now decide what her life would be. It would have been easy to pass off as a fevered dream if she didn't have the ominous folder sitting on the table beside her and the empty grocery bags tossed on her counter. Whatever Gabriel had put her through the day before had left her drained enough to sleep all day without a stir. The grogginess buzzed through her.

A knock on her front door made her jump, her phone launching in the air. Before it could land on the worn hardwood floor, Nora nimbly grabbed it mid-air. Her arm had reached out faster than should be humanly possible, just as she had done with her impressive tumbling display with Gabriel. She tossed the phone on the bed as if it had shocked her and looked at her still normal hand. Another knock, louder, had her on the move. Pulling on a robe, she looked into the peephole, unsure of who, *or what* could be waiting for her. She was allayed to see it was only Jenny and happily opened the door, not noticing her landlord's irritation.

"Hey, Jenny! I," Nora stopped, clamping her mouth shut when Jenny held her hand up between them.

"I don't want a 'hey Jenny' from you, Nora. I gave you the benefit of the doubt about this new job possibility and here you are in your pajamas in the middle of the day. I come home to find your car in the same place you left it yesterday," Jenny sighed, reigning in her anger, "I'm trying to be patient with you, I am," Jenny said gently, crossing her arms across her chest. Nora knew it was hard for her to get tough with her tenants.

"No, it's ok! I got the job," Nora grinned, glad to see the relief wash over her only friend. It was horrible to put her in the uncomfortable position of being the tough guy. "Hang on, one sec," Nora's smile grew as she hopped over to her bag. Giving Jenny the money was the most satisfying thing she had done since she had decided to strike out into the world on her own and moved to Aumbry Valley. Even if it was just paying money that she already owed.

Jenny was taken aback by the wad of cash that Nora handed her. It was her back rent and the next month, as well. It didn't leave Nora with much left, although she didn't mind at all. At least they would have their tiny home secured for another month and that was enough for her and Silas. The extra cash would be more appreciated by Jenny and Olivia, anyways. Nora knew she wholly owed her more for the kindness and patience she had shown her since she had arrived.

Giving snippets of her new employment, she tossed around generic terms that she hoped would be enough information to have Jenny leave happy and believing her.

Assistant, office work, coffee fetcher, mostly night shift...

Jenny was still sharing wishes of congratulations as Nora was closing the door, saying she needed to prep for her first big shift. It was best to get rid of her before she started to look for details of what that office, and its employees, were. She listened at the door until she heard Jenny's click shut and knew that she was in the clear of any more questioning. For now.

The new world that had been revealed to her would now involve a lot of lying if she was going to make it. She was now an employee of the *BITN Agency*. Along with a nutter of a vampire, a dapper demon, and the Supermodel Squad of fairy guards. It was hard to believe it was not a dream.

Turning the water on as hot as she could manage, she stepped into the shower, pulling the curtain tight to contain the heat. The day before ran in a loop, just as it did until she had fallen into a dreamless sleep. It was all so simple and complicated all at once. She still had a largely calm acceptance of it all that felt so out of character for her. Nora always had questions and she always asked them. It was seen as a character flaw by some. She didn't care as long as she got answers.

Why didn't she ask more questions yesterday?

Why didn't she turn tail and get the hell out of there?

She wondered if it was whatever the serum had done to her reflexes. Maybe it had done something to her brain. She shivered under the hot steam thinking of what Gabriel had said the serum was. There was supernatural fairy blood flowing through her. She looked at the veins in her arm, half expecting to see them glowing or shimmering. Everything looked as it always did. She rubbed her tongue along the tooth that had been cracked to feel it smooth and healed. No wonder fairies kept themselves and their secrets in the dark. If humans knew about them, they would probably find a way to set up fairy farms and sell their miracle blood to the masses.

Silas sat beside the tub, meowing his discontent that he had still yet to be fed.

Pulling on her robe, she left wet footprints across the floor to the kitchen to fill his bowl. He purred and rubbed his ribs along her leg in thanks. Nora barely noticed, still lost in her thoughts. Starting her fire hazard of a coffeemaker, she scooped in some grounds and went back to the bathroom while it brewed. A brand-new tube of toothpaste, from her indulgent trip to the grocery store, sat in a glass on the sink and she squirted a generous amount on her brush.

Nora stopped scrubbing her teeth, the toothbrush hanging from her foaming mouth, and when she caught her reflection in the foggy mirror. The look on her face caught her off guard. She was smiling, with a glow in her cheeks that hadn't been there in months. The grey shadow of the depression that had been overtaking her since she had arrived was starting to lift.

She was *excited*.

Gabriel had been right. For the first time in years, she was looking forward to starting her day. The very idea of what she was being told was ridiculous, yet she allowed herself to believe it because it was truly exciting. Vampires, demons, fairies, an entire world of unbelievable beings, not only existed, but she was also now a part of their world! There was something in the world outside of cubicles, staring at her laptop, worrying about bills, or if she had to go groveling back to her parents. Yesterday, she had spent her day talking to an actual vampire.

An actual vampire!

She felt her neck where the needle had left its mark and found there was now nothing to be found. She was still stunned that she had allowed a stranger to inject her with an unknown substance. The stranger being a damn vampire, at that, probably carried the most weight. The tickle of worry that she was persuaded more than she had allowed returned. There was a good chance that had happened to Ezra when his initial refusal was considered. Something had to have happened to him to change his mind, whether it was on his own or by force. He was dead set against it all when he was dragged into that little room. Nora grimaced when 'dead set' repeated in her thoughts. Dead just like the vampire that she was nose to nose with. Gabriel could have done anything to her. Put any thoughts into her mind, and she would never know. He could have convinced her to do anything.

The sunlight that shone on the edges of her curtains caught her attention. Slowly, she moved closer and stared at the beam running across her floor. Her arm rose haltingly towards it until she waved her hand quickly through the warm light. Relief washed over when nothing happened. No smoking flesh or Nosferatu destroying bursts of flames. Whatever had happened in that room had not turned her into a vampire. Gabriel seemed to have kept his word. As far she could tell.

She pulled open the drapes and looked out onto the street below. It all looked as it always did, with no notice of how everything had changed for her. The world she lived in now was one where she wasn't crazy to check if she had been turned into a card-carrying member of the undead. She laughed at the absurdity of it all and was starting to feel dizzy from the swift emotional shifts between happy excitement and paralyzing fear that had been her emotional norm for the past two days.

Or she had gone utterly crazy. That seemed a lot easier to explain.

Not that she would risk walking into a therapist's office with her concerns The very real file that she could see sitting on her nightstand was quite clear of what could happen with that. It was almost a blessing that her grandfather had passed on because it would have been impossible to not tell him about it all. He was her most dear confidant and on top of that, more so than Quinn, he had been very open to the unexplained and paranormal mysteries of the world. Noah Goodman was always flush with stories of curses and unexplained happenings from when he was on digs and Nora was always captivated by them. A lot of what she knew about supernatural lore came from him. Not that she ever assumed any of it was truly real.

Until now. And he was gone.

She pulled out her laptop to look at old pictures she had posted of him. Nora wasn't one to post many things online, especially since his death and Quinn splitting on her. Social media for her was mainly to live vicariously through other people's filter-perfect lives. The few images that she did share were her own private safe space. Before the computer could boot up, the memory-induced melancholy was thankfully chased away when her cellphone rang loudly. The number that flashed was only a mystery for a moment until she remembered the same one scribbled on her file. Ezra.

"Hey, fella. How are you coping today? Any fangs or tails pop up?"

Ezra grunted a laugh, "No, not so far. You?"

"All good over this way," Nora replied. "Did you read what was in that file?" Nora wondered if he had been given the same papers and information as she was. When he brought up the points that seemed to catch his eye the most, it seemed as if they had.

"What do you think they'll have us do tonight? At this point, nothing would surprise me," Ezra chuckled, poorly covering his nerves for the coming night.

A familiar was more or less a housekeeper and errand-runner in any story that she had read. The intense time in those chairs and the fact that they had been so insistent on the serum made her think it could be a little more complicated. "No idea. Hopefully something mundane. Hopefully for another fat envelope of cash, too," Nora mused. Either way, they were all in now.

"Yeah, about that. Doesn't it seem like way too much money to pay us to run errands?" Ezra's voice was low as if the big bosses at BITN could hear him. Being super-natural beings, Nora wondered if they could.

"I've been thinking that myself. I guess I'm not going to look a gift horse in the mouth, Ezra. That's a worry for another day." If they wanted to pay her that money, who was she to say no? She wasn't looking to get rich from whatever it was that they were about to get tangled in, but a comfortable life was not going to be something she would turn down. She wondered if she would be able to move into one of the larger apartments upstairs. The one on the third floor beside Norman's had been the one that she had originally wanted. High ceilings, with the original hand-carved moldings. A separate bedroom and a sundrenched space for a full couch that she and Silas could stretch out on. At three times her current rent, Jenny would certainly welcome the extra income.

Thinking of Jenny, she pulled her laptop onto her lap to see if she had posted any cute new photos of Olivia. Clicking onto the web and then Insta, she was surprised to see she was logged out.

"I guess they probably have unlimited funds, be-ing...you know, what they are," Ezra murmured.

"That's true," Nora answered, with her attention on her computer screen. She tried to log in three times and each time she was told that her account was not found. Switching tabs between each of her social accounts, she was met with the same response. "Hey, Ezra, are you on Insta?"

"That photo app?" Ezra asked with a laugh, "No, not really my thing."

"Okay, anything like that? FB?" Nora clicked over to her email and found it was still there.

"I had an account. I guess I still have an account. I don't think I've used it since," he cleared his throat, uncomfortable, "I haven't used it in a while."

Nora didn't notice the change in mood with his answer, her attention fully on the mystery of her apps. "Do me a favor. See if you still have the account," Nora asked and re-booted her computer.

Whenever something doesn't work, turn it off and on, right?

"OK, hang on. It's on my phone," his voice left for a moment when he checked, "Huh, I guess I did delete my account. Weird that I didn't delete the app, too."

"I don't think it was you, Ezra. All of my accounts are gone. All of them!" She re-checked each one when her screen switched on again. There was no sign of her online, except for her one email account, "They're just...gone."

"What are you saying? That *they* deleted them?" Ezra said with disbelief that lasted only as long as his words. Of course, they would. "I mean, do you think they could?"

Nora tossed her laptop onto her bed in frustration, "I'm thinking there is nothing that they can't do. Even slowly erase us from our lives."

It felt overly dramatic to say, but she was talking about demons and vampires. The only way to know was to show up at 1365 Beech Avenue once again. Nine PM was getting close, fast.

CHAPTER SEVEN

The rest of the nervous energy of the afternoon was spent on her laptop, falling deep into a research spiral. There was nothing to be found of The Firm and nothing more of Aumbry Valley. It made sense that they would not advertise what they were and the valley that hid them. A bright, exciting town page inviting humans to holiday in Supernatural Central seemed a bad idea all around. She took a break to douse her hair with the bright hair dye that she was beyond happy to have again, a break that lasted a little longer than she had hoped thanks to the mess she made of her bathroom. Tucking her hair up in a plastic bag, she made herself a sandwich and dove back into the internet.

Fairies were the most intriguing to her at the moment. Nora considered the fact that she had their blood mingling inside her. Gulping the last of the soda from her glass, she tossed it in the air. Her hand effortlessly grabbed it just as it fell to eye level. She didn't know how long her new physical skills would last, or why they deemed it necessary to give her what Gabriel called a gift, but they were fun to have for the time being.

Typing 'fairies' into the search bar felt ridiculous and intriguing all at once. The images that popped up were nothing like the Fashion Week lineup that she had witnessed. Iridescent wings, cherub faces, and flowing chiffon gowns were pictured beside the twisted and cruel faces of squat creatures brandishing long, razor-sharp fingers. Nora wondered if they could choose how humans saw them. Supermodels would be an excellent choice if they could.

A mystical-looking blog entry told of the fairy realm between heaven and earth, where the source of their pure energy is protected. She scanned the illustrations and paragraph after paragraph of stories of the folklore. The fae, according to that site, were beings that could harness their power to a specific area of the universe, including earth, and have been known to walk among us unseen. Nora shivered at how many beings had been living beside her unseen her entire life. Clicking on the next site, she read of the connections between demons and fairies, or what that writer deemed to be one and the same. The drawings provided there were much darker than the last and had zero resemblance to the ones she now knew of. The next site provided a list of dozens of different types of fairies, with none of those having an ounce of likeness to the Glamor Guards.

Taking a break, she rinsed her hair and plugged in her hairdryer. The mirror reflected the bright red locks that she loved. Running her brush through as it dried, Nora was surprised at how shiny it had turned out. So much that it almost sparkled. The same dye had never been so good to her in the past. Once it was fully dried, she took notice of her skin. Not that she had ever had bad skin, apart from the time when pimples were gifted to her in her teens. Now, however, it seemed to glow from within. Her cheeks naturally flushed, her lips rosy and plump. A day at the spa wouldn't be as generous.

Could fairy blood be the reason?

Clicking the words into her computer, eyes-wide, she was surprised to see so many websites that spoke specifically to the topic. One site stated that fae blood was irresistible to other supernaturals, which certainly was not the case with Gabriel. It also stated that it can improve the beauty and abilities of humans. Those boxes seemed to both be checked. Each site had its unique theory of the power or lack of according to some. Clicking away at every site she could find she was left more confused than when she started. She considered looking more into vampires, so she would feel more prepared for her next meeting with Gabriel, but decided that she read the word blood enough for one day.

Exhaling her frustration at the screen, she closed the laptop and tossed it to her side. Researching the supernatural online seemed like a fool's route. Anyone could say anything their heart and imagination wanted on the web, with none of it needing to be proven. If she wanted answers, she could go to the source. No matter how terrifying that was.

Checking the time, that was going to be sooner rather than later. Dressing in black leggings, a black tunic top, and a jean jacket that had seen better days, she decided it was as good as it would get. What she and Ezra would be doing was completely unknown and Nora tended to choose comfort and function over flash. She realized that she didn't even know how long she would be gone and poured extra kibble and water for Silas who watched her with disinterest.

"Wish me luck, buddy. Hold down the fort while I'm gone," Nora said, pulling her bag's strap over her head. He jumped up on the love seat, circling the cushion before plopping himself down. "No, no, don't miss me so hard, Si," she said flatly. He was certainly not a clingy roommate.

Pulling Cherry Bomb up to a free spot along the curb in front of 1365 Beech Avenue once more, the nervous energy that had been pooling in her stomach lessened when she saw Ezra's blue Jeep a few spots up. Nora didn't notice how she grinned when she saw him leaning against the wall beside the door to the building. His attention locked on whatever he was reading on his phone. He seemed to have had the same effect from the serum and Nora had to tell herself not to stare. She hadn't noticed how broad his chest was the day before, or how his arms filled out the sleeves of his t-shirt so well, either. His eyes twinkled brightly at whatever had captured his attention on the screen.

"Looks like we've survived to see day number two," Nora whispered when Ezra looked up, noticing her approaching. His attention darted about, making sure no one was around.

"So, far we have," he gave a half-smile and pulled open the door to the office building. He didn't seem as relaxed as when she had left him. The adrenaline of the day before was fully replaced with the reality of what they were walking into. Even so, it felt odd to ask him if he was okay. They were about to take an elevator up to the office where they had just met a vampire, a demon, supermodel fairies, and whatever the hell Pearl was.

Things were clearly not okay in the healthy sense of the word.

Watching him walk across the lobby with her, it was obvious that he was struggling with the same nerves that she was. Even though he was still mostly a stranger, it was comforting to have him side by side with her and just as scared.

The elevator took its time coming down to fetch them, staying on four. Nora stared at the frozen number, wondering what could be up there. Elijah's office seemed to dominate most of the building. Ezra pushed the button several times. He grew more on edge with each passing second that they waited. He looked her over, his lips tight, his eyes blinking a little too fast until he gave her a once over.

He tilted his head and smiled, "You look different. Your hair is redder, isn't it?"

Nora ran a hand over her ponytail that sat over her shoulder, feeling shy at the way he was staring, "Yeah, I was finally able to touch it up."

"I like it. It's cool," Ezra nodded as he spoke, the smile staying in place.

They both jumped when the elevator pinged its arrival and the doors slid open. They stepped inside and Nora pushed two.

"Thanks. I was hating how it was getting so pink," Nora picked up a lock of her hair and held it up to the light of the elevator. Small talk was always so uncomfortable, "Have you picked a name for your Jeep, yet?"

"You were serious about that?" Ezra grinned a little, a dimple pulling into his right cheek.

Nora feigned dismay at his lack of effort, "I was. I told you, every good car needs a name."

Ezra scratched the scruff along his jaw, thinking, "What's yours, again?"

"She's The Cherry Bomb," Nora declared, with pride.

"Because she's red, right?" Ezra asked as the door slid open. They stepped out onto the worn beige carpet that led to the office.

"And she's the bomb! The most loyal anything that I've ever encountered," Nora declared with a broad smile. They lingered in front of the elevator when it closed behind them, not in a rush to get to whatever lay beyond the office door.

"Maybe I should name my Jeep Blueberry, then," Ezra offered, looking pleased with his creativity.

"Blueberry?" Nora snorted, "That's a little plain, don't you think?" She could tell that he was humoring her and thought the idea was silly. That wouldn't stop her from finding the perfect name for it.

"What? I like blueberries," Ezra said, offended, "and it's a perfectly good choice. If a car must have a name," He seemed to have put all of his blueberries in one basket with that name, not offering anything else other than a shrug.

Nora laughed and shook her head and started to move down the hall.

Ezra frowned, following behind, "Okay, what's a tough name? Let's do a badass one. Dragon? How about dragon fruit, then?"

Nora shook her head, "Dragon fruit is pink, not blue."

"You seem to have a vast knowledge of fruit, Nora. Was that something they gave you with your brain scramble yesterday?"

Nora opened the insidious office door that changed their lives forever, her nerves building again, "No, I just had pretentious parents that stocked the house with likewise food."

The fluorescent light above them still flickered weakly. Pearl was nowhere to be seen in the dingy office, her desk stacked with papers and a plastic cover over her computer monitor. Her ashtray was still filled with discarded butts. The large sliding door to Elijah's office was open and Ezra stopped halfway to the opening in the wall. If small talk was good for anything, it was good for stalling.

Ezra's face twitched, obviously proud of his next suggestion, "I've got it. Blue Brie."

"Bluebree? Are you just saying blueberry quickly or are you saying brie? Like cheese?" Nora pursed her lips, trying to understand why he seemed so proud of his idea.

"No, Brie after the toughest girl I know," Ezra stated with surety.

"And who would that be?" Nora asked, amused with the precocious grin on his face.

"She was a girl I went to school with," Ezra paused, his face crumpled a little with embarrassment, "In kindergarten, I thought it was a good idea to pull up her skirt to make my friends laugh. Brie proceeded to give me my first black eye."

Nora's hand shot up to quiet a loud cackle of laughter, "Way to go, Brie!"

Ezra looked to his shoes that he shuffled, "I agree. She taught me a tough lesson that day."

"Any time, folks. I have places to be," Elijah's voice called from the vast marble office.

They found him sitting behind his opulent wooden desk, giving them a wave to enter without looking up from the documents that he was scanning.

"Sorry, Mr. Beasley," Ezra said quietly as they approached him.

"No need for apologies, and please, call me Elijah," he looked up from his work with a friendly grin, "I'm glad to see you both are getting along. I had a feeling you would find more in common than you thought."

Nora noted the flick of his eyebrow and humor in his voice but didn't get the joke. Even with what little she knew of Elijah, she was aware that he knew more than he said at all times. They sat when he gestured to the plush wing-backs across from him.

"So, what did you want us to do tonight?" Ezra's voice was unsteady. Who knew what the answer to that loaded question would be?

"Today will be a quick visit from you both. The plans I had for you seemed to have been quashed by the powers that be. Tomorrow will be a more official start date," Elijah lifted the receiver from the phone in front of him and pushed a few buttons wordlessly before returning it to the cradle. "I assume you read the files and have a few questions?"

A *few* were far less than what she had. Nora didn't know where to start. Being back in that room, eye to eye with who she now knew to be a demon, found her throat dry. She could sure go for some more of that serum if that's what had calmed her the day before. Ezra sat quietly beside her, his mouth starting and stopping with questions, leaving him with the look of a breathless fish out of water.

"I can only imagine how overwhelmed you both are," Elijah stood, moving to lean on the front of the desk. He looked more casual than he had in the past couple of days. His expensive suit jacket was hung on the back of his chair, and he had delicately rolled up the sleeves of his dress shirt. "I am here to help you with whatever you need to make your first days with us comfortable."

"Are you really a demon?" Nora blurted, her voice finding a mind of its own, "Sorry, but Gabriel said..."

Elijah smiled softly, amused with her embarrassment, "I am, Miss. Goodman. More specifically, I am a drude." He paused, waiting for a reaction. Silence had overtaken them once more. Elijah continued when they didn't offer a response, "There will be time for us to get to know each other better in the future and I look forward to you learning more about all of the beings that you will come to work with. But as I said I have places I need to be, and this will be a quick meeting. So, let's get down to it, shall we?"

A towering Glamor Guard, built like an Amazon, walked in from the front office. The juxtaposition of the *beige-on-beige-on-dirt* décor that she walked from, and her stunning appearance was almost laughable. Her golden hair was twisted into intricate braids atop her head, her black utilitarian uniform looking more runway than night watchman. She carried a chest about half the size of a shoebox that she tightly held onto.

"Kingsley, I would like to introduce you to our recruits," Elijah raised his hand with a flourish to present them. "This is Nora Goodman and Ezra Davis."

"I'm pleased to meet you both," Kingsley replied, her voice almost musical. Her skin shimmered, even with the dim wall lighting in the room. The mouth-watering scent of sugar cookies swirled around her and grew stronger the closer she got to them.

It was the Glamor Guards that smelled so delicious!

Nora and Ezra, mesmerized, could only smile in unison.

"I think we will just take care of this and then we'll send you on your way, until tomorrow, yes?" Elijah carried on, ignoring how gob-smacked the two were. He stepped aside when Kingsley moved to stand in front of them. Opening the box, she revealed a long, thin, dark blue crystal that had a streak of tiny sparkles which looked as if it had captured the stars from a clear night sky. Holding it up to Nora, she asked her to take off her jacket and hold out her left arm, palm up. When she complied, Kingsley pushed up the sleeve of Nora's cotton shirt and held the crystal to the inside of her wrist. It was a cold like she had never experienced at first. Sharp, cutting. It made her veins feel like the blood was freezing in place, and it ached up her arm. Before she could utter her discomfort, Kingsley had removed the crystal and was repeating the process on Ezra.

The chill to her skin lessened as a warmth moved its way from the surface right down to the bone. She stared, her face flooded with awe, as a mark began to appear with the heat. She recognized the main shape as an Ankh, the Egyptian hieroglyph for life. The cross and looped tear-dropped circle on top were branded, jet black, onto her skin. Down the center, was a tiny sliver of a line that Nora could not take her eyes from. It looked as if a stripe of pure gold dust had been embedded on her wrist, bisecting the Ankh and it glimmered as if lit from within. When she looked up at Ezra, he was staring at his own, and Kingsley, the Glamor Guard fairy was now nowhere to be found.

"Pretty neat, aren't they" Elijah commented, pulling their attention back to him. He had taken his seat behind his desk.

"What is this?" Nora asked, running her fingers over the mark. There was nothing to feel.

"It's a mark that is used by vampires and their people," Elijah said, sitting back comfortably as if it was an every-day thing for him. Being a demon, it must take a lot to shock him, after all. "It is a symbol of your belonging."

"As in, we belong to you?" Ezra chimed in, finally finding his voice.

"You could say that, yes," Elijah shuffled some papers, "So, between your nice new fresh marks, and your Ascension modifications yesterday, I think we are ready to have you out in the world." He stood and looked from the pair to the open door as if that was all that needed to be said on the subject, "I would like you back here again at nine pm. You will be shadowing some of our staff on an assignment to the nightclub Mystique. They will be inquiring about a gentleman we have been having issues with. Dress accordingly and please do attend to every and all requests they have of you," Elijah picked up the phone and began to dial.

"That's it?" Ezra asked, standing when they seemed to be dismissed. Elijah set the phone down. "I mean, you just tattoo us and send us on our way?"

"I have nothing further for you today, Mr. Davis. Is there something more you would like from me?" Elijah asked, polite yet more interested in the files before him.

"I have quite a few questions that I haven't gotten to ask yet, sir," Ezra added the last word nervously.

"I'm sure you have a list of questions, and they would be better suited to the people you will be with tomorrow. Believe it or not, the Ascension process gave you more information than you know. A millennia's worth of knowledge was passed on to you through that gift, as well as new muscle memory to help you protect your-selves. To help protect each other," Elijah offered the answer as if it were that simple.

"What exactly happened in that room? The Ascension, I mean. What all happened?" Ezra leaned forward, pleading for information that would explain everything.

"Now, Mr. Davis, a magician never reveals his tricks," Elijah winked, "and that is the easy answer. A magical gift was given to you, by incredibly magical beings. And we all know it's impolite to question a gift."

"It's not unheard of to ask just what the hell a gift is, Elijah," Nora exclaimed and quickly clamped her lips closed. Was it rude to say hell to a demon?

"That may be true, Miss. Goodman. That is the only answer I will provide, though," he leaned his head to-wards them, looking from one to the other, before gently clapping his hands once, "Okay, let me show you some-thing that may help."

Nora stared back at him, waiting to see something.

Elijah narrowed his eyes in thought before continuing, "Miss. Goodman, how do you identify a vampire?" He casually folded his arms across his chest.

"Pale skin, fangs, a crystal glow in their iris, a strong smell of copper about them, and the ability to move faster than the eye can follow." Nora slapped her hand over her mouth after the words poured out as if by their own will.

Elijah nodded and turned to Ezra, "And, Mr. Davis, how do you kill a vampire?"

"UV light or direct sunlight, a silver-tipped stake anywhere in their chest or a plain wooden stake through the heart, removal of the head, or burnt to the point of ash. The older the vampire, the quicker they will turn to ash." Ezra's eyes widened as he spoke, seeming as shocked as Nora was.

Nora tried to find other information that was new to her mind, "What the... What was that? How do we know that? "

need to know and will know it when you need it." The phone on his desk rang. Answering it he turned in his chair and spoke quietly, out of earshot of Nora and Ezra who were still reeling from the outburst of knowledge. The excitement wore thin as Elijah's voice raised tensely to whoever he was speaking to. The hot vibration of energy started to ripple from him as it had when he was angry with Gabriel. Nora realized she was watching an angry demon in action. Looking at Ezra, he was just as uneasy with the change in mood. Elijah slammed down the receiver and kept his back to them until he was calmed and the heat of the room lessened.

"Apologies, but as I said, I am a busy man, and getting you marked was the most important thing for you today, believe me."

Nora didn't like the edge in his voice and wondered what the important things were that he was in such a rush to get to. The reality of what was going on behind the scenes was probably far too terrifying for her to grasp. The longer she was near Elijah, the more she felt uncomfortable. It wasn't that she felt he would harm her. It was that he had a vibration of danger about him; an underground that he dealt in. It reminded her of a trip she had taken with her grandfather when he had acted the same way. After an exciting day exploring a site in the desert, she had been quickly shuffled into the van by her grandfather who was muttering about needing to get going and the sun going down. It was much later in life that he had one too many glasses of scotch and confessed to her that they had been robbed by bandits and he had hidden it from her. Whatever it was that preoccupied the mind of the demon before her, it was probably much more dangerous than petty thieves.

She would gladly get home to the safety of her apartment if that was all he required of her for the day. The idea of being out at night had lost its charm in the past two days. Checking the time on her phone, it was almost nine-thirty. The phone made her remember the missing accounts from earlier.

"Hey, this might be crazy," like anything could be considered crazy at this point, "but did you guys somehow get rid of my social media pages?"

Elijah stopped focusing on the paper and gave her his full attention, "Yes that was indeed us. We do require a certain level of discretion. It was alluded to in the file you were given."

Nora couldn't remember reading anything about online socializing. Who knows what *legalese* wording she missed in those papers? She worried about what else was alluded to. She made a mental note to read them again when she got home. There were too many things that just didn't make sense, "So, no more Insta-creeping?"

"No, Miss. Goodman. At least not from an account," He smiled gently when he saw her look at her phone, "I know you must be aware that your life is now far more interesting than quizzes on what cocktail you are and puppy dog filters?" He spoke the words as if they were foreign yet amusing.

"That is beyond the truth," Nora said quietly, looking at the brand on her wrist.

"You both still have your email accounts and the ability to have mail delivered to your homes. We are not looking to have you disappear," he tucked the files under his arm, picking up his jacket, "One of the best attributes you both have is that your social lives are almost nil!" he said with cheer, not realizing that Nora felt burnt by the observation. He wasn't wrong, though.

"So, nine again tomorrow?" Ezra asked, moving towards the front office. He seemed keen to get the hell out of there, as well.

"Yes please, Mr. Davis," Elijah replied cordially. The door he had left from the day before slid open, "Oh, and one last thing. Miss. Goodman, Mr. Davis, what happens if you tell anyone about us or betray us in any way?"

Nora and Ezra answered automatically in unison, "We will be put to death on site."

Nora's eyes widened at the words that poured from her mouth, "Wait, what?!"

Elijah Beasley disappeared into whatever demon business lay behind the wall and the door closed quickly behind him.

Nora slung her bag across her shoulder and quickened her pace to meet Ezra's. "Are you freaking kidding me? What do you think they're going to have us do?"

Ezra held the door to the hallway open for her and let the door slam behind them, "No idea. Whatever it is, it seems we'll have to do it," he grumbled, rubbing at the brand on his arm.

Nora knew he was right. They didn't have many choices anymore. They made their way silently to their cars and pulled out into the night. The ride home seemed too long, too dark, with too many shadows. The space right in front of her building was still empty and she gratefully pulled in and made her way quickly to her apartment.

Her key was halfway in the lock when she noticed a dark mark on her door. Looking closer, it appeared to be a smudge of ash right at her eye level. Tentatively touching it, some came off on her finger and she rubbed it with another finger. It did look and smell of ash. How it got there was beyond her. She quickly opened her door and slammed it, locking it behind her.

The words rolled over and over - *we will be put to death on site.*

And this was only her first day. Maybe Dirtbag Derek wasn't the worst.

Who was she kidding? Of course, he was.

Chapter Eight

The day dragged on with every slow tick of the clock. Deep cleaning the apartment helped Nora work away some of the nervous energy that kept her on her feet. The small space did not take long to scrub down, so she soon found herself doing a second cleaning of her kitchen to keep her hands busy.

'...be put to death on site.'

Silas lounged on the couch, watching her with minimal curiosity as she moved about him. When her hands were raw from scrubbing, she looked from cupboard to cupboard, knowing she should eat.

'...be put to death on site.'

Her mind would not stop repeating the words she had spoken. The not knowing what the night would hold tightened her stomach and she gave up on food, sitting beside her cat with her laptop on her lap. She searched for Mystique nightclub for the hundredth time and just as before, nothing came up. Nightspots for supernatural beings probably did not need to advertise. She now understood why the woman who answered the door, when she had tried to apply for a job, slammed it shut in her face.

The clothes that she had scattered on her bed didn't produce anything inspiring each time she tried to decide on what to wear. The outfit that she had worn to the interview seemed like the best option. A few bangles and a necklace would dress it up a little. After forcing down some soup and pulling her hair in and out of the bun countless times, she deemed herself ready. It was only just past eight, a little early. If she was to arrive before she was needed to head out with the others, she may have a few minutes with Elijah to make sure she was prepared. Not that he had appeared eager to provide her with any information. Gabriel was more of the type to share and overshare at that. Maybe he would be there this time.

"Wish me luck, Sy," Nora waved. Silas stretched out with a yawn and turned his back to her in response. "Don't worry too much, bud." She shook her head at her worriless cat.

Locking her door, she noticed the smudge of ash on the door. The mark had been smeared by Nora's finger the night before and now it was a perfect teardrop again. It didn't sit well that she hadn't heard anyone in the hallway all day, yet the mark was set in place again. She stared at it hoping that a burst of information would come to her as it had in the office. Nothing but the words that she was trying to smother came to mind.

'...put to death on site.'

Nora took a deep breath, pushing the notion away again. Maybe other than that terrifying thought, it was information only about vampires that had been given to her.

"Working the night shift or heading out for some fun?" Jenny's voice rang out from her own door, making Nora jump.

"It's work for me tonight," Nora said, trying to keep her voice casual. She reached out quickly and rubbed away the ash. Jenny peered at her, silent. "Well, I better get going."

"What is it they have you doing?" Jenny pressed and took a step outside of her door.

"You know, this and that. They don't tell me a lot," Nora couldn't tell her why, obviously, and thought quickly on her feet, "They do work for all of those posh-peeps up in the money hills. Errands, and looking after their every spoiled need and such." As far as Nora knew, that could be the truth.

"Hopefully they won't be running you ragged twenty-four-seven," Jenny said, thankfully seeming to buy Nora's story.

"I think a lot of my shifts will be at night. You know how those Richie-riches keep crazy hours, always demanding the dumbest little thing," Nora started for the door hoping to evade more questions.

"Well, good luck to you. I'm glad you found something that may be steadier for you," Jenny opened her mouth to add to her well-wishes and stopped speaking when Olivia, snug in her teddy bear pajamas, peeked her head around her mother's leg.

"Good luck, Norma!" the little girl squealed and disappeared back into the apartment.

"Thanks, kiddo!" Nora shouted and took it as a chance to exit, heading out to the street.

Ezra's car wasn't in front of the building when Nora parked, so she took the elevator up to the second floor alone. She sent out a silent prayer that he would be there soon. She hadn't called him all day as a way to give her mind a break from the new reality they had fallen into. He hadn't called her either. She hoped it was for the same reason.

Pearl was back behind her desk, smoking up a storm with her sweet smile, and told Nora to go on into Elijah's office. Instead of the demon, she found Gabriel with his feet up on the desk holding court for a group of six people dressed in varying black and white suits. If they were the ones she would be shadowing, her outfit was perfect to fit in with them. The extravagant silk pajamas that she had last seen Gabriel in had been replaced by a cream dress shirt that was covered by a red velvet smoking jacket. The feet he had set upon the desk wore matching velvet shoes. It seemed that Gabriel always kept it casual and fabulous in the office.

"There she is! You all are in for a treat with this one," Gabriel said, before sipping from the crystal chalice that he held. The deep red liquid in the glass stained his lip for only a moment before he licked it away.

"Hey, Gabriel. I'm a little early, I hope that's okay," Nora offered, giving a quick look over to the group. Two women, four men. One of the men was gorgeous and she gave his tall, blonde, and yummy a twice over, but none of them were quite up to glamor guard standards. They seemed to be mere humans just like her. They looked her over, as well.

"Early is fine by me, darling. Come, sit, meet the team," Gabriel beamed, "You'll need to leave as soon as Mr. Davis arrives."

Nora took the same seat as she always did and looked up to the people that seemed more curious of her than she was of them.

"So, what is it you'd like me to do tonight? I guess, just follow you?" Nora asked, looking from one face to the next. Ezra walked into the room, dressed in a fitted off-white dress shirt and dark grey slacks, clearing his throat to interrupt. Thank God he showed.

"Perfect timing, Mr. Davis. Go ahead and fill them in, Miss. Vincent. Just as you were told," Gabriel directed the woman closest to him, his eyes on Nora. He gave her a playful smile when she noticed he was focused on her, his eyes sparkling with secrets.

The woman he addressed, tall with broad shoulders, stood at attention and gave vague details of a vampire that was being problematic with providing proof of residency within the valley and required questioning. They were to follow the crew, say nothing, do nothing, and stay out of the way. They were there only to observe. The crew she spoke of, stood as stiffly as she did. When she finished her spiel, Gabriel gave them wishes of good luck and advised the recruits to behave in a sing-song voice. He was gone in a blink, as he preferred to do.

Nora didn't understand how this would help her learn the ropes of being what she thought was going to be an office lackey. Maybe it was just a way to expose them more to the underworld that they were now a part of, or maybe just to see if they could follow directions silently. It all kept adding up to more than she was being told.

Elijah had made her think that these guys would be far more informative than he had been. So far, shutting up and paying attention seemed to be the help she was being given. If they were going into a den of partying vampires, it was probably the best plan.

When they made their way to the street, they found two long, black SUVs with darkly tinted windows. The woman Gabriel had addressed as Miss. Vincent directed Nora and Ezra to one, while she and a stern, squat-looking man in his thirties loaded into the other. Nora watched them through the rear window until the other four members and Ezra had loaded in with her. Miss. Vincent and the other fellow must be important if they got an eight-seater vehicle to themselves. A woman with cherub cheeks on each side of a shy smile introduced herself as Melissa when she sat beside Nora in the far back. She spoke for the beast of a man in front of her, whose head grazed the roof of the SVU as he sat quietly with his huge hand wrapped on the roof's grab bar beside Ezra, and said he was Zeke. A wily man who never seemed to stop moving slid behind the wheel and introduced himself as Angus, and the lean, man with perfectly quaffed blonde locks beside him as Rowan. When he turned to the passengers to give a wave, Nora leaned to the side to get a better look at him. Even in the dark vehicle, just the glow of the streetlights was enough to see how attractive Rowan was. Nora couldn't be sure now that he wasn't one of the Supermodel Squad. There was no sign of the sweet smell of sugar cookies in the air. Maybe he was just a perfectly gorgeous specimen of a human. As if he could read her thoughts, he flashed a movie star smile of pearly whites before turning back in his seat. Nora shrunk down in her seat, feeling the heat of embarrassment on her cheeks. Who knows if there were mind readers among them? Two days ago, paranormal was just that — not the norm.

"How are you guys doing? A little nervous?" Angus asked, pulling out behind the lead SVU when it passed. Nora didn't know if she could speak or not. She was directly told to keep her mouth shut. Ezra turned and shared a questioning look with her. "It's ok, guys. At ease," Angus laughed. Zeke's mountainous shoulders shook slightly in front of her. "Davina is a bit of a hard-ass robot, but you can relax here."

"That's why we make her and Dan ride solo," Melissa chimed in, "They stress us out and kill the vibe."

It was beyond Nora what the optimal vibe was for going out into the night to hunt down a *vampire* to question him would be. The relaxed, friendly energy in the car was certainly more ideal.

Ezra was the first to chime in, "So, you guys work for The Firm, or BITN, or whatever you call it?"

"We do. We're an intel crew. It's pretty much just gathering what the High Council needs to know to get their important, secret monster work done," Angus replied.

"Who are the High Council?" Nora wondered how many levels of power were involved. It was starting to sound like she was working for a supernatural government.

"They are at the very top of the food chain. The highest-ranking member of each group of creatures and beings. They oversee everything. And I mean *everything*. In this world and beyond," Angus spoke with reverence and awe, which was fitting. Nora was still trying to wrap her head around this one same corner of a new world, and he was telling her that their reach was into realms beyond. Elijah said these guys would be able to give her information and they sure could.

"We're a Bump in the Night crew," Zeke's said quietly, and his shoulders shook again. He was playful for such a giant. "Get it? BITN?"

"Yeah," Nora laughed, "Seems a bit more suiting than Bureau of Identification of whatever it is."

"Identification and Tracking of Non-mortals," Melissa corrected, "Bump in the Night crew is just the fun name we use. Do not let Elijah hear you call it that. Or Davina for that matter."

"If this department is all about vampires, why does a demon run the place?" Ezra inquired, leaning forward to Angus.

"He's the best man for the job, man. They all intermingle within themselves. Pretty wild to meet a demon for the first time, right?" Angus said excitedly while he looked back at them in the rear-view mirror.

"It's all been pretty wild. Pretty unbelievably wild," Nora offered. She didn't add that's been entirely terrifying, as well.

The drive to the club was only a few minutes and her hands felt cold when they pulled up to the neon lights that signaled the front of Mystique. A few slow, deep draws of air helped prepare her for whatever lay within those walls. Knowing what she now knew, she was glad the door was shut in her face when she tried to apply for a job there. Who knows what would be required of the employees there? She hoped they had the same no-feeding clause that she now had. She shook away the memory of Gabriel's blood dripped lips.

Ezra looked out the window at the nightclub filled with vampires that sat just feet away, "Are you guys like Van Helsings hired by the vampires themselves?" Ezra questioned.

"Oh man, no. We're just on the street info-jockeys gathering intel. That mark on your wrist gets you enough respect from these guys to get more out of them than you think," Angus answered with a serious note in his voice, "They're mostly pretty terrified of the High Council."

"Killing vamps is a huge no-no," Rowan said, turning in his seat to them, "An absolute no-go zone for us. They have a separate squad for that."

"See, vampires are not allowed by their own laws to kill another vampire. Even in self-defense, whoever won would still be put to death. Other beings don't like to get into death dealings of other groups, so they leave it up to humans," Melissa said too lightly for Nora's liking.

"They have a group of elites that give the order to take one out. It gets around the rules, you know? To have us humans do their dirty work," Angus said, watching Davina and Dan slide out of the SUV in front of them. "Dan says he knows a guy that's on the squad who's killed over a dozen himself, but I call bullshit that he even knows the guy."

"Why don't they just change the rule so they can handle it themselves? It has to be easier for a vampire to handle a vampire than one of us?" Ezra asked, turning to see if Nora agreed. It did make more sense than bringing humans into the mix.

"Why change what's worked for them for thousands of years? And this way they don't get their hands dirty,"

Rowan said, adjusting something he had just inside of his jacket. A glint of silver flashed in the light. Would a gun be of any use against vampires?

"What you need to understand is that we're expendable. Humans. We're just worker ants to them. And if someone fucks up and kills a vamp without permission either because they want to or had to, all it means to them is a fresh meal," Angus said flatly, turning off the truck, "A chicken or a cow can't claim self-defense when it doesn't want to be eaten, can it?"

Nora shifted in her seat, not in a rush to get out of the truck.

'...put to death on site.'

"That being said, they aren't sending us out like lambs to the slaughter. Like Angus said the mark does mean hands-off. And if there ever is a time that we are put in harm's way, we all have these," Rowan said, pulling out what was concealed in his jacket. A smooth stake, made of a dark, rich brown wood with a polished and razor-sharp silvertip balanced on his palm. "They get rid of vampires that won't toe the line and they get to decide what they do with us after. If we're the ones that make it out, that is. They give us a fighting chance, at least."

Nora was horrified that they were so settled in that possibility as if it was a risk of a papercut. These people, these creatures more like it, used humans as completely replaceable objects and these four seemed perfectly okay with the situation they found themselves in. It had to be Stockholm Syndrome, or at the very least they were all insane.

"How is that fair?" Ezra barked, and checked his tone when Zeke turned to him with a stern glare, "I mean, how can they just use us like that?"

"Hey, fella. You get to be a part of the secret now. You don't know how lucky you are. You're safer working for them than going through life not knowing that you're literally one of their food groups, aren't you? It's better to be a tool to utilize than a blood bag to be sipped on," Zeke said, putting his massive hand on Ezra's shoulder. "We have a chance this way."

Rowan tucked his stake away when Davina knocked on the driver's window.

"Alright, let's go. Stay close, stay quiet, and stay alert. Fresh meat is always a novelty to these bloodsuckers," Angus directed before he joined Davina and Dan on the sidewalk.

"Remember, if anyone approaches you, show them that mark on your wrist," Melissa added.

Before she had a chance to let her nerves get the best of her or ask a million of the questions she still had, Nora found herself walking into Mystique and face to face with more vampires. Maybe it was better to know less about the dangers of the job if there was little more than a tattoo on her arm to protect her. Ignorance really could be bliss, no matter what Zeke said.

The same woman she had encountered when trying to find work was standing at the door. She had a comically straight black bob that hung just below her ears. The severe, too-short bangs drew a straight line across her forehead highlighting muddy brown eyes that were framed with deep crow's feet. Her stubby nose was held in the air with an exhausting level of arrogance when Davina whispered something in her ear, the pounding music covering any trace of what. The woman nodded, stepping aside. As Nora passed her, a look of recognition washed over her face for a flash of a moment before her mask of indignation returned. She pulled a slight, young man to her side and barked something at him. Nora couldn't make out what was said but it had him turning his heel quickly into the club towards the back.

"That's Muccia," Melissa said, seeing Nora stare at the austere woman, "We call her Mucus. She's been hanging off the vampires for decades. Poor thing thinks they're going to turn her," Melissa shook her head with pity in her eyes, "She thinks she's close enough to them to look down on us, but she's used even more than us by these guys."

Making their way into the club, music thumping between dark, mirrored walls, it looked just as most clubs in the city did. Not the fanged, blood and leather-clad sex scene that Hollywood was keen to present. Looking at the faces in the mirror, some caught up in conversations, others swaying to the beat of the DJ, Nora was surprised at what she did see that was unexpected. Reflections of the vampires. Hollywood and the lore seemed to be wrong about that one too. The only thing that gave them away in this space was that all of the glasses were filled with the same deep, crimson liquid. It was easy to tell that it was blood.

Served at 98.6 degrees, never frozen, and never stored for more than thirty days.

Nora shivered when the information popped into her head. That was not something that would normally present itself in her thoughts. She knew it was from the bizarre plant of knowledge that Gabriel had somehow dumped in her brain. She made a mental note to ask the crew what they knew about the Ascensions.

Sticking close to the group, she watched them scan the crowded space, at times stopping to speak with one club-goer or another. They seemed to be received fairly cordially and it made her a little more comfortable seeing Angus' words in action. There was a sense of respect between the human crew and the vampires which was unexpected. Humans acting as an authority over beings that could turn them into a juice box was not what you would expect to be welcome guests; especially when they were the minority in the room.

A pale man with fangs that hung over his bottom lip pointed towards the bar when approached about the vampire in question's whereabouts. Rowan motioned for the group to follow him over to check out whatever tip the rabbit-faced vampire had provided. The space between the rows of midnight blue banquettes was narrow and they fell into a single file to make their way through to the bar that stretched the length of the opposite wall.

It was only about fifteen feet before Nora found herself separated, a group of giggling sorority-sister-type vamps pushing their way in front of her. Stepping off to the side to make way for them, she bumped into a table. A wine glass filled with what was noticeably not wine started to tip and she snatched it up and righted it before it could spill a drop. The vampire that sat in the booth didn't notice, her face buried in the neck of a man whose head lolled back against the banquette. His head dragged up for a moment and he looked to Nora.

"Oh my god. Seriously? Ew!" Nora stepped back quickly from the dazed eyes and lazy smile of Dirtbag Derek. It was no surprise that he would allow himself to be a vampire's snack. His hand groped towards the vamp's lap only to have it slapped away and his head slammed against the high seatback for her to continue her meal. She grimaced at the sleepy, satisfied expression that melted over his face. Apparently, Dirtbag Derek was aware of the paranormal underbelly of Aumbry Valley and was a fan. She wondered if he was one of the humans that were used and abused by the super-natured or if he himself was something else. He was creepy enough to be something otherworldly. His eyes slowly turned back to her with a look of recognition. His lips turned up into a half-smile before his head was pushed back into place by the ravenous vampire. Nora stepped away from the table and the most disgusting meal she had ever seen.

Standing on her tip-toes, she could see that the crew had yet to notice she was not close by. Ahead of her, a gap between two booths led to a clearing where she would be able to meet back up with them. A metal sign etched with BATHROOM pointed in the direction she was going. Not having a mile-long lineup to the ladies' room was not something that Nora had ever seen before. If vampires didn't need them, it just left the few humans who either worked there or were *served* there to put them to use, and with no one lined up, she was quickly making her way along to the other side of the room. Unfortunately, when she made her way alongside the crew, there wasn't another break in the booths to allow her back through. Nora watched Ezra look over the group to find her missing. He scanned the crowded club, but waving her arms was not getting his attention. She decided to try to go back the way she had started and had only taken a step before a woman blocked her path.

"I know you," the woman purred. Her platinum hair fell in perfect curls to her waist, and her dark eyes were lit with the distinct glow of a vampire's iris. She took another step forward, close enough for Nora to smell the sickeningly metallic scent of blood on her breath.

"I don't think you do, sorry," Nora tried to move past her. The vampire blocked her again, her stance letting her know that was not going to pass. "I'm sorry, I'm just trying to get back with my group." Looking over to the bar, there were too many people to get eyes on where they were. Her hand shaking, she pulled up her sleeve, exposing the BITN mark.

"That doesn't mean shit to me, sweet little thing. I know exactly who you are and the trouble you're going to cause," she sneered, grabbing Nora by the jaw, locking her in place, "or maybe we can shut this all down, here and now."

Nora was sure that it was a case of mistaken identity and tried to get the irate vampire to listen when she was dragged towards the dark hallway that led to the restrooms. Her pleads for help were unheard through the pounding music. The woman tightened her grip on Nora's face and pulled out a cellphone that she shouted into. Nora tried to make out what she said, ignoring the stars she was seeing from the pain in her crushed jaw.

"Hey! It's Harper. I found her...Yes! It's her! I'm telling you, one hundred percent this is her...are you kidding me? We've all seen those stupid photos...I don't care...no, fuck her...that little bitch doesn't get to tell us what to do just because she's fucking him...she's going to get him killed...," she snarled into the phone, ending the call.

"I don't know what this is about or who you are, but I swear to you, I am not whoever you think I am," Nora could barely get the words out as the vampire's hand moved lower and tightened on her throat.

"Get your hands off of her!" Ezra's voice boomed through the hallway.

The vampire loosened her grip, turning to him, "Oh, look at this! A two for one! Let's get rid of you first," she said, her voice trembling with excitement. Nora tried to pull away from the vampire when she started towards Ezra just to have the grip tighten again and tug her along.

Rowan appeared at Ezra's side, his expression tight with concern, and his hand hovering over the space in his jacket that held his stake.

"That's enough, Harper. This isn't a fight you're going to win," Rowan spoke evenly, his other hand outstretched to Nora, indicating for her to stay put.

"You can't all be that dumb, can you? This isn't about a single fight. This is bigger than all of us. This is a war!" She pulled Nora against herself with lightning speed, her hand still on her throat and her fangs to her cheek, "This pathetic sack of flesh is as disposable as every other human life. Do not kid yourselves. You know it, I know it, everyone in here knows it. We will rise!" the woman cried out and bared her teeth, "Say goodbye, boys."

Nora closed her eyes, frozen in place and resigned to the helplessness of her neck being ripped out by this psychopath. So much for the superhero moves Gabriel had said she now had.

"Nora! Move!" Ezra screamed and Nora's body responded. A fist to Harper's face released her grip allowing Nora to spin away against the wall.

"Oh, shit! Oh, *shit*!" Rowan screamed just as Nora felt a flash of heat behind her.

Opening her eyes, the vampire was no longer there. In her place was a stake that sat upon a fresh pile of ash. Bright orange embers rose up and twisted in the air.

Nora's breath caught in her throat as she jumped away from the remains toward Ezra and Rowan. The other five members of the crew turned the corner to find the chaotic scene.

"What the hell happened?" Davina raged, her eyes bulging with anger.

"He just grabbed my stake...right from my jacket...she was about to pounce on Nora...and he...," Rowan blew out a tight breath, trying to put together what he just witnessed.

Ezra stood beside him, his arm still outstretched from throwing the stake, his eyes on the ashes.

Angus let out a surprised whoop and punched Ezra on the shoulder, "Goddamn! The new guy just took out a vamp!"

CHAPTER NINE

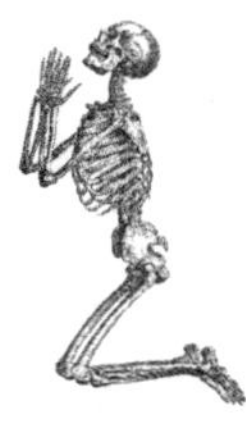

"Angus, seriously?" Rowan scowled at the glee radiating from his fellow crew member. The excitement of a vampire's death in a room filled with vampires could be a death sentence to them all.

Nora stood at Ezra's side, staring at the ashes which were still drifting in the air above what was left of Harper. Before she could utter a word, the team sprung into action. In a flurry of activity, the hallway was blocked off, keys were pressed into her palm, and they were ushered outside to an alley. When they made it to one of the SUVs, the door to the driver's side was opened to shove Nora in. Looking to her right, she saw that Ezra had been put in the passenger seat. His face was pale, his eyes far away and lost in the replay of what had just happened.

"Are you okay? Do you understand? Nora!" Melissa's voice pulled her back into the moment, "I need you to take him to his house and then I need you to go right home and stay there until you hear otherwise, okay?"

"Ye...yeah, okay," Nora nodded, fumbling the keys into the ignition. Her jaw throbbed and her throat was raw from screaming against Harper's death grip.

"You're okay to drive, right?" Melissa asked, urgency in her voice. She put her hand gently on Nora's shoulder, "Nora, look at me. It's going to be okay. Just get him home, and then you go home. Got it?"

When Nora nodded again, Melissa turned and was gone back into the alley. Pulling the truck into the street, Nora gunned it for Ezra's place. The squeal of the tires brought Ezra out of his daze and into a newfound panic. He pulled at fistfuls of hair on his head and rocked back and forth in the seat.

"What the fuck, what the fuck, what the fuck?! Oh my God, what the fuck did I do?" he shouted as his body madly trembled.

"It's okay, Ezra. It's going to be ok. It's okay," Nora reassured him, not believing a word of it. She repeated the words over and over, trying to soothe herself, as well.

"I don't know why I did that! I just reacted. You looked so scared and before I knew what I was doing, it had happened," Ezra stared at his shaking hands in disbelief, "They're going to fucking kill me, Nora!"

She tried to focus on the road while the words from the office screamed in her head, prophesizing what she was sure to come.

'...put to death on site.'

The very first assignment they were given, and it would be their last. Ezra had acted on her behalf; he had saved her life. There was a good chance he was now going to pay with his. Nora knew that there was an equal chance that she would suffer the same fate. Would the rest of the crew, who were currently cleaning up their mess, also be in danger of losing their lives because of a blink-of-the-eye mistake? Nora cursed the moment she laid eyes on Elijah in the elevator, she cursed letting herself get excited about being a part of something so dangerous, and mostly she cursed the moment that she had decided to pack up and start over in Aumbry Valley. It had been nothing but hell on earth since she arrived.

Screeching to a stop in Ezra's driveway, Nora turned to him. He was still rocking in his seat, unaware they had arrived at his house. "You need to go inside. They said we need to go inside and wait to hear from them." He turned to her, his face pinched with worry. "We're going to be ok, alright? It's okay."

She wished she could believe her own words.

"I never should have come to this fucking nightmare of a town," Ezra punctuated his anger by punching the dash.

"I need you to get inside your house, Ezra," she took a deep rooting breath when he didn't move, "Why don't I stay with you?" Nora started to unbuckle the seat belt that she didn't remember buckling in the first place.

"No! That's a bad idea. You almost died once tonight. You need to put some space between us in case something happens." Ezra held up his hands in protest before jumping out of the truck without another word.

Even though she had been directly told to go home, Nora didn't like the idea of leaving him on his own. She waited until he was inside before pulling back out of the driveway. Pausing on the street, she wondered if she should stay parked in front of his house. Now was not the time to break any more rules. It was smarter to follow Melissa's instructions, so she hit the gas and made record time to her apartment.

Locking the door behind her, she peered through the peephole. There was no sign of life, just as always in her quiet building. If someone were to come after her, she hoped that the others who lived within the old walls would be spared. Heavy guilt bled through the worry that pressed into her chest. Ezra could be in serious trouble for protecting her, and now she had put Jenny,

Olivia, and her other two tenants in danger. Tugging the curtains closed, Nora hopped onto her bed and pulled up Ezra's number on her cell phone. Silas, seemingly unaware of her fright, curled up on her lap to demand attention. Each ring made her heart jump until Ezra answered.

"Are you okay?" they asked in unison.

"Yeah, I'm home. Are you good?" Nora asked, relieved to hear his voice.

"So far so good," Ezra replied, sounding more in control of his facilities than when she had left him, "A half glass of scotch has helped."

Nora rubbed at a headache that was settling in, "What do you think is going to happen?" She got up from the bed to look at her neck in the mirror. Deep red streaks of bruising striped across each side.

"I don't know, but I'm guessing nothing good," Ezra murmured.

Nora could hear the clink of ice in his glass.

Sitting back on her bed, she stared at her closed curtains, her imagination running wild at what could be on the other side. Her heart jumped a beat when her phone buzzed against her cheek. A text message from Elijah. Seeing his name atop the message let her know that he, or someone, hell – some*thing* – had put his number in her phone. She wondered what aspect of her life they hadn't meddled with yet. The message left her mouth dry.

`9 am sharp. In the office.`

Ezra, having received the same message, read it out, "Well, it looks like I've been given a stay of execution until at least 9 tomorrow," Ezra's laugh was hollow and echoed in his glass.

"We don't know what's going to happen, and there's no use worrying about the worst," Nora offered. It was foolish to try to pretend everything might turn out alright, but all they had left was hope. Leaving them until morning did give the impression of possibly getting out of the current situation alive. The warning in the office had seemed that it would be an instantaneous and permanent punishment. She tipped-toed to her door, peering out the peephole. Still no signs of anyone.

"Maybe I should just get the hell out of here. Run for the hills," Ezra sighed. Nora could hear him sloppily pouring another drink.

"I don't think there's a hill that you could run to that would hide you from vampires and demons, unfortunately," Nora said and quietly moved across the apartment to peer out onto the street. "I know you don't want to talk about it, but why did you come here, anyway? How did you even know about it?" She had found so little information on Aumbry Valley when she received

Quinn's letters with that postmark. Since her aunt had always been drawn to places off the beaten track, Nora hadn't even thought to ask her how she found this one. If she had known any bit of what she was now privy to, she would never have pointed Cherry Bomb in the direction of the dammed valley of the undead.

"It was weird," Ezra started. He paused with a disquieted chuckle when Nora did the same, "I guess weird is life now."

"Ain't that the truth," Nora mumbled. She curled up on her bed, taking comfort in Silas' steady purr.

Welcome to Aumbry Valley. A voice told me it was the right place to start over. It told me that every night until I packed up my car and headed towards the pin on the map that I dropped when I finally found it."

Nora sat in the silence he left for a moment. There was no way that those dreams were a coincidence. Especially now that she knew a vampire who liked to play around in people's heads. Why on earth would he find a random guy and lure him to Aumbry Valley to be a vampire lackey? There had to be more to how they found him. "What was so bad back home?"

"What wasn't?" Ezra breathed sadly. Nora could hear him sniffling into his sleeve. "I had nothing left. I had my sister Laura, and her wife Aria. End of list. They were just starting their own family and didn't need me there being a shadow of depression over their happiness." Nora could hear ice cubes clinking into the glass again. "So, it is what it is, and I ended up here. It's fine. It will all be fine, just like you said. We're gonna be okay," Ezra slurred, "They just had a baby last month, you know? Lucy. They've sent pictures. She's really sweet. Looks like my mom."

It tore Nora apart to hear him so raw and broken, "Ezra, I...," she started.

"No, it's all good. I'm good. I think I'm going to try to get some sleep. We'll see what tomorrow brings when it brings it, right?" He sniffled loudly and let out a hollow laugh.

Nora wanted to say something that would console him. The man had just saved her life and he sounded completely defeated. She pleaded with him to stay on the phone with her, that they didn't have to talk, just have an open line in case anything happened. He declined her offer and hung up.

Nora stared at her phone, wondering if she should call back, or if she should go over to his house. Not following Melissa's, and especially Elijah's, instructions seemed like the worst idea in the world. She set the alarm on her phone for eight AM and was lucky that she did. At some point in her swirl of worried thoughts, her brain gave her the courtesy of letting her nod off for a spell. She awoke with her phone still in her hand, the alarm pinging.

She immediately called Ezra back, and she was relieved to hear his voice, still raspy from a scotch-induced sleep. He did not continue the conversation from their last call and instead said he was jumping in the shower and would meet her at Elijah's office. When she offered to come to pick him up, he said his Jeep was somehow back in his driveway and that he would drive himself. After making him promise over and over that he would indeed show up so they could face what lay ahead together, Nora quickly got ready and threw on some sweats. If she was walking into something dangerous, she was at least going to do it comfortably. She was pleasantly surprised to find the pain in her jaw and the marks on her throat were gone. Fairy blood for the win again.

A quick peek into the hall found it still to be empty. Listening, she could hear Olivia loudly singing a made-up song about cereal from the safety of Jenny's apartment. Quietly closing the door, she clicked the key in the lock. It would be best if she didn't have to see Jenny or the other residents of the crumbling Dunhope Manor that morning. Her hands were still shaking, and she could think of no plausible excuse for her frazzled and uneasy appearance. She frowned at where the remnants of the ash she had wiped off of her door the night before were and the fresh mark in its place. She gave it a quick swipe with her sleeve and headed out to her unknown future.

Pulling her wet hair into a tight bun on the top of her head, she stopped where she had parked the SUV the night before. In its place sat Cherry Bomb. Reaching into her bag, she found the keys to the truck.

"Well, how's this supposed to work?" Nora asked the universe, frustrated. When she tried the handle, she found the door open and the keys sat at the ready in the ignition. Throwing her bag onto the passenger seat, she slid into the car and started it up. It seemed that vampire killing came with free valet service. Either a good sign or a last courtesy. She didn't know which but hoped for the best. There was no time like the present to find out.

Pulling up to 1365 Beech Avenue, she parked behind Ezra who was waiting in his car. His black ball cap was pulled low to the dark sunglasses he wore. He stepped out when he saw her approaching in his rear-view mir-ror. He had taken the opposite attire choice with a crisp white shirt and matte black tie as if he was headed to court. He looked as uncomfortable as he must feel with the unknown ahead.

"Well, we've made it another day," he said, his smile tight.

"Let's do this," Nora tried to sound brave and steady.

The elevator ride up one floor was too quick for their liking and soon they were standing in front of Pearl's desk. The hidden door to Elijah's office was closed.

A muffled snicker shook Pearl's tiny shoulders. She had put aside her work to watch the two, "You two seem to be getting along like a house on fire, aren't you. Quite the team," she said, her sweet voice gravelly. Ezra and Nora looked at each other, unsure how to reply. "You two are going to give me endless entertainment. I'll tell you that for free."

They didn't have a chance to find hope in her words before the large door slid open. Gabriel, in his luxe pajamas and a face twisted with displeasure, pointed a long, manicured finger at them.

"You two, in here. Now," Gabriel hissed.

Chapter Ten

Uncertainty weighted their stride as they followed him in. They found Elijah was inside the office, leaning on the front of his desk, arms folded, one ankle crossed casually over the other. His face was unreadable when he nodded towards the chairs for the two to sit. When they complied, he looked them over wordlessly. The room was silent other than the squeak of Gabriel's velvet slippers when he shuffled over to lounge on one of the sofas along the wall. Nora watched him toss himself onto the cushions and was sure she would pass out if someone didn't say something soon.

"Well. You two sure had quite the first night," Gabriel announced, fussing with his silk pajama coat, "I can't say I'm surprised."

"Gabriel, please," Elijah scolded him, his impenetrable eyes never leaving the apprehensive pair. The wait overnight seemed to pass more quickly than the ticking clock of the moment.

"Don't *Gabriel please*, me, mister. This could have waited for tonight and I could be resting peacefully right now," he growled, "I had to spend all night cleaning up their mess, just because *you* wouldn't be honest with these two from the start. For someone who proclaims to avoid drama, this is all on you, Elijah. I'm exhausted and grumpy," he pouted and crossed his arms like a petulant child, "Make this quick."

Elijah ignored him with a sigh before turning his attention back to them, "Miss. Goodman, I have been informed that you were not badly injured last night. I do hope that is correct," Elijah inquired gently.

Not what she was expecting. Gabriel's anger seemed to be directed at Elijah and not her and Ezra, and Elijah's tone seemed genuinely caring. That would be unexpectedly, and incredibly welcome, good news. Ezra sat rigidly in the chair, eyes on the floor, his leg bouncing rapidly. Nora put a hand on his arm, hoping to comfort him.

"Yeah, I mean yes, I'm okay," she said quietly, cutting herself off before she could add thanks to Ezra. It seemed best to not draw attention to the elephant in the room.

"Fucking Harper. She's always been such an aggro-bitch," Gabriel sneered, "She wasn't going to last long with them anyways. Big fucking mouth, that one."

The energy in the room was not the fire and brimstone that she had been expecting, and hope of reprieve started to grow. The red-hot, pressurized anger that could roll from Elijah was not making an appearance. At least so far it hadn't. Ezra looked up from the floor, meeting the demon's eyes, "Sir, I'm..." he stopped when he was silenced by Elijah's raised hand.

"Mr. Davis, let me begin by allaying your fears," he began, calmly walking around to his seat behind the desk, "You are not in trouble, *per se*. In a way, you reacted exactly how we hoped you would," he punctuated his message with a sly smile.

Ezra sat up, back stiff, and took in the demon's words. Nora couldn't believe there was a possibility of being let off the hook so easily, especially in Ezra's case. The rules of the supernaturals were not easy to comprehend. *Put to death on site* seemed to need something more serious than killing a vampire seeing as they were both still alive and kicking. What could be worse was unknown. She hoped there was an ancient manual tucked away somewhere that could educate the foolish mortals on the ins and outs of these crazy beings. She gripped Ezra's arm with the strength of her building relief.

"You just staked the wrong one, dum-dum," Gabriel laughed and smiled broadly when Elijah glared, "Say the word, Hot-head! I can leave at any time. This is your mess, not mine."

Elijah again didn't reply to him. "Gabriel is right that I should have been honest with you from the onset of your inclusion in our business. It is unfortunate that Harper lost her life, and it rests on my shoulders to deal with that. It is sad but the loss of life in battle is required to win some wars."

Nora thought of Harper's rantings of war and how they would rise. These were not the words of basic business. There was no way she could believe that they were there as human lackeys anymore. Just as relief had started to wash over her, fear of the bigger picture revealing itself demanded to be acknowledged. Nora scowled at the voice in her head that grew louder and more insistent.

If it's too good to be true...

She tried to silence it by focusing on the fact that they didn't seem to be there to walk the plank. Whatever was going on, they were going to live another day in the middle of it. The word live was the most important element.

Confusion sat on Ezra's face, listening intently to the riddles that Elijah preferred to speak in, "So, am I...?"

"Off the hook for bitch-slaying? For now, yes," Gabriel answered, carelessly picking at his nail.

"I think it's fair to say that we weren't clear with your roles as our employees. The reason for that is we were not sure ourselves, in how you would best be of use. If I'm to be completely honest with you, you are not our employees at all. You would be more aptly called tools for our current assignment. One of the most difficult and worrisome issues we've had to deal with in some time, frankly. Having you complete an Ascension was required for us to utilize you in the ways that we have. Or how we had planned to, I suppose," he paused, looking over Nora and Ezra's overwhelmed expressions, "You can not be surprised that you were selected to be more than the work of a familiar."

"Like we'd bother gifting a basic-bitch Familiar with a salary, let alone an Ascension," Gabriel chimed in. "Humans are not something we are in short supply of, and Fae blood is not an easy access welcoming gift that we toss around to the help."

Nora wanted to know what the deal was with the blood and secrecy. The connection between herself and the supernatural beings that saw fit to turn her life upside down, and what she and Ezra could possibly have in common with each other to find themselves side by side in the whole mess. She started to let the questions pour out for only a split second before a pointed finger and warning glare from Elijah silenced her.

"Please, allow me to speak," his eyes were black as night until she clenched her jaw to stop herself, "Regardless of what your role would end up being, we wanted to give you the highest level of protection before utilizing you," Elijah spoke at a dragging pace that let her know he was choosing his words carefully, "The one thing we all have in common is free will. You both have free will, regardless of what influence we have over you. Even a memory wiped from your mind is accessible if your will is strong enough to retrieve it," he sighed, frustrated with his explanation, "I didn't want to involve outsider humans in any of this. The fae were even more adamant about that. Last night was supposed to be the beginning of the end of all of this. Nice and easy, over before you even knew what had happened. Unfortunately, it has just gotten us all in deeper," he shook his head at whatever he was trying to explain to them, "The good news is that you are willing to and capable of doing what needs to be done if we need you to. That means you have a better chance of surviving this mess."

"Elijah, you're rambling again," Gabriel piped in, "What he's trying to say is that he hoped that you wouldn't have to use it but, we gave you the skill to kill, and you chose to ash that bitch. Very good news for us."

"So, you *do* want us to be vampire killers?" Ezra questioned. The unease and confusion of what was being poorly explained crumpled his face with a frown.

"Dear me, no," Elijah said, opening a drawer and pulling out a stack of files. He had more manila folders than answers, that's for sure. "We didn't want you to have an active role in any of this at the onset. I hope that Harper is the last one harmed in what has become senseless aggression."

"Don't get any ideas about going all Helsing around here, Mr. Davis. Some of us are the good guys," Gabriel barked out a laugh, "Not all of us are as useless as Harper," he turned a serious glower his way, "and we're certainly not as weak."

Ezra looked to Nora, wordlessly. She mirrored his discomfort.

"Okay, enough is enough. It's time you knew why we sot you out," Elijah said, handing them each a file and brushing his hands as if freeing himself of the bother of it all, "These are the reasons you are of use to us. The reason why you are of importance to our current unfortunate predicament."

Nora slowly opened the cover to reveal a single photograph placed inside.

It was a photo of her Aunt Quinn.

Before she could speak, Ezra screamed, throwing the folder on the ground. He jumped away from the chair, knocking it to the side with the power and speed of his movements. He stared down, looking at whatever was in his folder as if it could set him ablaze, "There's no way! There's no way he's a...," his eyes were crazed, and his chest rose and fell quickly as he tried to catch his breath, "Where the fuck did you get that?" he screamed.

Nora leaned down to pick up the photo that had tumbled from his file. It was a dark-haired man who appeared to be in his thirties, whom she had never seen before. He was well dressed and smiling a lecherous grin of fangs into the camera.

Ezra knew a vampire?

Nora held the photo up to him, "Ezra, calm down! Who is this?"

He pointed a shaking finger at the photo, rage consuming his face, "That's the sonofabitch who killed my wife and daughter!"

Chapter Eleven

Nora stared at the photo of the snide-looking man. The arrogance in his eyes made him instantly detestable, even without Ezra's revelation, "Your wife and daughter? What are you talking about?" she turned to Elijah, "Who is this?"

"My wife and my baby girl. He slaughtered them and got away without a trace," Ezra glared at the picture, his eyes locked with fire that made his tears glisten.

"I'm so sorry, Ezra. I didn't know," Nora whispered. She couldn't imagine having a husband and child at her age, one that seemed close to Ezra's, let alone losing them so violently. The horror that he was trying to escape was worse than anything she could have imagined, and it turned out he was following it while thinking he was escaping it.

The tears that welled in his eyes streamed down his cheeks when he spoke, "Where did you get this picture?" he seethed before ripping the photograph from Nora's hands, "Are those really... he's a vampire? You're telling me a vampire killed my family?" he spat the words in Gabriel's direction, making him sit up at attention on the sofa. The photo had left Ezra understandably unhinged.

The door that led further into the depths of the offices opened. Four of the supermodel squad of fairies walked in and stood at attention along the wall. Gabriel sat stiffly, his attention quickly alternating between Ezra and the new arrivals.

"It's alright, Mr. Davis. I can explain everything once you calm down," Elijah said, giving a quick nod to the guards.

Nora took in the shimmer in their skin when they approached. The closer they came, the more detailed the glistening of the pastel rainbow became. She sunk back into her seat and smiled at their beauty while she watched them approach Ezra. How could anyone be angry with such gorgeous creatures in view? The sweet fresh bakery smell that accompanied them warmed her nose. She looked lazily down at the photo in her hand. She blinked her eyes into focus on the image of Quinn. Her aunt's eyes staring back at her forced her to fight through the effect of the fairies and gave her head a shake. It was easier to concentrate when they focused fully on Ezra, who had calmed down and sat when they circled him. If what she was experiencing was just a contact high from being so near them, Ezra must have been turning into putty, yet tears still quietly made trails down his emotionless face and onto his jacket. His chest which was pumping from rage was slowing as he sunk further into the plush wing chair that one of the guards had righted with one hand. Nora didn't know how long they could keep him in that state, so she took advantage of his silence to get some information.

"How do you have these pictures? What does my Aunt Quinn have to do with all of this?" Nora pressed quickly. There was no way that she would have had anything to do with killing a mother and child. Quinn was wild, but she was not a murdering monster and she certainly had never been violent. There had to be another connection. How could she fit into this mess?

"Your Aunt has terrible judgment and even worse taste in men," Gabriel spat, cautiously moving around the four fairies and perching on the desk. His eyes narrowed on Ezra, and he waved his hand in front of his face to make sure he was still zoned out. Being that Ezra exploded with rage upon finding out a vampire killed his family, and the fact that he had just killed one the night before, it made sense for Gabriel to be leery.

"Quinn would never do anything like..." Nora pointed to the photo Ezra now held loosely on his lap, "She would never harm anyone, especially a child."

"No, she did not have anything to do with the tragedy that befell Mr. Davis," Elijah said quietly, "She does, however, keep intimate company with the man who did. She is not the same woman that you knew, Miss. Goodman. Not anymore."

Nora stared at the face in his photo and back to the one in her hand. Quinn was dating a murderer? An undead, blood-sucking vampire? She was vegan, for god's sake! "Is she, I mean did he..."

"She is now vampire, yes," Elijah nodded softly

"An illegal at that!" Gabriel said, baring his fangs.

Elijah silenced him with a flick of his eyes in his direction, "You can see now why I was utilizing you under false pretenses. I had hoped to keep all of this from you both. It's only right to tell you the truth now."

Nora was dazed with the shock of everything that she had been hit with but tried her best to follow along with Elijah and Gabriel as they tagged teamed the explanation of why they were there. The man in the photo was Judiah. At some point, he had modernized his name to Jude.

"As if anyone thought that was better," Gabriel butted in.

Elijah ignored him and continued to explain that he was believed to have been a vampire for around a century and a half after being turned in his late thirties.

"As if that blink of time makes him a big deal," Gabriel sniffed. He closed an invisible zipper on his lips when Elijah turned an annoyed frown his way. The story was laid out for her without further interruption.

Jude had been a very successful human in Aumbry Valley, making his fortune working closely with the beings that had been settled there for thousands of years. The ties that he had to the town had been broken when he was made vampire by an unknown make and his departure shortly after his turning. He had briefly attempted to live among the other vampires and disappeared just as quickly, with no reason given. Until a year ago.

He had reappeared and almost immediately started to push back against their authority. He had returned to shut down the high council as he believed it to be archaic and unnecessary and made a point to go against every law that they had in place to maintain the peace among all of the beings that resided in the Valley, as well as the universal treaties that have been held up for millennia. Jude believed that if there had to be one power, that power should be his if he was able to take it.

One of the rules that he despised most was needing to ask permission from the council to turn a new vampire. He loudly preached that the power of a vampire lies in that vampire, and he should be able to use it as he pleases. Since his return, he had already turned dozens that they knew of, and each new vamp followed him without question, creating a cult-like army that would continue to upset the balance of creatures for as long as he could. The most worrisome issue was that he had broken one of the most sacred of covenants by turning other supernatural beings to vampire. This was rarely done and deeply looked down upon by the High Council, especially the fae members. It was never something that a vampire could take upon themself to decide.

Elijah spoke at length of the need for the High Council to keep control over those that could destroy the peace they had found with creatures and humans alike, and that they were responsible for keeping each species alive. They also had the power to destroy if they felt threatened. There hadn't been a threat like Jude in a very long time and he needed to be stopped. Elijah spoke pointedly for once and Nora listened in silence. Ezra stared at him through sedated eyes.

"Jude has been building this army with the pure intention of living outside the confines of rules and justice with himself as judge, jury, and executioner of all vampires," Elijah's wrung his hands with the thought of it, "He finds it unnecessary to create peace among creatures and kills any and all without prejudice."

When he finally stopped speaking, Nora thought through her remaining questions, "How is Quinn involved with this other than he made her a vampire? And what does any of this have to do with me?"

"You're the bait for the bait, honey," Gabriel chimed in. No matter the gravity of a situation, nothing could quash his glib way with words, "This little weasel is too good at hiding and at being hidden by his minions. *So*, you're going to draw out his little side piece, namely your Aunt Quinn, and he'll be drawn out by her." He punctuated the plan with a smug look of satisfaction.

Disappointment washed over Elijah's face when he explained, "When your arrival here was noted, it was decided that you could be of use and a plan was formed to draw you into our fold to assist in locating him. Even with such a small area making up the valley, he has enough of his followers to shield him from us that getting him safely into our custody has been impossible. Sadly, simply having you in Aumbry Valley has not been enough to draw them out. We were hoping that last night would have been the end of it all. Our intel had them making a rare public appearance at Mystique and we had hoped that seeing you in such an environment would have been enough of a distraction to be able to detain them without incident. However, Jude did not appear as expected," his lips pursed for a moment with frustration, "The hope was to keep enough of the details from you that there would be very little to wipe from your mind. We wanted to be able to send you on your way with as little involvement as possible. Once Jude had been taken care of, that is."

Nora's brow tipped up, "Are you kidding me? I'm literal vamp-bait? What would make you think any of this would work, anyway?" Nora was incensed at being used, her life meaning nothing to them other than as a means to an end. They wanted to use her to get to her aunt, without any question of if she would want to help. Without any notion that she would not want to put her aunt in danger. She could understand why Jude would push back on them.

"Our information was clear on how much your aunt loves you. We knew she has been desperately missing you and would jump at the chance to see you. Unfortunately, the longer she has been turned and remains with that nest of followers, the further away she will slip from her humanity," Elijah insisted, "So, time is not on our side."

"You want me to help you draw my aunt out so you can, what? Kill her? Oh my god, do you expect me to do it?" Nora's voice cracked, horrified at even the idea of it.

"Oh, calm down," Gabriel barked, "Your aunt is not the target. We have no intentions of harming her if we can help it."

Nora slammed her hands on the arms of the chair and started to let Gabriel exactly what she thought of him when Ezra's low voice interrupted them.

"Adalyn was only five," his lip quivered with a small smile, "She had Rose's bright green eyes," the room was silent as he mumbled, "They were sure it was me. They were sure I had done it. As if I could ever...they wouldn't listen about that sonofabitch," Ezra started to sit up, looking at the photograph on the floor in front of him. He was still calm but becoming more alert as he picked it up, "When they stopped looking at me, they said the trail was cold and he'd never be caught. Just like they were sure that Rose and Adalyn would never be found. They put them in a box and shoved it on a dusty shelf."

Nora covered his hand with her own, her bitterness turning to heartbreak. She looked to Elijah who, to his credit, looked just as moved, "And what is his purpose? Is he just bait, too? Hasn't he had enough taken from him already?"

Gabriel smiled widely, not reading the room, and leaned towards her, "No, sweetheart, that's my fun little twist. He's the hook!"

Ezra's eyes slowly focused on the gleeful vampire, "Meaning what?"

"If anyone should get a chance to wipe that garbage from the earth, it should be you," Gabriel playfully clapped his hands at the idea. Nora stared at him slack-jawed. As earth-shattering as Elijah made the situation seem Gabriel played it off as a game to be played. A game that he found quite fun.

"It was you, wasn't it? I know your voice now. It was you in those dreams that showed me this godforsaken town," Ezra blinked his eyes, trying to wake himself from the fairies' influence. Nora remained speechless.

"It was," Gabriel's brow wiggled with excitement.

"And you can help me track him down and destroy him?" Ezra said with steel in his voice. He was coming out of the fae's haze with a renewed rage and purpose. Nora could practically see the target he was picturing on Jude's chest. She prayed that was the only one. There had to be a way to get Quinn safely away from them.

"I can and I will," Gabriel declared, and Ezra stood quickly, his legs once again strong. "Not today, though. After the excitement of last night, it would be best to lay low."

Elijah gave another nod to the glamor guards, and they filed back out of the door. The calm remained over Ezra, thankfully, and they weren't needed to contain the explosion of emotions any longer. Gabriel gave an exaggerated stretch, complaining about the late hour, and excused himself after thanking Ezra for ridding the world of Harper. He strode from the room as if everything was right and well in the world. Nora wondered what it would take to get that vampire to take anything seriously.

"Well, that all went better than I had hoped," Elijah said with an uncomfortable smile when they were alone. Ezra tossed the photo onto the desk with a low growl. He was still worked up about it all but holding himself together.

"Those people, the fairies, they did that to Ezra, didn't they? They put him under a spell," Nora asked watching Ezra.

"Yes, one of their many fine traits is controlling the emotions of humans. It comes in quite handy," Elijah added.

"Is that why they work for you?" Ezra asked tersely, "So you can control people?"

"I wouldn't say they work for us. We have a mutual arrangement due to the nature of this valley," Elijah pressed his lips tightly as if that was all that needed to be said. He continued when they stared back at him silently demanding more, "You see, Aumbry Valley is a very special place for many different types of beings. There is a power here that is ours and ours alone that is filtered into this world through a very sacred portal. The fairies have their use, as do I, as do the vampires, as do other beings that you don't need to trouble yourselves with. This area goes back centuries upon centuries, even before humans were a blink in our eye. We all have very hallowed...," he paused searching for the word he could share, "*things* in the valley. We help each other guard them with our own unique capabilities."

"What do you have that will protect Quinn?" Nora asked flatly, "You do plan on protecting her, right?"

"I do, Miss. Goodman. You have my word. The very threat that Jude is creating is a threat to all vampires. Unfortunately, he will not believe us," Elijah stopped. He blew a small breath while trying to decide if he should go on, "You see, one of the things that the vampires have protected by the fae is their original maker. He is the lifeblood that runs through every vampire ever creat-ed, your aunt included. If he is destroyed, all vampires would follow suit. The fae have threatened this very outcome if Jude continues to create chaos within the valley. There is little more that I could tell you without putting you at further risk but know that the entire High

Council will do their best to protect you, Ezra, and your aunt," Elijah spoke with conviction and kept his gaze on her until she gave him an uneasy nod.

"If Jude isn't stopped, they would just kill all of them? They would seriously do that?" Nora's stomach lurched with the thought of her aunt losing her life because she fell in love with a psychopath. If they carried through with their threat, that would be the end of Gabriel, as well. The pomp and playfulness of Gabriel didn't align with the fact that the fae could wipe him from existence at any moment. Living with that threat every day would be enough to drive anyone mad. Maybe that was why he appeared to be the embodiment of *carpe diem*.

"They would, yes. The fae tend to have the final word with most matters on this plane and they have not existed as long as they have by accepting less powerful beings stirring the proverbial pot," Elijah sighed and stood from his desk.

Nora was in the thick of it now. Life was a lot easier not knowing about wars among supernaturals, even just moments before when she was still shaken by the simple knowledge of their existence. Going forward, lives were on the line.

"So, what now?" Nora forced her voice steady but wavered when she stifled a yawn and saw Ezra doing the same. The fairy hangover was setting in and they were feeling the drain. The emotional upheaval of the last twelve hours didn't help, either.

Elijah insisted that they go home to rest and when they asked if it would be safer to stay within the walls of The Firm, he was clear that he thought it was unnecessary, insisting that the issues of the night before had been resolved and that they were perfectly safe to go home. He believed they would be more comfortable in their own spaces and let them know he would be in contact when they would be needed again. The rush to get them back outside and on their way made Nora wonder if there was a threat to them within the walls of The Firm. She had no idea of what and who was beyond the sliding doors that they would appear and disappear through. If Jude was turning supernaturals, who was to say that he did not have some of his followers working in that very building.

For now, Elijah insisted on rest and time to process what they had been told. His awkward body language and lack of eye contact seemed out of character, making Nora nervous, but she decided who was she to decide what was the normal behavior of a demon. There was nothing more to be said when Elijah whisked himself from the room, so there didn't seem a reason for them to stay in the dark office. They let themselves out, minds still reeling. Nora could not stop thinking about Quinn, wondering where she was and if she was safe.

Nora remembered that she didn't put food out for Silas and knew that an angry kitty was waiting for her to come home. Ezra declined her offer of sticking together at her place, saying he would rather be on his own to sort through what he had learned. He had some things that he wanted to look into, and no offense meant to Nora, he would rather be alone with his thoughts. She offered to swing by his place after she fed the cat, and again he declined. He insisted that he would call her and, after they told each other to be safe multiple times, they parted ways. In as much as it didn't feel right to be alone, it felt wrong to force her company on him after what he had been told.

Dunhope Manor was silent when she slipped in, just after noon. Jenny and Olivia would probably be having their after-playschool park play. Before she could get the key in the door, she stepped back, shocked to find the same smudge of ash right in the middle of her door. There was no way that it was not being put there intentionally if it kept reappearing. Who was doing it and why were the newest of frightening mysteries to add to the growing pile. She left it be and walked into her apartment. Silas was waiting to curse her out before she even shut the door. She wished her only worries in life were demanding food and snuggles. Silas didn't know how good he had it. He certainly didn't have to deal with the nightmare that her life had become.

After putting down his food and switching on the coffeemaker, there was a rap on her door. She hoped it was Jenny with a request to look after Olivia. The wholesome normality of that little girl's silliness was just the thing she needed to try and clear her head. A quick look in the peephole showed the back of a man's head, the short blonde hair taking up the space of what she could see. She opened the door to find Rowan and Melissa, still dressed in the agents' garb of black and white.

"Hey, Nora. We wanted to swing by and see how you were doing," Melissa said. Her happy face was a relief for Nora to see, "We were glad to hear that they decided against any serious repercussion, but we still wanted to stop by and make sure you're okay."

"Wow, that's kind of you. Come on in," Nora said, stepping from the door to allow them to pass. Rowan was even better looking in the light of day when she could see how well his tailored suit wrapped over his well-defined body. He didn't smell like the sweet sugary fae, but he could easily pass as a glamor guard, "I just put on some coffee, did you want some?" She hated the flush that heated her face when he smiled and declined the offer.

Way to keep it cool, Nora.

"I'm good, too," Melissa replied. She looked around the apartment with interest and knelt to Silas when the cat approached her, "We can't stay long. Angus and Zeke are over at Ezra's. Last night was crazy, huh?"

"You can say that again," Nora scoffed, pulling a mug from the cupboard.

"Last night was crazy, huh?" Melissa stood from the cat, laughing at her own joke. Nora and Rowan chuckled at how pleased she was with herself.

"I can't believe how well you both handled yourselves. I've never seen anything like that before, especially from new recruits," Rowan said with obvious awe.

Nora poured the coffee and a sprinkle of salt before leaning on the counter to blow at the steam rising from the cup, "I don't think I've ever been so scared in my life and that's saying something with what I've been through in the past few days."

"The way you both moved so quickly with such precision. If you stick it out here, I see you both rising through the ranks above our lowly jobs and fast," Rowan said, turning to Melissa for agreement. She had pulled out her phone to read a message and her attention was now on whatever she was quickly typing in reply.

"That part was kind of cool," not the part where a vampire's flaming ashes exploded around her, she thought, "I guess that's why they do the Ascension thing."

Rowan's brow furrowed at hearing the word, "The what?"

"The Ascension. You know, with the serum," Nora replied, watching Rowan's confusion deepen, "Didn't you have the Ascension thing, in the creepy room?"

Rowan gave an uncomfortable laugh while he tried to process what she was saying, "I have no idea what you're talking about, sorry."

The curious look on his face told Nora that he honestly didn't know. The Ascension, the menacing side room, the serum, and its capabilities didn't seem to be common knowledge to the other humans that were under The Firm's employ. Just another reason for Nora to suspect they still weren't being given the real reason why Elijah and Gabriel were so keen to have them on board. Even to the point of forgiving Ezra for the death of a vampire. Something that she believed any of the agents, the two in front of her included, would have been executed for.

If Rowan and Melissa weren't aware of the Ascensions, it seemed prudent to not say anything more to them about it. Thankfully, whatever Melissa was doing on her phone was important enough for the need to rush out. Rowan was still looking at her, intrigued, while

Melissa pushed him out the door. She called out good-bye over her shoulder and pulled the door closed behind them.

Nora sat on the couch to enjoy her coffee, the caffeine having no effect on the deep fatigue that was setting into her, both body and mind. There was too much being put on her at once to easily sort through. Quinn was a vampire. Her favorite person in the whole world was a vampire, and it seemed that Nora was going to helplessly put her in danger because of a supernatural political pissing match. If only Quinn hadn't come to Aumbry Valley. If only Nora hadn't followed her. The what-ifs swirled in her head until she tossed herself onto the bed, exhausted by the last few days and the leftover effects of the fae's mood-altering influence. She soon fell into a deep sleep of vivid nightmares. Hours passed while she tossed and turned, her mind overwhelmed with the shocking revelations and violence that she had been exposed to. Dreams of Quinn, fanged and fierce, kissing the lips of Jude swirled around others of Ezra hugging a woman and child whose faces were just out of sight. The mirrored irises of Harper, nose to nose with her was the image that woke her with a start.

Silas was curled up against her side, purring. A heavy knock on her front door had her sitting up. Looking at the time on her phone, it was after seven at night and there were five missed calls from Ezra in the last half hour. Another rap on the door had her on her feet. In case it was Ezra, worried that she hadn't answered the phone, she called out apologies to him as she shuffled across the room. Opening the door, she froze. It wasn't Ezra standing there, but she did recognize the man. The slithering smile that had looked back at her from the photograph was on full display in the hallway of her building.

"Hello, Nora. I think it's time we meet. My name is Jude."

Chapter Twelve

Before Nora could move the door even an inch to slam it in his face, his impossibly strong hand was pressed against it. He held it in place as if made of steel, forcing Nora to step further back into the apartment desperate for space between herself and the newest danger to appear in life.

"Nora, Nora, Nora. Don't be afraid of me," Jude cooed to the terrified woman. He raised his arms to flatten his palms on either side of the door frame, leaning in towards her. Silas slinked over to sniff Jude's well-shined boot. "Hello, pretty kitty," he said to the cat before Silas hissed, the hair on his back spiking in response. Jude's eyes followed the cat as he scurried to Nora's side.

"What do you want?" Nora stepped back further, hoping to reach her phone without taking her eyes off of him.

"I'm guessing you already know who I am," he cocked his head, his smile grew, "I'm flattered." He took a step inside the tight space of Nora's home. As he went to take a second, he noticed the ash smudge on the door he stood beside. His nose twitched in response. "Looks like everyone has taken notice of *you*, huh?" Jude's face drew close to the mark as he closed his eyes and inhaled. His eyes opened quickly, and he faltered in his step before stepping back to the entrance. His feet remained just inside the apartment. "Lucky you, to be of such interest."

Lucky was something that Nora hadn't felt in a while. Hearing a deadly vampire speak the words inside her tiny space was something that would have made her laugh if she wasn't so utterly frightened. She looked at the ash on the door. She wanted to know what he knew of the mark on her door, but more so, she just wanted him to leave.

"How can you be in here? I thought you all had to be invited into someone's home," Nora asked, searching her mind for any trace of vampire folklore that she had ever learned. She wished that she knew how the information that would magically appear was triggered. There was no sudden answer that came to the front of her mind like before. The answer to getting him to leave as quickly as he appeared was not popping up.

"Why would I need to be invited into my own home?" Jude questioned, reaching in and dragging his finger along the chipped, plastered wall. Nora had backed up against the window and had no further space to create between them. "I was the original owner of Dunhope Manor, Nora. It has seen better days, though," he studied the room before focusing on her again. His eyes felt like they could see right through her making her feel uncomfortably exposed. Silas stood between them, hissing.

Nora pushed herself to find her voice, "But I know you don't own it now," she accused. There was no way Jenny could be a vampire. She had stood beside her in the blazing sunshine too many times for that to be true. Nora steadied her stance and put on the fiercest face she could muster, "So, I want you to leave."

not have let it fall into the shape it's in now. This is just appalling," he ran his nail down the many layers of paint on the trim he lounged on, "I sold it to a tasty little tart of a human shortly after I was turned. Sadly, she became quite boring, you know? After I became vampire, her simple little life bored me to tears. Lucky for *me*, she never had a chance to uninvite me, nor have any of the other owners since."

He had a different idea of what luck was. Nora silently called to Jenny, willing her to appear and ask him to leave. The mug that she filled with the pens of her failed jobs was within reach. If she were to smash it hard enough, there was a chance that Jenny would hear. It was the only solution she could think of, even though it wouldn't be fair to drag her into the mess she found herself in. Picturing Jenny running out into a potentially deadly situation had Nora changing her mind as quickly as she had thought of the hapless plan. It was not worth risking Jenny's, or worse Olivia's, safety. She wished that she had collected pencils instead of pens. She could at least have a sad excuse for a stake on hand. Why hadn't they been given any form of protection other than brainwashing and perfect tumbling skills? One of those fancy silver-tipped stakes would be more helpful at the moment.

"Nora, I'm not here to frighten you. I'm here to help you," Jude said with a gentle voice, pushing the loose, deep brown curls back from his face. "Quinn misses you. She's worried about you getting caught up in all of this. With all of *them*."

"Where is she? I want to see her," Nora mindlessly took a step towards him at the mention of her aunt and caught herself before she went further.

"She's safe," he nodded as he spoke, his voice warm and smooth, "I'm keeping her tucked away from the danger that those tyrants present to us. To *her*."

Nora would have felt better if Quinn had come to see her instead of Jude. Was she locked away because she was in danger from the people she had been working with or was she locked away because Jude wanted it that way? Nora wondered if her aunt was even still alive. Or still undead, as it was.

"I want to talk to Quinn. I want to hear what she has to say."

"Did you know this used to be the sitting room of Dundurn Manor? I miss the way the beams of sunlight would dance across the floor in the morning," he rubbed his hand along the wall again, his attention on Nora.

She had no interest in Jude's trip down memory lane. "I want to see Quinn! I need to know that she's okay."

He bent forward an inch into the doorway but didn't take a step closer, "She is, I promise you that. I love her, Nora. You need to believe that. And she loves *you*." Jude focused in on her, "From what she's told me, you're a very smart young woman. You need to know the whole story of what's going on. Don't you know that everyone likes to create a villain? How else can they control you if you know that they are the enemy?" his voice was velvety smooth, "The problem is, who is a villain to me may not be the villain to the next guy. His villain may not be one to you. *You* could be the villain in someone's story, and you wouldn't even know, Nora. You trust Quinn, don't you? She knows I'm not the villain in this mess."

"I want to hear that from her!" Nora felt a surge of bravery with the worry of her aunt burning in the pit of her stomach. She did not want to take a stranger's word, a vampire's word, that she was alright and safe.

Jude straightened, he was taller than she had noticed, and his eyes flashed with red-hot anger, "Well, you're the one that is trying to lure her out for them, aren't you? I'm the one keeping her safe," he took a broad step into the apartment. Nora widened her stance to hold her ground.

"Get out of here!" Nora shouted, her brow snapped together. She gritted her teeth when he laughed.

"I don't think so, little girl. I've been here a lot longer than you, as I will be in the future. This is still as good as my home. Take a look on the fourth floor, sweetie. It's my little pied-a-terre in town when I need to get away from the old ball and chain. Perfect place for a midnight snack," he slicked his tongue over his deadly fangs.

The fourth floor had been boarded up for years, according to Jenny. The original ballroom of the house had been in such a state of disrepair that they had cut it off from the rest of the house. Could he have been living above her? Her stomach rolled thinking of the midnight snacks he may have been having up there.

"What do you want from me?" Nora stammered, swallowing the acrid taste of her stomach that was trying to move up her throat.

"I want you to know that you're on the wrong side of this. You need to stop listening to the fools in that so-called Firm and join us. They are trying to control things that they have no right to control, and they are causing irreparable damage," his eyes became hooded, an attempt at looking like he did care, "Bloody hell, Nora, they would slaughter your aunt if she got in their way! Does that sound like they're the good guys in all of this? They will use you to kill her." Jude accused, taking another step towards her. Silas stood between them, a low growl vibrating from him.

"I want to hear that from Quinn, I want to hear it from her mouth. I mean it," Nora cocked her chin up defiantly.

Jude's face twisted, exposing his fangs, "Why, so you can lead them to her? You don't call the shots here, little girl. You will speak with her when I allow you to. Just like I am allowing you to have a pulse!" he shrieked and pointed to the ankh mark on her arm that she was nervously rubbing. "Just as they are. Do you think that they won't get rid of you as soon as you aren't of use? That fucking picture on your arm doesn't give you any protection. Don't you understand that? You get the respect of the fools that bow down to the High Council. To those that see through them? That's nothing more than a fancy tattoo." Jude stepped back towards the door, his fury dissipating like a fog from his face. "It would be a shame to waste such a pretty little thing," he purred, "Just think about everything that I've told you. That's all I'm asking of you. For now." The relaxed smile he gave her couldn't disguise the threat in his eyes.

"Nora?" Ezra's voice called out from the hallway.

Jude gave her a wink and moved in a flash out of her apartment. Nora made it to the hallway just as he slammed past Ezra in the entry, disappearing into the night in a blur.

"What the hell was that?" Ezra blurted, the short hair on his head settling after being lifted by the speed of Jude's departure, "Nora, are you okay? Who was that? Why didn't you answer your phone?"

Nora didn't know how to tell him that it had been the man who had destroyed his family.

Chapter Thirteen

Nora stood shivering at her apartment door, Jude's words ringing in her ears. Ezra shuffled her inside and shut the door.

"Who was that? That was another vampire, wasn't it?" Ezra asked, peering through the peephole.

Nora pushed him aside and locked the door, not that it would bring any protection against a vindictive vamp. "Not just another vampire, it was Jude," Nora replied, watching as Ezra's face reddened with fury. He flicked the lock and opened the door wide, eyes wild at thought of the man who had murdered his family being so close for such a brief moment, "He'll be long gone by now, Ezra," Nora tugged at his sleeve and pointed to the couch, hoping he wouldn't run off into the night and get himself killed. He stayed in the doorway, glaring at the entrance to the building.

"Why was he here?" he stared toward the street, his feet shuffling, unable to stand still.

"I don't know, he was going on about how Elijah and all of them were the bad guys and I was taking the wrong side," Nora pulled at his shirt again, "What are you going to do? Chase him? He could be two towns over by now with how fast he hauled ass out of here."

"He thinks he's the good guy?" Ezra scoffed, and gave one more look towards the street, "That piece of shit thinks he..." he closed his eyes, pulling in a slow deep breath that started to calm him with the focus he had earlier at the notion of putting an end to Jude, "Anyone who is against that, that...thing...is the right side to be on."

Quinn was on his side. Nora kept that thought to herself. Ezra was still staring towards the street, shifting his weight from one foot to the other and back. At least he didn't look like he was going to run out into the night any longer.

Her composure returning, she knew they needed to let someone know that he had made contact with her. She wondered if they already knew since they made it seem of utmost importance to find him, yet he just strolled on up to her door and gave it a knock.

"I'm calling Elijah to let him know," she said to the back of Ezra. He didn't acknowledge her.

When Elijah answered, he seemed distracted and made her repeat herself. She questioned how they didn't know that Jude could enter her apartment whenever he wanted, how they could know so little about him if they were trying to hunt him down? His simple answer, that they were well aware that he could, was appalling to her. It was clear how little they were trying to protect her if she could be accosted in her own home with their full knowledge. She tried to protest being involved with any of the schemes going forward, knowing that she was already too tangled in the roots of it for that to be a possibility, and was interrupted by Elijah who only wanted to know what he had said to her. She wanted to throw the phone when she listened to his unaffected tone.

"What he said is that maybe I'm on the wrong side of all of this and maybe I'm starting to see what he means!" Nora shouted into the phone, pacing back and forth, her hand pressed to her head in frustration.

Elijah paused with a sigh, his attention finally on what she was saying, "I know you must be frightened, and I am sorry that you have been dragged into this mess," the sounds of raised voices moved closer to him in the background until she heard a door click and he continued, "I don't have time to defend myself, to defend what we do, at the moment. I wish I could, but I cannot. Jude is very good at twisting narratives. That is exactly why he has been able to surround himself with those that believe the dangerous nonsense that he has been spouting. I do wish there was more that I could tell you, but again, I cannot. A lot is happening outside of your view of the situation, Miss. Goodman."

His voice had turned from empathetic to bothered in a matter of words. Nora was left uneasy by the blasé reaction Elijah had to her most recent encounter with danger, even if there were other problems at hand for him. Gabriel had easily compared her to fish bait, and Elijah had called them tools, so she shouldn't be surprised that her issues were not top of the list for the important supernatural beings of the valley. Her fears, Ezra's anger, none of it was anyone's problems but their own, it seemed. She hung up when Elijah told her that he was on his way to her apartment to discuss things further. Most likely just to set her up to be dangled in the wind again. Tossing her phone on the counter, she relayed the minimal information given to Ezra. He didn't seem to be listening. No one seemed to be listening to her. If only she could talk to Quinn. She would always listen to Nora, no matter what.

"Do you know what this is?" Ezra asked, pointing to the smudge on her door.

"Nope. It appeared a couple of days ago and it comes back if I clean it off. And for god's sake, close that door!" Nora moved to do it for him.

"I have the same thing on my door. I noticed it today when I got home," Ezra gave it one last glance and clicked it shut, turning the lock, "What do you think it is?"

"No idea. Some supernatural nonsense that I'm sure they won't tell us about," Nora muttered, going to the kitchen to pull out a bottle of wine. Holding it up to Ezra, he nodded and sat on her couch. His energy had slipped from attack to pensive, as he stared at the door, his face pinched in thought. Silas wound around his leg, purring up at the new arrival. "I mean, if they can brand us, I'm sure there's a lot of other ways they have us marked," Nora didn't like the feeling the word *marked* left with her.

Marked for death.

Ezra mindlessly tickled the fur on Silas' back, not sharing the thoughts that clouded his eyes. Nora could see the want for revenge burning through him and was glad that he was smart enough to stay put. If Jude had been a regular old human, Nora did not want to even imagine how Ezra would be ripping him into pieces at the moment. She didn't want to try to picture what Jude could do or what he had done to his family. She handed him a glass of wine and he gulped it half down as she sat beside him.

"What exactly did he say to you?" he murmured into the glass.

Nora parlayed the gist of what he had said, trying to keep it as least inciting as she could. She needed to keep him calm and in the relative safety of her apartment until Elijah arrived. She told him of her worries for Quinn. That she could not even get proof that she was alive anymore, and if she was, even if she was a vampire, she could be a pawn in all of it. Just as they were. Ezra's lip snarled and his eyes burned into the floor in front of him when she repeated Jude's message to not trust anyone in the agency. He turned bitterly to Nora when she suggested that he may be right.

"We can't trust anyone anymore, but if I have to side with anyone, it's going to be with the ones that want Jude dead," he fumed, "You need to know that, and I need to know that you feel the same way."

"It's more complicated than that. My aunt is with him. She's the only flesh and blood that I have," Nora bit her cheek to stop herself from going on. Pain twisted Ezra's face at her words.

"Maybe she's not the great woman you thought she was, Nora, or maybe she's not the same woman that you knew before she met that murderer. A good person would not stand by him," he swallowed a gulp of wine and cleared his throat, trying to tamp down the emotions that were welling up, "Rose was my first and only girlfriend in high school. The love of my life by the time we graduated from college. The only girl I have ever truly loved," his eyes glistened with the memories that he was briefly allowing himself, "until Adalyn came along." Nora sat motionless, unsure if she should offer comfort or just listen when he dragged his sleeve across his damp eyes, "She was only five years old when that monster took them. We were sitting on the hood of the car in the park. We'd spent the whole day there. It was Adalyn's favorite place. She was asleep in the back seat of the car when ...he came out of *nowhere*. Slashed Rose's throat right in front of me and buried his face in the blood. I didn't know what he was, other than a psychopath at the time. I didn't know those *things* were real," his lip quivered until he pressed his mouth tight and swallowed deeply before continuing, "I tried to get to Adalyn, but that motherfucker slammed my head into the car, and I was out cold." He took slow, methodical breaths as his grief returned to rage, "When I came to, they were gone. Just *gone*. He left me on the ground, covered in blood, and my family was nowhere to be found. He left me and took them. I have no idea why he left me. Maybe it gave him a sick pleasure to know what that did to me. Taking my wife...my sweet baby girl," he dragged his sleeve under his nose and Nora grabbed the box of tissues from the side table to pass to him. He took another mouthful of wine before he continued, "The police did what they could. There just wasn't a lot to go on with what little I could tell them and eventually it became another cold case that was forgotten to them and gossip to everyone else. Not that everyone didn't think it was me all along. Like I could ever do *anything* like that to my family," his face tightened with heartache, and he cleared his throat before finishing the wine in a gulp.

Silas bounced away from Ezra and took off for the bathroom in a blur of fur just before a rap at the door made them jump to their feet. Nora moved silently to the door and peered out, "It's Elijah," she said with relief and opened the door.

Elijah stood in the hallway, holding a handkerchief up to inspect it, "It seems as if I'm not the only one looking out for you, Miss. Goodman," he announced, nodding his head towards the ash on her door.

"Do you know what that is? Who put it there?" Nora asked as he walked past her into the apartment, "It's on Ezra's door, too."

"How are we doing now?" Elijah inquired, ignoring her question. His eyes narrowed for just a moment when he saw Ezra attempting to straighten the sorrow from his face, blowing his nose quickly and wiping at his eyes.

"Just super, Elijah. I love being yummy human bait," Nora fumed.

"Technically, you are vampire bait, not human," Elijah smiled uncomfortably at his attempt at a joke, "You...ah...you are the human, so you would be the...," he smiled tightly when Nora glared back at him. Gabriel was most certainly the one that could diffuse tension, not Elijah.

Nora moved towards him, standing tall and fierce as she could, "Did you know he was coming here?" Demon or not, she was pissed.

"We had hopes that he would, yes. I'm surprised that it was so soon," he raised his eyebrows, and his tense grin grew wider.

Elijah was being Elijah and as usual not providing any worthwhile information to the silly little humans. Nora felt like nothing more than a novelty to him. Their lives were being used as pawns in a game she didn't understand, and he didn't seem to have a care in the world about how she felt, "He told me that I shouldn't trust you. Why should I believe you and not him?"

Elijah nodded, taking in her words before giving her a shrug, "I cannot give you a reason why you should do anything, Miss. Goodman. You have no reason to trust me. Especially when you are well aware that we need you to put yourself in danger for our cause."

"I just don't see how you're using us is any different than Jude using humans to make his vampire army. You're the two sides of the same coin, Elijah. We're just tools for your secret supernatural world. I want you to tell us what's going on and what you plan on doing with us!"

"Therein lies the problem. There are far too many facets of our world that you cannot comprehend, Miss. Goodman," Elijah said with a knowing look until Nora interrupted.

"Stop with the Miss. Goodman, Mr. Davis bullshit, Elijah. I know we're just lowly humans to you, but we deserve better than being strung along and terrorized. If you want us to help you, you need to be straight with us," she erupted. The breaking point had arrived, and Nora couldn't take anymore. The world had gotten too dark and dreadful to go on as they were.

"You're right, *Nora*," he said her name gently and paused to gather his thoughts. "I can understand how frustrated and helpless you feel. I *do* understand. If it were safe for you to see the wider picture, you would understand that what Jude is attempting to accomplish would put you and all those that you care about in danger. Not just the beings of my world and of my community. Whether you were ever aware of the situation or not, the threat is there. I am keeping information from you that would put you both in grave peril if you had access to it. I know that does not sound like an answer, and maybe not even an excuse, but it is the truth that I can give you," he gave his head a shake, looking less the dapper in control demon and more a tired man in need of a break, "I have not handled this well from the beginning. I can admit that. The level of threat that Jude has brought us is much broader than I expected, and it has all blown up quickly. What I can do is that I can promise you that we are doing everything in our power to protect you as best we can, even if it doesn't seem that way," Elijah leveled his eyes to hers, "I promise you that," he said firmly and turned to Ezra, "I promise both of you that."

"So, it comes down to believing a vampire that is in love with my aunt or a demon that has lied over and over to me?" Nora spoke harshly, but her anger toward Elijah was already weakening. For a demon, he could seem quite sincere; or he was at least adept in trickery. That seemed more like the actions of a demon. Looking into his eyes, Nora couldn't decide.

"I can give you a couple of reasons not to believe that waste of skin vampire," Ezra cut in. He didn't need to speak the words. The pain was still washed over his face from reliving the worst day of his life.

"Yes, well, I have mixed emotions about Gabriel bringing you all of this, Mr. Dav...," his eyes flicked to Nora and back, "*Ezra*. However, you are here now, and...oh my, I am so sorry," Elijah said, stepping away from the windowsill. Nora's collection of barely alive plants was instantly withered and brown, the leaves all drifting sadly to the floor, "One of the disadvantages of being a demon, I'm afraid," he added with a grimace. He patted his jacket pocket when his phone began to ring. Retrieving it, he gave an apologetic smile and answered, "Gabriel, tell me you have some good news for me," he held up his hand to Ezra and Nora, gesturing he would be a minute, and stepped the few feet away into the galley kitchen.

The apartment wasn't one with an abundance of areas for privacy but even still being near, they could not hear what Gabriel was saying on the other end of the call. Elijah listened silently except for a few murmurs of *yes* and *I see*.

"Are you ok?" Nora asked Ezra who had taken a seat on the couch again, his eyes still red.

"Yeah, I'm good. Sorry about that, uh, outburst. It's all a little overwhelming, you know?" Ezra said, watching Elijah.

Nora understood how it was simple for Ezra to see clear sides in the situation. If she was in his shoes, she would probably do the same. There was no reason for him to worry about Quinn after what he had been through. The terror and tragedy of his loss had caused irreparable damage to his life, to his entire existence.

It would all be so much easier if she could see Quinn. To know that she was okay and what she had to do with all of it. How she got involved with vampires in the first place. If Quinn was able to care for Jude, could he be that bad? Hearing Ezra's story, it was hard to believe he was nothing but a creature of destruction and cruelty. That was the opposite of Quinn and what she had always stood for.

It was impossible to pick sides in supernatural politics as a human who didn't even know they existed until a few days before. She stepped closer to Elijah, pretending to clean up the remnants of her plants to try and hear the conversation.

"How could that be? Davina assured me that they had swept that house last week and there was no sign of him...yes...yes...and they're sure it's the one at the end of Westbury Road?" Elijah sighed and nodded to whatever Gabriel was adding, "All right then, if they're sure, this is indeed fantastic news."

Nora made her way back to the couch as Elijah said goodbye. Hanging up the phone, he slapped his hands together happily, "Well, I have some excellent news to share. It seems the little visit you had today may have been the thing to have brought this all to an end!"

"And how is that?" Nora questioned. That's all it took? Sitting in her apartment until Jude popped by to introduce himself? Supernatural crisis averted?

"We knew that Jude had taken an interest in you when you arrived. He has always had an eye for young ladies, even while he has taken up a relationship with your aunt. I'm sorry to sound crass, but a fresh, young version of the blood he has bonded with would be irresistible to him," Elijah averted his eyes when he spoke.

"That fucking piece of..." Ezra seethed and ground his teeth to stop himself.

"Yes, well, we were hoping that it would be enough to get him to come out of hiding. As you know, it was not, and we needed to up the ante. When he found out you were cooperating with us, he was put off balance as we had hoped and got a little sloppy with his security measures. Thanks to his misstep, he was too distracted to notice our people tracking him from your apartment to the nest he and his followers have been hiding out in. We know exactly which house up in the hills he is running things from and first thing in the morning this will all be over," Elijah informed them with relieved glee.

"What does that mean? Over? What about my aunt, will she be alright?" Guilt flooded Nora at the thought of Quinn being harmed or worse because of her.

"We will do everything we can to make sure your aunt is kept safe," he assured, with the air of proper business once again in place. He tucked his phone into his pocket and headed for the door.

"When do we go? Why do we have to wait until morning?" Ezra was on his feet.

Elijah stopped, "*We* won't be going. The agents in charge will be handling it first thing in the morning when the lot of them are asleep. You both need to stay tucked away safe. Your work here is done."

Ezra started towards him and the door, "You get me all this way, dangle the man that destroyed my family just out of grasp, and you think I'm not going to be there to see him die?"

"As I said, Gabriel may have made a mistake..."

Ezra cut him off, "No! You can't take this from me!"

Elijah put a hand on his shoulder, "Stay here, or go home, Ezra. Either way, your part in this situation is complete."

Nora didn't know if he meant to go home to his house across town or to go back to where he had come from.

Neither seemed like answers that would satisfy him or her, "So, we're just supposed to go back to life as usual? Our lives have become hell on earth because of you! Can't you even see that?" Nora snapped. Was she just supposed to sit around and hope her aunt was left unscathed? That she and Ezra were going to be safe?

Elijah's demeanor softened just a touch when he turned his attention to her outburst, "We all have our own versions of hell, my dear and unfortunately I know yours as poorly as you know mine," the words sat in the air before he continued, with his business-minded attitude shifted back into place, "When this is concluded, you will have the choice once again to continue on with us, or to be wiped of the memories of the past few days. Both of you. We owe you a debt and it will be honored. You received your Ascension as a blood oath to this promise, from the fae," he pulled out his phone and typed quickly as he spoke, "and the blood oath you gave on the contacts, along with the marking we provided you with, are promises between BITN and yourselves," his attention was more divided to whatever he was typing as he pulled open her door and stepped into the hall, "We can discuss this tomorrow evening. Unfortunately, I must go and deal with the matter at hand."

Ezra followed closely behind, still arguing his case to be involved. Nora watched the two until they stepped out onto the street.

"Everything ok?" Jenny's voice called out, startling Nora. Jenny looked from Nora to the front door and back.

"Yeah...fine. It's just a, ah...work thing," Nora half lied. Just a demon and a new buddy arguing about killing a vampire. No big deal.

"How has it been going?" Jenny questioned. Her voice was light, but her eyes were investigating. It was the same look she would give Olivia when she asked who had taken a cookie from the jar.

"It's good, don't worry. It's good, steady work," Nora flat-out lied.

Jenny stared at her for another moment before a small smile set on her lips, "Good. I'm glad to hear. Take care of yourself, Nora, okay? I'm always here if you need me, or you need to talk."

Nora wished upon wishes that she could talk to her about how the world was turning on its head. Letting Jenny in on what she knew would only put her and Olivia in more danger than they already were, so Nora just nodded and started back into her apartment before she stopped, "Hey Jenny? The fourth floor. It's still boarded up, right? No one can get in there?"

"Yeah, why?" Jenny gave her another inquisitive stare.

"Oh, I...," *I think there may be a vampire using it as a snack shack*, "I was thinking of maybe moving into a bigger space with the paychecks I'm getting now," Nora said with an uncomfortably forced laugh. Her lungs began to tighten with panic. Jenny was still looking at her questioningly as she backed into her apartment and shut the door.

The weight of everything that had been thrown at her in the past few hours once again rained down on her as her chest continued to tighten. She just made it to the couch as her legs let out and everything spiraled down on her.

Jude's visit. Ezra's horrendous story.

Quinn may be dead in the morning, and it would be her fault.

If they didn't kill Jude, what would that mean for Ezra? And who's to say that Jude wouldn't march right into Dunhope Manor and slaughter everyone he sees as an act of revenge against Nora's involvement? Gail and her songbirds. Poor, shy Norman. Jenny and Olivia. Nora knew she would be on the top of the list if he managed to survive.

On the other hand, if they were successful, how did she know that Quinn would be alright. Nora still didn't know if she could believe that her aunt was now a vampire and if she was, did she choose for it to happen or was she forced? There was only one thing that Nora could do. Find Quinn herself, and before morning. She remembered Elijah's words to Gabriel.

The one at the end of Westbury Road.

She grabbed her keys and was out the door in a flash.

Chapter Fourteen

Pulling Cherry Bomb onto the dimly lit Westbury Road, she wound her way up through the hills. She had only driven up into that posh area of Aumbry Valley a few times when she first arrived. There was little to see with the expensive cabins and mini-mansions set so far back into the trees and eventually, scenic drives became gas that she didn't have the money for. The main use of her car became limited to errands and round trips to the assorted crappy jobs that weren't quite a walkable distance.

When the road ended towards the top of the hill, there was only one driveway to be found. According to what she had eavesdropped on, this had to be the house Elijah was talking about. It had intimidatingly large iron gates, like so many of the other expensive homes she had passed, but these were surprisingly open. Nora wondered how it could be so hard to track down Jude if he didn't even feel the need to fence himself in from the threat of the BITN crews.

Parking her car on the side of the road, she made her way up to a clearing that revealed a stone pathway. There was a steep drop on one side that marked the end of the road, and intimidating darkness that deepened the further sleek asphalt led away from her on the opposite side. She talked herself out of getting into her car and high-tailing it home, knowing that there was no other option than to seek out Quinn, and started up the stone path. Following it further, she found herself standing in front of a sleek, mid-century modern house made of clean lines of timber, concrete, and steel. The tall windows, that reached from floor to ceiling, were blacked out and reflected the low lights that shone down from their dotted spots along the roofline. Elijah had referred to it as a nest, causing Nora to picture a nest of hornets swarming dangerously around to protect their Queen, or in this case, Jude.

The gothic castle you would expect a power-crazed vampire to live in was nowhere to be found either and this house seemed more suited to hipster architecture buffs. It had a fun vibe that Nora could see Quinn loving.

Even with the friendly façade of the building, her stomach rolled as she approached the door. A part of her was hoping that it was the wrong house so she could turn on her heel and rush to the relative security of her apartment before anyone found out what she had attempted to do. Unsure if it was the possible confirmation that her aunt was now a vampire or the threat of being on Jude's turf that was her biggest fear, she told herself Jude had made it clear that her own safe space was also his turf, so it made no difference to her safety if she was here or there. Seeing Quinn was the only thing that could bring her a semblance of peace and she pictured her warm, smiling face to give her the courage to ring the bell.

The door opened, and instead of her aunt, she was face to face with the door bitch from Mystique: Muccia aka Mucus. She glared at Nora in the same manner that she had the previous two times they had crossed paths.

"What is it?" she asked indignantly as Nora stared back.

"Hi. I...I'm sorry to bother you, but I'm looking for Quinn Goodman," Nora said, trying to ease a friendly smile onto her lips that were jittering in time with her hands.

"I'm sure I don't know who you're speaking of," Mucus spat, shutting the door.

Before she could click it closed, Nora took a page from Jude's playbook as her hand shot up and pushed it back open a crack, "Please, she's my aunt. I need to find her."

Nora had pushed herself to come this far, she was not going to let an unpleasant, vampire wannabe keep her from seeing Quinn.

"Muccia, let her in," a voice that Nora knew well instructed.

Mucus stepped aside, her jaw steeled with the displeasure of having to comply, and she avoided Nora's eyes when she made way for her to enter.

Quinn stood in the cavernous entryway, looking just as Nora remembered her. Short, cut-off denim shorts, an open floral kimono that hit just above her knees and covered a lace tank-top, and far too many beaded bracelets, necklaces, and crystal rings. Classic Quinn pseudo-hippy quirkiness. She rushed to her aunt and pulled her into a tight embrace. She slowly let go and stepped away when she felt how unnaturally cold her body felt. When Quinn smiled, she noticed her fangs, and then the mirrored glow in her pupil. It was true. She had been turned. Quinn Goodman was now a vampire.

"This must be quite the shock, huh?" Quinn mused and pulled her in for another hug. "I've missed you so much, Squirt!"

She guided Nora further into the house, pointing out this piece of artwork and that architectural detail as if they were simply having a happy, normal reunion after one of her sojourns around the world. Around each corner and from the shadows cast here and there, she could make out the distinct mirrored pupils of the vampires that must also live in the expansive house. They watched curiously and withdrew into the darkness as Quinn walked through the space with the flourish of a Queen holding court. Nora moved alongside her, feeling as if she was floating thanks to the numbness that accompanied shock and when they made their way to a cozy sitting room, Nora wordlessly sat opposite her on plush velvet couches. She shifted uncomfortably, thinking of how it must be hard to keep cream-colored velvet clean when your diet consisted of blood. She braved another glance at Quinn's fangs that smiled happily back at her.

The floor-to-ceiling wall of windows on the far side of the room had a round, open fireplace with a black metal chimney that stretched high to the roof. The flames made the room uncomfortably warm and cast shadows that flickered in the corner of Nora's eyes, no matter where she looked. The view over the mountains was breathtaking, with the village below only twinkling dots of light, but Nora could not get over the feeling that it was she who was being viewed by prying eyes, even though they were alone in the room.

Quinn sunk back into the pile of cushions, perfectly at ease, "Isn't it beautiful here, Squirt?"

"It really is," Nora replied, forcing herself to look at her aunt.

"Who would have thought I would settle down in one place and be happily domesticated," Quinn laughed.

Nora didn't join in, "That's obviously not the most shocking thing, Quinn."

"Well, you know me, go big or go home, right?" Quinn snickered, "If you're going to be a vampire, why not be practically Queen of the Vampires?"

"Is that what this is? Are you and Jude seriously that important to the other, you know, vampires?" Nora knew they were important in the sense that BITN had deemed them dangerous, but did the vampires that followed Jude consider him a true leader of them all?

"I'm pretty sure you know the answer to that," Quinn's smile did not match the darkness that filled her eyes. In a blink, it was gone, "And I'm so happy you're here with me now!"

Nora swallowed, trying to be rid of the dry mouth and tight throat that tried to silence her, "How did this all happen? I was so worried when you lost touch."

Quinn dramatically frowned a pout and pulled her legs up under herself, "I know, I'm sorry. I wish I could have reached out to you. Things are all happening so fast, and I didn't want you to get mixed up in all of it, you know?

It's been so hectic with Jude and all of the shit he's been going through for us."

"Quinn, I don't get it. How did you become a vampire?" Nora felt both frightened and absurd to speak the words to her aunt.

Quinn smiled at the memory the question invoked, "Well, I was at a meditation retreat in the desert, the one I told you about. Remember, the one Delilah from London told me about?" Quinn regaled her story as if she were describing a vacation that led to a sweet, little meet-cute. Nora just nodded along trying to comprehend how they had gotten to where there were, "On my second night, there was a guided full moon mediation. It's all about self-reflection and where you fit in with nature and stuff. Anyways, I micro-dosed some ayahuasca, and I was halfway through, my mind was blissfully clear and quiet, and a voice filled my head. It was asking me if I wanted *more* out of life or if I wanted to *be* more in life. My eyes shot open because you know what? That was exactly what I wanted, and I didn't even know it! I never felt like I was enough, you know, and I was always searching for more when I wanted to *be* more, myself. That's when I noticed Jude sitting beside me," Quinn's fangs shone in the firelight, "I mean, you've met him. He's gorgeous, right?"

Nora wondered how much she knew about her meeting with Jude earlier that day. It would be a lie to say he was unattractive, but terrifying was a better-suited description. It didn't escape her that there was a good chance that he had used his influence to plant the seed of self-awareness in her mind to get to her. Gabriel had made it quite clear how easy it would be. Quinn carried on without waiting for Nora to answer.

"So, we got to talking and I told him about my epiphany, and he said he totally understood and that he knew how to make that happen," Quinn's voice was filled with amazement, and spoke of Jude as if he were a god on earth. Nora had never seen her aunt so wrapped up in someone before and she had watched her survive three separate communes that were cults in disguise.

"And you just agreed to be turned into a vampire? Just believed what he said and let him make you into a vampire?" Nora asked. It was too much even for her to jump into something so inconceivable.

"No, it wasn't like that, Nora. It was a spiral of revelations that brought me to his truth," Quinn waxed on about thinking it was just the psychedelics that were making her see what Jude was and he had explained how her eyes were opening to the things in the world that we chose not to see. In time, the tea had worn off and all that was left was the truth of what Jude was and how the universe had chosen her to be at his side.

She had always been a bit of a hippy-dippy, but this was beyond her usual sage and crystals. She had cut herself off from her former life and given it over to a vampire after knowing him for one night. One drugged-fueled night. Nora wanted to throw her over her shoulder and make a run for the door. The shimmer of unnatural light in Quinn's eyes flashed as she spoke of Jude trying to free himself of the shackles of his people and how she would help him conquer the world.

"He was born to lead, Nora. I swear, he's the most incredible being," she smiled, softly nodding at Nora, "and I'm telling you, you should join us. You need to join us! It would be the best thing for everyone."

"Join...be a vampire?" Nora felt herself pushing back on the couch away from the idea and looking for the door. When she imagined whisking Quinn away from the vampires, she hadn't had any thought of becoming one of them and it didn't seem any more enticing with Quinn's long canines shining four feet away from her.

"When Jude can rid us of the tyranny of The Firm and the High Council, when we're away from the unnecessary nonsense of the other creatures, who let's be honest – are subpar – when he accomplishes that, he will practically be a king among vampires. That makes me his queen!" It was Quinn's voice, but those words had to be coming from someone else. She was not someone who sought out power over others. She communed with the trees, and talked to birds for god's sake! Quinn smiled mischievously, "And let me tell you, you haven't fucked until you've fucked a vampire," she laughed when Nora's eyes widened above newly flushed cheeks, "And as a vampire yourself it's even more intense. I'm telling you, if I wasn't already technically dead, Jude would kill me with his...let's say, stamina," she giggled.

Nora was not exactly overly experienced with sex, not that she hadn't had a few boyfriends and some decent times between the sheets with them, but to imagine having sex with a vampire was too much. It seemed strange to do that with someone who also considered you a meal. Talk about playing with your food. Quinn, on the other hand, was well versed in the beast with two backs. Although some of her stories involved more than two backs. At one Burning Man, the way she told it, there were about twelve backs and she loved every single moment with every single one at once. As surprised as Nora was that Quinn had become a vampire, it was not that surprising that the sex had been a key selling point to her.

"When you're made vampire, you'll see what I'm talking about and you will not be able to thank me enough," she winked, "The world is not the same as one of us, Squirt. It's bigger and brighter and deeper. It's like spring, you know? In the beginning, you can smell the rot and death from the autumn before, but if you pay attention, you can smell newly bloomed flowers and fresh rain dancing in the warmer breezes. You become at one with what the universe wants you to be. You are going to love it."

"I don't think I..." Nora stammered, watching her aunt bounce happily at the idea of her niece joining the ranks of the undead. The glow from the fire lit up in her eyes, making her pupils seem too deep and inhuman. This was not the woman that she had spent her childhood with. She had become someone else in the short time they had been apart.

Quinn leaned forward on the sofa, "Don't think. There's nothing to think about. Humans are beneath everyone, Nora. They are nothing more than food. Food to creatures like me and food to each other. Worthless to themselves,"

Nora's heart pounded in her chest. Quinn had never had a cruel word for anyone. Hell, she was kind to her brother Adam, even though he could care less about her. Nora's father was far more suited to be a cold-blooded vampire than his sweet little sister, "I don't...I think we should...," her eyes darted around. A lanky man, in ripped jeans and shirtless, peered around the corner at her before disappearing. He was there long enough for Nora to notice the anger in his eyes and fangs that framed his scowl.

Quinn cut her off, "Squirt, it's ok. I was overwhelmed too. It's scary at first, I get it. I can only imagine what you thought when you found out about all of this," Quinn's energy softened, and she stretched forward to take Nora's hand into her ice-cold palm, "Jude will make everything better. Just like he did for me."

"Is he here?" Nora willed her voice to steady. If he was, she wanted out of there and fast. There was no way that Quinn would protect her from him if he chose to do anything. It was clear where her loyalties now lay.

Quinn tilted her head, eyes dark and locked on Nora's, "No, not at the moment. Why?"

"Why?" Nora looked to the door and started to slide sideways on the couch, "I mean, you make him sound so great. Maybe I misjudged him."

"Misjudged him," Quinn's grip tightened on Nora's hand as she scoffed at her words, "Or maybe you just want your new friends to meet him?"

Nora tried unsuccessfully to tug her hand away, hoping to be ready to move if she needed to. The predatory heat burned in Quinn's eyes when she waited for an answer.

"What? No! I don't want to have anything to do with them, Quinn. I made a mistake when I showed up there. I thought it was just a job. I swear to you I didn't know anything about *any* of this. You have to believe me."

"So, you're looking me in the eye and telling me that you're honestly not here to lead them to him?" Her voice was low as she slid her legs out from under her, planting her feet on the floor in front of where she sat.

Nora's stomach lurched in response to her threatening posture, "No, I'm not! I swear! They already know you're here! That's why I came, that's how I know you're here. I wanted to warn you. I want to help you," Nora blurted, squirming at the painful pressure on the tiny bones in her hand.

"Help me? Bitch I could eat you!" Quinn bellowed, the words echoing from the walls around them. The hateful words coming out of the mouth that had only provided kind words and encouragement were too much for Nora to hear and she couldn't hold back the tears that rushed down her cheeks. Her best friend had been replaced by a vile, unstable monster. Aunt Quinn was now Jude's. It had been a mistake to follow her to Aumbry Valley and a worse mistake to seek her out.

"Please, Quinn..."

Quinn threw Nora's hand back at her and sat back on the sofa. A smug grin crawled across her face, "Don't you realize that they're using you? They'll toss you aside just as soon as they're done with you," in a blink, the twisted mask of the vengeful vampire was gone without a trace and Quinn's serene smile and soft tone had returned, "I missed you, Squirt."

Nora opened her mouth to speak, only to close it again. She wanted to scream at her for leaving her behind back east, and for handing herself over to Jude. To blame her for the danger they were both now in and she wanted to drag her from that house and never look back. She wanted to call her stupid and cruel and insane and more than anything she wanted to tell her that she still loved her after everything that had happened because she had been her whole world, but she wasn't able to utter a word with Quinn's soft gaze on her. Her lip trembled and she blinked back the tears that refused to stop.

"You're a smart girl. You know who's right here," Quinn casually pulled her legs up and crossed them in front of her, "Don't look at me like that. I'm not going to hurt you, Squirt. Leave if you want to. It's fine. When the time comes, I know you'll make the right decision."

Nora stood without another word and quickly retraced the way back to the front door. She could feel the eyes of the vampires in the nest on her, watching her retreat. Each step seemed slower than the next as she worried that any one of them could snap her like a twig if they felt like stepping out of the shadows. When she was out on the lawn, the night air being pulled into her gasping lungs, she bent over, sure she was going to wretch. Never in her life had she felt more alone or more confused. There weren't right answers anymore. There was nothing safe left in the world. Just nightmare after nightmare.

Pulling her keys from her bag, she willed herself to make it back to her car. Her feet moved automatically as quickly as her legs would allow. The stone pathway seemed to quickly rise up and it slammed into her before she even knew she had been pushed to the ground. Her arms were braced in front of her face just in time to save her from serious injury. Rolling onto her back, she watched as a small woman with long pin-straight black hair that dangled over each of her shoulders, circled her, laughing maniacally down at her.

In a split second, Nora was on her feet, crouched and ready for the next blow, just as she had done when Gabriel had rushed at her in Elijah's office.

"That's some fancy footwork, there, blood-bag," the woman sneered, her fangs rubbing along her bottom lip.

"Amber! Hands off," Quinn's voice rang out through the chilled night air. Nora looked up to see her perched on the edge of a second-story balcony, "not for you."

She was gone as quickly as she appeared, as was Amber when Nora looked back to where she had stood.

Picking up her keys, she ran as fast as she could down to the road and the safety of her car. Halfway down, bright headlights lit up the driveway, stopping just before they struck her. Ezra jumped from his Jeep and ran to her.

Just what she needed, more trouble.

"What are you doing here?" Nora asked, pushing him back towards his Jeep.

"What am I doing here? What are you doing here? I went back to your apartment, and you were gone. I remember Elijah mentioning this road and figured you were up to no good," he accused, "Why were you in there? And why the hell did you come alone?" he barked at her, standing firm against her hands pushing him back to his car. He looked over her shoulder towards the house. Nora gave him a good shove and he stepped back.

"I had to warn my aunt, Ezra. She's just as innocent as anyone."

"You have got to be kidding me. Vampires aren't innocent, Nora! They're cold-blooded killers!" he yelled and pushed her aside. Grabbing at a tree beside them he broke a branch off into a fine point, "Is that bastard in there? I'll take care of this here and now."

Nora knew that he wouldn't last a minute up against a house full of vampires, even if their deranged leader was not at home, "He's not here, Ezra. Please, let's just go."

Footfalls on the pathway echoed quickly towards them and Amber, now with two burly male cohorts marched forward, her finger pointed in Ezra's direction, "That one is fair game, fellas. No matter what the Queen Bitch says."

Ezra looked down at his slivered attempt at a stake and back to the three vampires approaching them. Throwing it down, he turned around to his Jeep and jumped behind the wheel as Nora jumped in beside him.

"Go, go, go!" Nora screamed as he backed quickly through the twists and turns to the road, hitting the gas and heading back into the valley as fast as the wheels would carry them. To their relief, there was no sign of the vampires following them when the wheels screeched onto the main road.

Nora's apartment, being the closest, was best for both of them to hole up in and they were there in minutes. Neither of them wanted to be alone after yet another near-death experience with vampires and they decided to stick together until sunrise.

When they slammed the door closed behind them Nora brought up the danger presented with Jude's ability to freely enter her apartment. Locking every window and pushing her dresser against the bolted door did little to quell their fears. Going back out into the night in an attempt at making it to Ezra's seemed just as risky. Who was to say one of Jude's lackeys didn't have the same ability with that house, as well.

Every noise outside made them jump at the thought that they had been followed. Nora suggested that they call Elijah and confess what they had done and each time she mentioned it, Ezra refused the idea, sure that it would only make things worse. There was nothing to be done until morning when the BITN crew did whatever they were going to do. Desperation filled Nora's chest at the thought of Quinn possibly being killed, but it swelled along with the grief that told her she was already gone. There was no way that Nora would be able to join her in whatever ill-thought coup attempt they were attempting, and there was less of a chance of allowing herself to become one of the undead followers of Jude.

Memories of the good times she shared with Quinn and the fearful thoughts of what the future would hold kept her occupied and rattled until her body was finally drained of adrenaline. Exhausted and tucked under a blanket on the loveseat, her head fell against Ezra's shoulder as the sun rose outside.

Chapter Fifteen

Six days. It had only been six days since Dirtbag Derek had grabbed her ass and she walked into the elevator that would change her life forever. In six days, she had learned that the world was nothing like what it had appeared, had supernatural blood injected into her own, witnessed the death of a vampire, and found out that Quinn as she knew her was gone forever. New realities upon new realities were instantly pounding in her head the moment she opened her eyes. They had only managed to restlessly sleep for a few hours before Nora and Ezra were awake and anxiously pacing the floorboards. Repeated attempts to call Gabriel were unanswered. Each time they called the office number Pearl would pick up but never had any information to pass on and would tell them to sit tight and have faith in Elijah. A million little possibilities of what Elijah could be accomplishing drowned Nora's mind with worry. Ezra's irritability and insistence that he should return to the house in the hills only added to her stress.

Quinn could be dead. They could have missed Jude once again and soon he would be at her door seeking blood-soaked revenge. They may have both gotten away and the cycle of this nightmare would continue until the fear of it all swallowed her whole.

"What's the point of staying here? What could they do to us in the daylight, anyway?" Ezra asked for a tenth time, wearing a path on the already scratched hardwood floor of Nora's apartment.

"We were told to stay here. We may have blown this whole thing up worse than it was by going last night. I don't think getting a demon pissed at us will help us out," Nora bemoaned. If they knew that they had gone to the house the night before, they could be in even more trouble than she could imagine. The chance that they did not know every single step that they took was slim and Nora hoped that it would not be as big a deal as it felt. She had risked everything to try to help Quinn and for what? She sat on the couch, head in her hands, trying to slow the avalanche of what-ifs. When whatever was to come had arrived, she knew she would have to grieve the loss of her aunt in one way or another. She had never felt so alone, even with Ezra a few feet away. Pain in the pit of her stomach burned with her worries.

Nora kept her still silent phone constantly in her hands, plugged in to prevent the chance of losing an ounce of charge. On the very first day of this nightmarish journey, Gabriel had been so keen to take her under his wing and now he didn't even bother to check in with her. The rise of the sun had never stopped him from flitting about the office, so that was not a plausible excuse to leave them high and dry. She pushed away the idea that something horrible could have happened to him. To all of them. If they didn't receive word soon, she was sure she would go mad.

Silas had just about enough of the two of them pacing and bickering in the small room. After picking at his kibble, he stomped into the bathroom and jumped in the empty tub to curl up for a nap. Like all cats, the weight of the world never settled on his shoulders. Nora wished she could go curl up with him and forget the last week completely. If there was still the option of having her memory erased when they were done with her, she decided that she would jump at the chance. She had gone almost twenty-five years without knowing about the things that lurked in the darkness and she would happily go another twenty-five and more. Ignorance truly was bliss. The things that she had been exposed to in the past week were too much for a mortal human's happily unknowing brain.

Ezra stared at his phone, willing it to ring while talking non-stop about all the different things they could be doing instead of staying inside as they were originally told to do, "I'm just saying, we can drive that way. Head up the mountain to see if there are any signs of what could have happened or what's going to happen," he stopped in the middle of the room, his newest ploy lighting up his face, "Don't you want to get your precious Cherry Bomb, anyways? It's sitting up there where anything could happen to it."

The car made her think of her aunt which sent another spiral of nerves twisting through her stomach. It may be best to just leave it up there and move on. Going forward, every time that she looked at it there would be a fusion of sadness, anger, and grief. Unless she was able to have the memories of Quinn wiped. If she didn't, would she want to be rid of the last happy memory that she had of her time with her? It seemed disrespectful to forget about the good time.

Nora knew it was a stupid reason to head into a possible battle zone, but she refused to admit to herself that she was also looking for any excuse to follow Ezra back up the winding roads. Sitting around without answers was going to make her go mad.

"Okay, but you have to promise me: We go get my car and get the hell out of there. We're not going into the house, we're not getting in the way, and we're not staying," Nora conceded.

Ezra was out the door before he could finish agreeing to her terms. The worst had to have been over with. The sun had been up for hours. There was nothing fair in leaving them caged up and ignored. The damage that she had done the night before was already done and she couldn't worry about it affecting the rest of their assignment. What was done was done. Well, hopefully, was done.

Taking a deep breath, Nora followed him to the hallway, locked her door, and said a silent prayer as they headed out to the street. Every inch of her body was buzzing with uncertain fear, and even though she knew she was making a mistake, she lied to herself to keep her feet moving forward. It was impossible to stay put not knowing what was happening, but more so she wanted to know what was going to happen next. She doubted that there would ever be a normal that she recognized ever again if she stayed in Aumbry Valley. That did not mean she couldn't take some control. If they did not offer to have her memories wiped in the next few hours, she would get her car, pack up Silas, and drive as far as Cherry Bomb could muster. Her use to the BITN Bureau had to have expired now that they knew where Jude was. There could not be that much of a fuss for tracking down a lowly human if she made herself disappear. Could there?

They both screeched to a halt when they made it to the sidewalk. Cherry Bomb had been returned and sat at the curb in front of the building. Nora's hand covered a yelp that tried to escape when she saw how it had been destroyed. The roof had been crushed, the glass shattered, mirrors knocked off, the wheels slashed. It was as if it had been ripped apart in a tornado and landed perfectly in front of her building.

"No! Are you kidding me? What the hell?" Nora fumed circling the devastation, "I can't believe...when...how...," she stuttered her disbelief as she took in the devastation that had torn her prized car to pieces.

"Nora, look," Ezra pointed to a stake through the collapsed hood, holding in place a torn scrap of paper. He pulled it from the car and read the note before passing it to her.

SEE YOU SOON, SQUIRT!

Seeing Quinn's nickname for her, made her heart drop. The only thing that kept her on her feet was that it was not written in Quinn's handwriting. Nora knew her looping, almost calligraphic writing like the back of her hand. Countless letters over the years between the two had made her handwriting as clear as her voice and that was not what was on that paper. Her fingers shook when she noticed the blood that streaked across it, and she dropped the paper to the ground, wiping her hands on her shirt.

Ezra pounded a fist on the crushed trunk, "How is this keeping us safe? They tell us to stay put and they'll handle things while we're feet away from someone who wants us dead?" he bellowed out into the street. A boy on a bicycle wove around him, eyes wide looking at the crushed car.

Nora managed to stay silent until he wobbled his bike around the corner, "Ezra, keep it down! We don't need the whole town out here asking questions." She looked up and down the street for more signs of life. The street was deadly silent apart from Ezra's shouts.

"Well, maybe they should be! Maybe they should know what the fuck is going on right under their noses!" Ezra yelled to the empty street and stomped down the sidewalk to where his Jeep sat, untouched, "Are you coming or not?"

The thought of running toward beings that could rip a car to pieces was now the last thing that she wanted to do. She looked back towards the door to the building and again to Ezra. Whoever was involved with the mess that Jude and Quinn had created was angry, and they were making it clear that they were angry with them. Staying to hide in the building was irresponsible, no matter what Elijah had directed them to do. Jenny and Olivia didn't need to get caught in the crosshairs of what was to come next, let alone poor, naturally frightened Norman or sweet Gail and her songbirds. It was a miracle that they hadn't been harmed already if Jude had been serious about spending time in the boarded-up ballroom. She looked up, squinting through the sunlight at the shuttered window on the fourth floor. Even with the heat of the day already building, she shivered. "I think if we're going anywhere, we should just go to the office and wait. It has to be the safest place," Nora said, picking up the note and shoving it in her bag.

"If you think they give a shit about keeping us safe, you're a fool," Ezra spat. Regret at his tone to her instantly settled in when he saw the hurt on her face, "Sorry, I didn't mean that. I'm just so fucking mad. I need to know if he's dead, Nora. I need that monster dead and gone for good," his voice vibrated as he pulled out his keys, "You have to know what this is doing to me."

"I do," Nora said gently, "It's a shitty situation all around and the sooner it's all over, the sooner we can get the hell out of here and never look back. I still think Elijah's office is the safest place for us for now. Who knows, someone there might know something by now."

Ezra sighed deeply and nodded, unlocking his Jeep, "Fine. You win. Let's go."

Nora stepped back towards the building, holding up her index finger to him, "I'm just going to grab Silas. It doesn't feel safe to leave him on his own."

"Sure, just hurry up ok?" Ezra said as he slid behind the steering wheel.

Nora hustled quietly back into her apartment and found Silas still curled up in a purring ball in the tub. Wrestling him into his carrier was never an easy task and today would be no different. When she finally did get him in and the small cage door was clicked closed, she moved quickly through the kitchen to get packets of food for him in case they were to be gone for a day or two. She looked over the tiny studio space forlorn. If she was being honest with herself, this could be the last time she was ever in her very first apartment. The home she created with all of the hope one had of starting a new life. Whatever lay ahead, she knew that she had to leave the valley if she were to have a chance at making a less dangerous future. She grabbed the trinket box that held the letter from her grandfather and added it to her bag. Sliding her key into her lock, she looked at Jenny's door and whispered goodbye.

Setting Silas on the back seat of Ezra's car, she slid the seat belt around the cage before hopping into the passenger seat.

"Okay, ready to go?" Ezra said, putting the car into drive. Before he could pull out into the street, his cellphone chimed, and he put it back into park. As he read the text message, the color drained from his face and his breath quickened, "Oh, god, no!"

He held the phone up for Nora to see. It was a message from someone named Laura:

Hey Easy-E! Guess what? Surprise! We're here to see the new digs and you can finally meet your niece! Where are you? We're waiting on the porch and Aria needs to pee! LOL!

"Oh shit," Nora gasped. It was his sister. They were in Aumbry Valley.

Chapter Sixteen

Ezra didn't wait to type a response to his sister and hit the gas. Nora had to hold onto her seat to fight against the speed he used to get home in mere minutes. They were barely parked when he jumped from behind the wheel and rushed up to his porch. His reaction was the polar opposite of the calm, friendly smiles the waiting couple gave him.

"Laura, what are you guys doing here? I told you this wasn't a good time for a visit," Ezra quaked, opening his front door and gesturing for them all to enter quickly. Nora gave him a pinched face of warning to calm down. Now was not the time for him to lose his head. They had two more people and a baby to worry about. Ezra nodded at her wordless warning and took a deep breath before following her in.

"Well, I'm glad to see you too. Geez," Laura laughed, dusting sawdust off a worn armchair before setting her daughter's car seat down. A flat-screen television on a console made of reclaimed wood was the only furniture in the room. Nora sat Silas' crate on the floor beside it and he yowled grumpily with the complaint of her not opening the door for him. She ignored him and stood to smile as best she could at the new arrivals.

Nora stepped out of the way for Laura's wife to pop into the powder room beside the front door before having a look around the space. The decor of Ezra's home was minimal, with more tools and workbenches than knick-knacks and personal touches. Broken spindles from the torn apart railing sat piled on the hallway table and sawdust had been swept into every corner she could see. The smell of freshly cut wood and paint filled the house giving it a homier feel than it appeared. Ezra may be a self-proclaimed klutz, but his craftsmanship was admirable. It was easy to see how beautiful the house would be when he was done. Nora tried to ignore the possibility that he may never get a chance to see the finished product if they had to hightail it out of town. She pressed her smile tighter to smother her thoughts and worried that she was starting to look insane to the ladies, who smiled back politely.

"Sorry, but I have a lot going on at the moment. It's not that I didn't want to see you, it has just been pretty crazy," Ezra offered before quickly adding, "at work.

Super crazy busy at work." He stared at the baby fussing in the cozy little travel seat, "So, this is Lucy?"

"Meet your grouchy Uncle Ezra, Lucy," Laura laughed, unbuckling the baby and hoisting her up into her arms. The baby cooed and smiled at the group. She reached for her uncle as if she had known him from day one. Ezra took her in his arms, straightening the blanket that wrapped her tiny body.

"I guess she has an affinity for grouches," Laura's wife said with a laugh, re-joining them in the front room.

His eyes glassed over with happy tears that wouldn't fall. "She's beautiful." Looking up from his niece with pride he found Nora standing awkwardly in the doorway to the room. The levity of the moment was dashed, and his eyes darkened with the quick trip back to reality. He handed Lucy back and introduced Nora as his co-worker.

"This is my sister Laura, and her wife Aria," Ezra said and moved quickly to the front door to twist the lock. He gave a glance out the window and stepped back into the room with them.

"Nice to meet you both. Your daughter is adorable," Nora said before Ezra grabbed her by the elbow and started to tug her further into the house.

"Make yourselves comfortable. We just need to finish up something and we'll have a proper catch-up, ok?"

Ezra called out to them as he and Nora slipped from the room. The women looked around at the lack of furniture and laughed at the limited options to settle into.

The kitchen, at the rear of the house, was wonderfully lit and warm with the afternoon sun and equally covered in half-finished projects and tools as the rest of the house. Nora looked around the room and waited for Ezra to stop pacing and speak. If he was waiting for her to come up with something, they were going to be there for a while. There was no way that they could walk in 1365 Beech Avenue with the new arrivals. They were going to have to stay put until they heard word from Elijah or Gabriel and hope for the best.

"What the hell are we going to do now?" he barked in a hushed voice. "I can't believe they're here right now! This is the last thing we need." He closed his eyes, tugging at his hair in frustration.

Nora could not imagine the fear that was surging through Ezra at the idea of anything happening to the only family he had left. If they were successful in taking care of Jude, the worst of the danger would seem to be over. It could also mean that the last of who she considered family, Quinn, was dead. She pulled out her cellphone.

"I'll call Elijah again. He'll know what to do," Nora said putting the phone to her ear. Eventually, the voicemail directed her to leave a message. She quietly gave him the update on the new arrivals and where they now were, begging him to call her back to let her know anything about what was going on, "At least I could leave a message this time. It just rang and rang earlier. That might mean something." She didn't know what it could mean. At least it was something, anything, other than an unanswered ringing, "Do you think they may just be done with us? Like, they did what they had to do, and they've just washed their hands of us?"

"And what, just let us go out into the world knowing what we know now?" Ezra gave her a look of disbelief. It did seem too good to be true. Ezra leaned forward on the counter, listening to the murmur of the ladies chatting in the front room. Lucy let out of a tummy rumbling laugh which her mothers joined in on. "I guess since they're here, it's better that they're here with us," Ezra said, pulling four beers from the fridge, which was most of the contents. "We may as well make the best of this until that fucking demon takes the time to fill us in." He checked his phone, swearing again, and plugged it in to charge with a cord that had been left on his table. He checked that the volume was up twice before returning to the surprise guests in his front room.

"Look at you back on your feet! The way you had described your leg, I thought you were going to be on crutches for months, drama queen," Laura teased.

Nora and Ezra flicked their attention to each other, then to his healed leg, and back, "Yeah, I...it wasn't as bad as they thought," Ezra bounced on his leg and offered two of the beers to her.

"Dude, I'm breastfeeding her still. I don't want to have to pump and dump and waste perfectly good milk when I'm traveling," Laura laughed and nodded down to Lucy who was cooing in her arms, "Especially on the crap beer you always prefer."

Nora looked at the bottles in his hands, Bitter Bruja, and swallowed a snort that tried to escape her nose. It was a good beer, but poor timing, she thought. It was best to keep mention of anything supernatural out of the conversation, either way.

Ezra's lips twisted into an uncomfortable frown when he also realized what he was holding, "God, right. I'm sorry. I think I have some bottled water in the closet. Aria, you good with beer?" He was already walking away with the bottles.

"Water would be awesome if you have it," she replied, digging through the diaper bag slung on her shoulder, "Thanks."

Ezra left down the hallway, muttering to himself, his heightened stress level easy to see. Laura and Aria gave Nora a sympathetic grimace when he was gone.

"He's a bit of a handful sometimes," Laura laughed, bouncing the baby in her arms.

Nora looked towards the kitchen hoping he would be back soon. She was sure that she would say something that she shouldn't if she started nervously small talking with them. A bad impression of being awkward was much better than a bad impression of seeming insane.

"So...you guys work together?" Aria asked, moving the baby's seat to the floor so Laura could sit in the armchair with Lucy.

Nora nodded with tight lips. They stared at her, waiting for more. "Yep. We just recently started at the, uh, same office," Nora said, unsure of what he had told them about what their new positions were.

"Office? I didn't know he's started work in an office," Laura said, confusion on her face, "I don't think I can even picture him sitting behind a desk," she said and shared a laugh with Aria, "He's always been Mr. Outdoorsman with dirty hands. We could never get him inside long enough to do an entire shift at our family's restaurant without him finding an excuse to go fix something or look into something outside. Does he wear a tie and the whole bit?"

"Yep. He's Mr. Business now, I guess," Nora smiled back at her, unable to press down the nervous grin, and sure she looked like a crazy woman.

Aria pulled out a pacifier and clipped it on Laura's t-shirt before popping it in Lucy's mouth. She sat on the arm of the chair beside Laura. The two looked back at Nora, waiting for her to elaborate, and received only her frozen awkwardness in response. Aria nervously scratched at her short dark curls and pressed an uncomfortable grin when Nora just stared back silently screaming for Elijah to call and end their worry. Thankfully Ezra returned with the water, handing one to each of them before twisting the cap from his beer and downing half of it in a gulp.

"How've you been, Easy-E?" Laura asked with the concern of an older sister, "My little brother is an office guy now?"

He glared at Nora who gave an almost imperceivable shrug, "I'm good. Good. Just crazy busy, like I said," Ezra nodded as he spoke as if it would make his edgy tone more believable. "It's good to see you, Laura. Both of you. Well, all three of you, now, isn't it? Really," he took another swig of beer, "I'm sorry I've been pushing off visiting. I just wasn't...you know. Setting up here has been taking a lot of time." He gazed at the baby.

Laura looked at her brother with sadness and concern. She would have been with him in the days after he lost his wife and child and would know what pain he had endured before he set off for Aumbry Valley. Worry shadowed her face when he shifted from foot to foot, clearly agitated.

"Well, we're here now and brought supplies," Aria said brightly to ease the tension and headed to the door.

"No, wait!" Ezra blurted, "I mean, let's just stay inside. It's too hot out today."

"Exactly why I don't want to leave the groceries in the car any longer, weirdo," Aria laughed at his outburst. Ezra followed her out the door, giving Nora a concerned look before stepping out onto his porch.

She quickly excused herself and scurried to the kitchen. Calling Elijah, and then Pearl, and then Elijah again with no answer had her sitting on the edge of madness. There was no reason to leave any more messages. They would call when they would call. It was ridiculous to her that they didn't feel the need to keep them in the loop after putting them in danger so many times. Being a human was truly unimportant to these creatures and she couldn't help but feel used and discarded. It was enough to worry about what was happening with Jude and Quinn, now they had three newcomers to protect from the unknown, one of which was an infant.

She checked Ezra's phone for any activity when he came in with grocery bags loaded in each hand. She shook her head when he looked at her hopefully. Taking each item out of the bags he placed them mindlessly on the counter. Laura watched him for a moment before giving Aria a troubled look.

"The house looks great, Ez. It's going to be stunning when you're done," she gushed, setting her hand on his shoulder, "I knew you could be handy, but this is something else to take on."

Laura seemed to know how to navigate her brother when he was out of sorts, even if she couldn't possibly know why, and she soon had him distracted with questions of the house and then childhood memories filled with sibling rivalry and teasing. The kitchen was quickly filled with the smells of home cooking and the chatter of Laura, who turned out to be a talker, unlike her brother. She described the recipe she was preparing and how it had been a favorite of their mother and how she had had a true passion for food. This was the main reason why Ezra had been an overly plump child, she teased.

The afternoon clouded over with the rainclouds the summer heat brought on and before long, the skies opened up. Even with the house in shambles and danger waiting behind every minute, the kitchen was almost cozy with the family scene in front of her. It was not what she had been raised with, and up until that moment, she had believed it existed only in sitcoms and movies.

They picked at the chicken and pasta that Laura had prepared, while Nora and Ezra checked their phones incessantly, being teased by the couple that they worked too hard. The comfort of the afternoon wore thin as the day burned on and the stress of not knowing what had happened in the house on the hill was getting harder to hide. Ezra insisted that his family stay overnight, and they pushed back saying it would be impossible, given his furniture situation. There was only one bed and it had been a long drive to see him. The amenities at the small inn on Main Street would be must better suited and much more comfortable with a baby in tow. Ezra pushed back harder, frustration manifesting in anger.

"Whoa, you're wound tight enough to explode," Laura said, watching him glance into the backyard that was slowly darkening with thickening clouds and the sun heading towards the west. "Is it this new job? A little town like this doesn't seem like it would have a lot of stressful work. I'm worried about you, bud."

Ezra and Nora's phones rang out in unison causing them to jump with frazzled surprise and Aria and Laura followed suit thanks to their reaction. Startled by the four, Lucy's bottom lip quivered before a tearful cry ripped from her. Before they could answer their phones, a heavy knock on the front door echoed across every surface of the house.

"You answer the phone, I'll get the door," Ezra directed Nora, "Everyone stay here," he shouted over his shoulder as he bolted for the door.

Nora picked up her phone, not recognizing the number, "Hello?"

"Where are you?" the voice on the other end demanded.

"Who is this?" Nora asked, her hands shaking from the sudden excitement.

"It's Gabriel! Where are you? Are you with Ezra?"

Nora started to ask what had happened when her blood froze her in place. The voices from the front door trickled into the kitchen. Voices that she knew.

"Hello there. Mind if we come in?"

Nora pushed herself to move and was at Ezra's side in seconds when she recognized Jude's voice. She grabbed his arm, pulling him back just as he started to launch out the door. Jude and Quinn stood on the porch, rage burning in their eyes.

Quinn snarled when she saw her, "Get your ass out here, Squirt."

Chapter Seventeen

Nora pulled Ezra as hard as she could muster from the reach of the vampires, relieved to see they weren't making any attempts to cross the threshold. Quinn stared her down beside Jude whose carnivorous grin was equally arrogant and vicious. The rain had soaked them and their hair was dripping down around murderous stares.

"Ezra?" Laura's voice called out to him from the kitchen and Ezra turned towards them.

"Stay there Laura! All of you, stay there!" Nora screamed.

It was easy to see that Ezra was torn between protecting his family and seeking the revenge that was at his fingertips. He looked back and forth from the kitchen to his ultimate enemy with crazed eyes. Nora gave his shoulder a shake, willing him to focus on the situation and not act rashly enough to get them all killed.

"Oh, how nice. You put out some snacks for us," Jude exclaimed, looking over her shoulder, "Is that fresh Davis blood I smell? Oh, Ezra, you shouldn't have."

Nora's grip on Ezra's arm tightened and she pulled him halfway down the hallway. She struggled to steady her breathing and calm the panic that had her mind spinning. Jude had some nerve to incite him with such disgusting words. The thought of that bloodsucker with his hands anywhere near that sweet baby made her sick.

She remembered the phone in her hand and lifted it to her ear, screaming for Gabriel's help. When no response came, she looked at it to find a blank screen. He was gone. They were on their own with the vengeful vampires that stalked just outside his door.

Ezra was still too filled with rage to think clearly. Nora knew she would have to take charge and decided it would be best if kept his remaining family safe, while she dealt with her own. Grabbing his face to center his attention on what she was saying, she shouted the words as clearly as she could, "Go, now!" Nora pointed to the kitchen, "Get them safe, now!"

Ezra's jaw was set firm with rage, his eyes locked on Jude, his feet planted in place. Laura's voice called out to him again and thankfully broke the spell that fury held over him. He bolted for the kitchen.

"Babies are just so delicious, aren't they? The blood is so savory and honestly just a treat!" Jude licked his lips as Quinn giggled and looked up to him adoringly. He pushed his soaked hair back from his face, slicking it to his head, with a satisfied grin.

"Jesus! What is wrong with you?" Nora spat, revolted by the pair of them.

"Looks like you're big, bad, bosses weren't able to take us out, Squirt," Quinn snarled.

Nora took a step towards the door, her heart pounding hard enough that she knew they could hear it. As long as they couldn't enter the house, she was sure that she could buy them some time. Squaring her shoulders, she balled her hands into fists, trying to convince them and herself that she was not frightened. Over and over again in her mind, she repeated to herself that the woman before her was not Quinn. Not anymore. She was Jude's now and there was no turning back. There was no way that she could fight them, even with the supernatural reflexes she had been gifted. She would just have to keep them talking until she thought of a plan or the BITN Calvary miraculously arrived.

"They're not our bosses, Quinn. I told you, we wanted nothing to do with this! Do you really think I would want to have someone put you in danger? Do you think I want to be in danger? I'm only here because of you! I'm only wrapped up in this mess because of you!" Nora shrieked.

"Don't put this on me. You chose to follow me like the broken little puppy that you are. The weak-minded, pathetic little thing you've always been. Always someone else's fault, right? Your mommy and daddy didn't love you enough, so you tried to take *my* father as your own. You're too awkward to make friends so you clung to me like a tick, thinking we were friends? You've been handed more than 99% of the world and you're sitting here still telling yourself that you're the victim?"

Nora willed herself not to break a sob when she steadied herself to speak, "Quinn, you don't mean that. I know you can't mean that. You and grandpa were the only ones that ever made me feel loved. The only ones that made me feel like I matter."

"Well, we're both dead now, aren't we? It's just my bad luck that I still have to hear you whine about your life," she paused to watch her hurtful words sink into Nora's soul before her voice softened, "You always listened to me before. I don't know why it's so hard for you to see what's happening here. I told you that you were on the wrong side of this. I warned you, Jude warned you. You made your choice," she leaned forward, her nose stopping at the edge of the door frame, unable to move closer, "I'm giving you one last chance to listen to reason."

Nora, her heart shattered, scoffed angrily at the idea, "Sides? I didn't pick a side! I wasn't given a choice. I haven't been given a choice in anything since the day I found out about the fucking monsters that live in this bloody town!"

Jude gingerly moved Quinn back from the door and to his side. He tilted his head and narrowed his deep, dark eyes on Nora as she stood helplessly trembling. "Tsk, tsk, tsk," he clucked at her, "Name-calling isn't necessary, sweetheart," he moved slowly back and forth along the space of the empty door, his foot never braving a step inside, "Your aunt is perfectly entitled to feel betrayed by you, little girl. How could she not? You have to see that now. You, coming into my town and helping the false leaders try to take the life of the woman I love? It's barbaric, Nora. Barbaric and foolish," he looked her over from head to toe and back again, his gaze thoughtful, "I also see your side, Nora. I do. You're right that you haven't been given a choice in many things, and that saddens me," his voice purred, low and level, "It's not fair, truly. I need you to hear what I'm saying to you, alright?" He stepped closer to the entry, his eyes shimmering mirrors that reflected light from within, "I'm standing here, offering you a choice right now. I'm asking you to choose us. Choose your family."

Nora recognized what he was attempting to do. It was the same look that Gabriel had given her when she had agreed to take the serum. This time, there was not a warm freefall in her mind, not a moment of lost control. Jude's stare faltered, confusion replacing his confidence. His influence did not affect Nora and that fact emboldened Nora who dared another step forward.

"You are not my family," she said, looking him dead in the eye.

Jude, unbalanced by the exchange, stumbled back just an inch, with a weak scoff. Quinn's face wrinkled with worry seeing her fearless leader have a momentary loss of the upper hand.

He quickly shook it off and came back at her, "Quinn is. Quinn is your family, Nora. From what I hear she was pretty well your only family when she left town. She doesn't mean to be so hurtful to you. She doesn't mean the angry things she says. The pressure we are under is too much sometimes and add to that her concern that something could happen to you, her only niece, it's all a lot to balance. Now that she is by my side, I'd like to be your family, too. We all do. Believe me when I say, if you give me the chance, I can make your life a lot more comfortable. Safe. Protected from the real monsters that are out there," Jude whispered and offered her his hand.

"Nora, please. I am so sorry that you have been through what you have because of me," Quinn said with a gentle sadness, crimson tears settling without falling, "I couldn't help it that I fell in love with him. I can't help that he is what he is. That I am what I am now. But I promise you, being a vampire is the most incredible thing you will ever experience." Quinn moved closer to Jude, hooking her arm with his, and rested her head on his shoulder.

The fallacy of the return to the soft, loving Quinn was easy for Nora to see now. There was a darkness, a cruel hunger that she was trying to hide. The only thing that baffled her now was why they would want her to join them. Even the serene, loving smiles they projected couldn't hide the thirst for revenge that burned in their eyes. They may have wanted her to be one of their mindless followers just a day before, but now they wanted her dead.

"Are you fucking crazy? I'm not going anywhere with you. Even if you do make me a vampire and not rip out my throat the second that I step out there, I'm dead anyway," Nora roared, blindly grabbing for the door, "You may think you're better than the ones in charge now, but I know for a fact that they will just take you all out! I know about the original maker. I know the fae are threatening to destroy his body and all of you with him. So, I'm dead if I do, dead if I don't."

Jude's face twisted with rage, "Don't believe their lies little girl. I am the only fucking chance you have."

"I'll take my chances without any of you," Nora slammed the door as Quinn launched forward, fangs out, screaming bloody murder.

They beat on the door as she ran into the front room to snatch up Silas' carrier. He sat wide-eyed and silent inside as she ran to the kitchen, calling out to Ezra. Finding no one there, she called out again, fearful that someone had been able to breach the house. She rushed towards Ezra's voice when he yelled that they were in the back room. He stood at the door and slammed it behind her when she entered. Laura and Aria huddled around Lucy who was wailing in Aria's arms. The room was empty other than a worksite lamp that cast shadows over the windowless space. It was better than nothing, as long as no one could make their way inside. Jude and Quinn's fists on the door echoed throughout the house and into the small closet of a room. Ezra crouched on the floor beside them and put his phone to his ear.

"She's here, she's ok," Ezra stammered and mouthed to Nora that he was speaking to Elijah, "We will. We will, okay," he finished and hung up.

"What did he say? What do we do?" Nora asked breathlessly. She tucked Silas into the far corner, his yowls filling the tight room.

They jumped with a fearful cry when the pounding on the door quickly spread, encircling the house and vibrating from the floor to ceiling. It seemed that Jude and Quinn did not come alone. They were trapped.

Ezra put an arm around his sister, trying to comfort her. Utter terror could be seen rippling through every inch of her as she tried to comfort Lucy.

"Elijah said everything blew up when they tried to take Jude in. There were way more of them than they knew about camped out in the house. Someone on the inside of the bureau had been lying to them about how many vampires Jude had been creating. It's bad, Nora."

Saying this situation was bad was the biggest understatement that she had ever heard. Bad was a cold, or a snowstorm. Vampires that were trying to take over the world and currently trying to rip his house apart nail by nail were a hell of a lot worse than *bad*.

"I'm sorry, did you just say vampires? What the hell is going on, Ezra?" Laura's quaking voice broke through the deafening thumps around them, "What's out there?

Ezra continued as the pounding intensified, "It's okay, Laura. We're all going to be fine. He said help is on the way, and we should stay inside. Someone's coming to deal with those fuckers."

"Will someone please tell us what the hell is going on?" Aria screamed, wrapping Laura and the baby in her arms. "Who are those *fuckers*? Are you seriously saying that there are bloodsucking undead trying to get in here? This is insanity!"

As she spoke the word, the flurry of thumps that shook the walls stopped and Nora's phone rang out in the silence. An unknown number flashed on the screen.

Nora held it out, answering on speaker, "Hello?"

"Do you see now, Squirt? How powerful he is? There is no running away, no hiding, no way out of this," Quinn said with deadly calm, "We don't want to fight, we don't want to hurt you. Just come outside and talk to me."

There was no way they would be leaving on their own and it was a very long time until the sun could intervene. They needed help from the agency, and they needed it fast. Nora hoped to keep them talking until then, "I don't believe you, Quinn. Please just go," Nora pleaded. "Why do you even pretend to want me so bad? I know you just want to hurt me. Please, just leave us alone."

"If you come out here, I promise the others won't have a hair on their heads touched. Just you and me. Let's sort this out together," Quinn offered with saccharine sweetness.

"I don't know what there is that we could sort out, Quinn. I don't know why I have to take the blame for a war that doesn't even involve me."

"Doesn't involve you?" Jude's voice screamed from the phone, "Those weak, incapable bastards will not make me look like a fool and I will not stand by and watch you help them try to destroy what I am building! They will not take what is mine! Now get the fuck out here before we tear this building down around you and take the heads from every single one of you, including that delicious little infant!"

"You mother fucker!" Ezra exploded, grabbing her phone.

"I did it once, didn't I?" Jude goaded, "I have a taste for your family now, bitch."

Ezra threw the phone, shattering it against the wall, and stormed from the room with Nora on his trail, screaming for him to stay inside. There was no way that the two of them would be able to take on an entire nest of crazed vampires, even with the extra boost they had received from the Ascensions. A few drops of fairy blood would be nothing against an army of murderous vampires ruled by a madman.

Nora tried to grab his arm when he snatched one of the railing spindles from the pile at the front door, snapping it to a point over his knee. He moved quickly and before she could stop him, he had thrown open the door.

Jude stood with Quinn in the center of Ezra's small yard, now surrounded by dozens of his newly-turned minions. The rain poured down in sheets on them as they stood looking ready to charge as soon as Jude gave them the word. He had his fangs on display when he spoke, "Ah, there he is. Hello stranger. Have you missed me?"

The group laughed along with their leader, amused by the palpable pain that radiated from Ezra. There was nothing inside any of them that could be seen as human anymore. The cruelty and bloodlust had swallowed them all. Whether it was as Elijah had said, that living as a nest had removed their humanity, or if they had just been horrible people in life, one thing was clear: they were willing to kill for Jude.

"Just me and you, you piece of shit. Don't hide behind your lackeys," Ezra bellowed, eyes crazed as he stepped out onto the porch. Nora tugged at his shirt, fearful of her arm being past the threshold of the house.

The crowd started forward, ignoring Ezra's demand, until Jude raised a hand, stopping them in their place, "What do you think you're going to do with that little stick, boy?" Jude asked, amused.

Ezra shook Nora from his arm in one fierce push, "I'm going to end you!" he bellowed, launching himself from the covered porch with the spiked spindled held high in the air. Before he could make contact, Jude had closed the space between them and plucked it easily from his hand. He looked at the DIY stake with snide delight before catapulting it into the side of the house. The sliver of wood embedded in the cedar shingles just inches from Nora's head. Ezra stood before him, his breath fast and deep, his now empty hand still held high. Despair started to replace the frenzy of hate that had moved him to action.

"End me? Ha! You're going to do no such thing, son," he reached forward, grabbing Ezra by the collar, "But I'll tell you what. I'm going to be generous. Instead of killing you on the spot where you stand, I'll offer you the chance to join us," Jude inched closer to him, forcing Ezra's feet to start stumbling up the steps behind him, "The same choice we gave Nora," he beamed, nodding to her, "You have a fire in you that I could put to work. Starting my own family has made me a bit of a softy, I guess. Do you remember what that was like?"

His heartless words snapped Ezra back into the moment, his fear being swallowed with anger one more time, "You can go fuck yourself."

Jude frowned and lifted a brow, nodding, "Choice made," he backhanded Ezra with the strength of a freight train, knocking him into the air before he landed in a heap on the porch floor, "This one is all mine," Jude growled to the circling group of snapping vampires. His fangs were on full display as he hissed, his mouth moving for the blood that poured from a gash on Ezra's forehead.

The spindle was out of the wall and into his back before Nora could notice it was in her hand. Jude turned, looking up at her in shock before his body collapsed into a pile of ash over Ezra's immobilized body.

"No!" Quinn's anguished voice pierced the night, "What have you done?"

Nora felt herself being pushed back towards the door and grabbed at the doorframe to steady herself.

"Invite me in!" Gabriel stood before her with one hand on her chest, the other holding Ezra over his shoulder. Nora looked from him to the approaching vampires on the lawn.

"You bitch! I'll end you!" Quinn's voice rang out in sobs as she moved in a blur towards them.

"Invite me in, Nora!" Gabriel screamed, nose to nose with her.

"Come in," she said and in a blink was on the floor behind a closed door.

Ezra hung motionless over his shoulder, blood dripping from his brow to the floor, looking like Gabriel may have arrived a minute too late. The pounding on the house resumed, matching the pounding of blood in her ears. She looked at her hand, the one that had pierced a sliver of wood through Jude, ending him as Ezra said he would.

"Where are the others?" Gabriel asked. Before Nora could answer he gave a deep smell of the air and was moving down the hallway towards the back room, still carrying Ezra. She was on her feet when he shouted for her to get off her ass and follow. She caught up with him just as he swung open the door.

Laura and Aria pressed themselves with Lucy against the far wall when Gabriel swept in with Nora in tow. Paralyzed screams twisted their faces with horror when they saw Ezra bloodied and flopped on the shoulder of the fanged man.

"Not the best time for introductions, ladies. Keep an eye on him," Gabriel instructed Nora before leaving in a flash, the door closed behind him.

The commotion outside was much louder than before. Screams of anger and agony were intertwined with the thumps of what had to be bodies hitting the exterior of the house. Nora rolled Ezra onto his side, looking at the gash that split across his forehead. Within minutes, the house was silent. The only sound was their ragged breath until Ezra started to moan, slapping Nora's hand away from his head.

"What..." Ezra reached up, blood covering his fingers.

"It's okay. We're all okay," Nora soothed, ripping a piece of her t-shirt to press against the torn skin.

His eyes started to focus on the room when he struggled to sit up, "Laura?" he called out, looking around for her.

"I'm here, Ez. We're alright. We're all okay," she said and moved to his side. She took the ripped cloth from Nora to hold it against her stunned little brother's forehead, "It's okay. I'm here."

They sat in the silence of the room, not knowing what had happened or if they could leave. Nora held Silas' carrier tightly in her arms, quietly babbling to him that they were going to be alright. There was no sign of Gabriel's return, or even a voice muffled outside. Shimmying themselves into the corner, they huddled together and waited.

Chapter Eighteen

It was Elijah who was the next one through the door, awash with concern. Nora knew that if a demon was worried, the situation was dire. When Elijah told them it was safe to go back out into the house, she helped Ezra to his feet, steadying him as they walked. The gash on his head had mostly sealed with the dried blood smudged and framing a newly forming scar. She assumed it was the fae blood still in his system that gave him the ability to heal so quickly, just as it had his leg and her tooth. It did nothing to help still her nerves. Every creak or bump had her jumping in place; her eyes scanning every dark corner for another threat. Her hands struggled to keep the strength to hold onto the cat carrier. She wondered if any of the Glamor Guards were waiting for them. A good dose of their calming sugar cookie juju would certainly hit the spot.

They walked out in a tight pack to the front room to find only Gabriel, who stood slurping on a medical-grade bag of blood.

"Excuse the low-rent meal, folks. Even with the disgusting sparkle blood stinking him up, fresh blood is just too enticing," Gabriel said with a wink to Ezra. He wiped his mouth, tossed the bag into a sawdust-filled corner, and pulled another bag from his pocket. He ripped the small opening with his teeth and went to work on finishing that one.

Laura grabbed Aria and Lucy, pulling them behind Ezra, her mouth slung open at the sight before them.

"He's alright, Laura. He's disgusting but harmless," he told her, letting her cling to his shirt, watching the vampire happily finish off his snack.

"Oh geez, sorry. This must be terribly frightening for you ladies. I promise you, I have no intention of harming you. Just the opposite, actually. May I?" he asked Ezra, gesturing him to step aside.

Even with the trust he had for the familiar vampire, he put his hands out to keep him at bay, "Stay away from them Gabriel. They've been through enough. They don't need your craziness on top of it all. I'm warning you."

Gabriel stepped back, apprehensive of his words, "I'm well aware of what you are both capable of now," he said with an uncomfortable laugh, "but I think it would be best if we helped them *cope* with what they've witnessed. Help them *move past* it?" His brow moved up as he nodded along with his words.

Nora knew he meant to wash their memories of what they had experienced. After a minute, Ezra did as well. It would be best to have all knowledge and memory of what they had just experienced washed away as quickly as possible. Aria's pale face looked on, watching the bizarre conversation. She looked as if she could clutch her chest and tip over dead at any second.

He turned to face his cowering sister, "He's not going to hurt you. I promise," he went on with his voice as gentle and calm as he could muster at the moment, "I know this is all crazy. I can't explain it, but he can, alright? He's going to take care of you guys," Ezra squeezed her hands and stepped to the side when Gabriel approached again.

"I don't think..." Aria trailed off as Gabriel gazed into her eyes. Color returned to her cheeks when her lips lazily curled with the comfort of Gabriel's influence washed over her. Laura opened her mouth to speak, and had the same reaction when he turned his attention to her, murmuring words of comfort.

"Nora, be a pet and take the baby for a moment. It would be best if you all stepped into the other room while I take care of this," he advised, not looking away from the women.

She took the baby from Aria's limp arms while the woman's eyes never left Gabriel's. It made her stomach churn at the ease with which a vampire could separate a mother and her child. At least Gabriel seemed to be a vampire with better intentions than the gang of beasts that had just had her surrounded. Daring a peek out the front window, the yard and street beyond were darkened by the unlit light standards that dotted along the sidewalk. There was no sign of the angry mob to be found. No movement or telltale signs of a violent battle that she had assumed had occurred. Just silence and darkness.

Moving to the kitchen, Nora sat at the dining table with the now calm baby while Ezra washed up at the sink, wiping away the crusted blood that remained on his face.

"Well, now. That was quite the day, wasn't it?" Elijah quipped as he strode into the room.

"You think?" Ezra replied, pointing to the wet paper towel in his hand that was streaked with blood. He gave his head one final wipe and tossed the wad into his overflowing garbage can.

Nora cradled Lucy as she started to coo herself to sleep, the effects of the brief encounter with Gabriel keeping her calm and spent, her chubby cheeks flush from fatigue.

Elijah stiffly sat at the table and began to provide details of the day, and what had led up to their near-death encounter. He told them that they had been unable to even make it to the house that morning thanks to the number of vampires who were willing to fight for Jude. There were far greater numbers than they had been told. Far too many than the human crews could handle, and they were told to retreat.

"We came very close to having the fae step in and end it all with their maker, but calmer heads prevailed. We, the demons and fae that is, were given special license from the High Council to intervene on behalf of the vampires when Jude made his escape. The gaggle of followers that descended on you in this house was of a much smaller number than the ones that we dealt with in the nest. I can tell you of your luck in that matter," he said with pride.

Ezra coughed a laugh at the notion of luck being associated with the night they had been through, "Lucky us. Only a couple of dozen vamps trying to kill us. Child's play, amirite?" he gave another tired chuckle.

Elijah ruefully nodded and continued. There was word that the remaining nest was planning on fleeing the valley for an undisclosed new location with Jude and Quinn at the helm. They were mad with anger that their numbers had been mostly annihilated during the raid and Jude was in a hurry to regroup.

"Is that why they came here? They thought we would join their ranks? I know they're undead, but could they be that dense?" Ezra asked, baffled. He pulled a beer out of the fridge, holding it up with an offer first to Nora and then Elijah, who both declined. He twisted the cap and tossed it on the counter before joining them at the table.

"A psychopathic vampire could be delusional enough to believe that you might. However, in this case, I believe it was Quinn who was here for Nora," Elijah suggested.

"Yeah, she made it clear that she was keen to finish me off," Nora said, the pain of that truth tearing inside her.

"Actually, from what we have gathered, it is quite the opposite. I think she genuinely wanted you to join her. Her love for you is still inside her. The only ember of humanity that Jude was unable to extinguish," he took her hand and gave it a quick squeeze of comfort. She was surprised at the intense heat of his skin; a slight red mark in the shape of his hand remained for a moment after he let her go.

She sat quietly with the possibility that Quinn could still care for her. That she could still be the same woman she loved deep inside the monster that had taken her over.

"Is she, I mean, did she...?"

"She is alive as far as I know. When the agents arrived, just after you assisted Ezra, the remaining vampires scattered. Quinn was among them. It seems there isn't much cohesion of the lot after they witnessed their fearless leader being staked," Elijah said, crossing his arms and leaning back in the stiff wooden chair.

"How much trouble am I in?" Nora asked. Going to see Quinn had to have caused the nest to know about the plans for the raid. Elijah did mention that there were moles inside the bureau that had been passing on information, and she hoped that they were to blame. Especially now that her use as bait was no longer needed and she was completely expendable.

Put to death on site returned to her thoughts with a hiss.

She nodded for Ezra to take Lucy now that he was cleaned up and seated with his wits about him again.

"Trouble? For Jude's death, do you mean? Oh, my dear! You are not in any trouble at all. If The Firm were medal giving folks, your neck would be heavy with praise," Elijah exclaimed, putting an awkward attempt of a comforting pat on her shoulder, before straightening up again. The heat from his hand warmed her shirt.

"I'm not in any trouble at all?" Nora couldn't believe it was that simple, "For anything?"

Ezra gave her a surprised grin when Elijah shook his head.

"Not at all. Jude was a lot more dangerous than you could ever imagine. We haven't seen the likes of such a perilous dissident in centuries," Elijah told them, sitting beside her at the table, "He had made enemies of every species on the High Council. Execution motions were being put forward just yesterday," he shook his head, in awe of what could have been, "Of all places to try to manifest a coup, he foolishly attempted on Fae soil! He was quite close to having all vampires wiped from existence and his disturbing ego wouldn't let him see it. His followers were just as blind."

"What's going to happen to everyone else? What's going to happen to Quinn?" Nora asked, knowing that the answer wouldn't be what she wanted to hear. If she even knew what she wanted to happen to Quinn after everything that had happened.

"I must be frank with you. There were...there *are* orders to stake on sight for her, Nora. When they were approaching the nest, she was lying in wait. Mr. Terrel did not see her coming. It was a brutal attack," Elijah said quietly, "and he did not survive."

"Mr. Terrell?" Nora asked, not recognizing the name.

"Angus, Angus Terrell. He was a member of our intel crew that was assisting us. I believe you met him the night you went to Mystique," Elijah said solemnly.

Nora's breath hitched and her heart fell to pieces. If her visit to the nest was what tipped them off to the planned raid, Angus' blood was on her hands as much as it was literally on Quinn's. He had seemed to be a truly kind man in the short time she had spent with him. An infection ball of happy energy. His bright smile flashed in her memory. It had been of no use to seek out Quinn after she had been directly told to stay home. She had gained nothing more than solidifying Quinn as an enemy. Thanks to her selfish decision, Angus was dead. Nora closed her eyes, willing the images of what her aunt could have done to him from her mind.

How could her sweet, hippy-dippy aunt have turned so vicious? At their core were all vampires cruel and quick to kill? Nora reminded herself that just moments before she had taken the life of the man Quinn had professed to love. That she had taken Jude's life to protect someone who had done the same to save her. The lines of right and wrong had been permanently blurred.

"Get the worry from your face, girlie. It's not your fault," Gabriel declared as he entered the room, "There are people to blame, people who we know are to blame, and you're not one of them," he picked up Ezra's beer with curiosity before setting it down with a grimace. "We were on borrowed time from the High Council to shut Jude down. Doing away with our maker wasn't taken off the table, so I guess I do owe you thanks, missy," Gabriel stopped to smile at Laura and Aria who were pleasantly and cluelessly grinning when they appeared from the hallway. He turned back to Nora, "You in a way, saved me too."

"In a way?" Elijah asked, with mock bewilderment, "If they had followed through on their threat and destroyed the maker, you have been ash right alongside him. You all would have. You never seem to realize how fragile your life is in the bigger picture, Gabriel."

Nora tried to weigh the balance of lives given and taken so easily with the creatures of the paranormal world. It was all business as usual to them. The vampires say that they won't kill their own, yet they have an order to kill Quinn on the spot. Was it for what she did to Angus, a dispensable human, or did she do something worse? The rules of this new world were too layered for her to wrap her head around in such a short amount of time. It seemed in poor taste to enquire further about her aunt with the news of her murdering Angus. She watched Gabriel silently turn over Elijah's words. His lips were tight holding in a response that he willed himself to hold in.

"Yes, well, it is what it is, and I thank you for that," Gabriel shifted uncomfortably in the moment of emotion. Nora was surprised that she could sometimes find ways to relate to the absurd man. "Anyways, these two are here for their little juice box and need to be on their way, don't you, ladies?" he snipped, nodding to the infant in Ezra's arms.

And there went *that* sentimental moment. Awkwardly relatable or not, the man was a vampire.

"Gabriel!" Elijah scolded the moniker that he had chosen for Lucy.

"What? It's cute," Gabriel shrugged with a wink, "Isn't that right, you sweet little snack pack?"

Ezra moved the baby away from him as he cooed down to her. He looked at his sister and her wife, who swayed in the doorway, "Are they, you know, are they good to go?" Ezra asked, settling Lucy in her car seat. Her parents stood on either side of her without any sign of distress or knowledge that the man in front of them had fangs.

At least they didn't have a chance to find out that the other man was an actual demon.

"They are. Sad to go, but perfectly well, right ladies?" Gabriel assured.

"It was great seeing you, Ezra! I'm so glad you finally got to meet little Lucy," Laura said with a tight hug for him, "Sorry we have to be on our way, but it's time to get home."

Aria slung the diaper bag over her shoulder and passed the car seat to her wife, "I'm so glad you're settled in here. It's going to be gorgeous when you're done." She gave him a quick hug and the trio started for the door with the rest following behind giving their goodbyes.

Gabriel called out to them as they stepped onto the porch, "Wait, what do we say to our new friend, ladies?"

In unison, they turned to Nora with wide grins, "Nice to meet you Dumb-Dumb. Keep an eye on Ezra for us."

"What the hell, Gabriel?" Nora knew it was his handy work through the brain scrambles he had given them.

"Gabriel!" Elijah shouted, pressing a hand to his head, "Can you ever control yourself?"

"Come on, that's funny!" he replied, waving happily at the women climbing into their car and pulling out onto the road. He turned to face the judgmental faces of the remaining three, "What? You guys need to get a sense of humor. I'm hilarious and you love it."

Nora rolled her eyes at the childish vampire before scanning the yard. The rain had stopped, and fog had started to drift up from the ground as the night air breezed through the grass. There was no sign of the raucous attack that had been pounding around and against the house. Not a trace of Jude was left on the porch or even a sign that anyone had been there. Vampire or otherwise. Everything moved fast in the supernatural world, it seemed.

"So, what now? They don't remember anything. Jude is gone. It doesn't seem like you need us anymore," Ezra asked, hope in his voice, "Is this insanity finally over for us? Can our minds be wiped now, too?"

Nora wanted nothing more than to have the last few days long behind her with all memory of what she had learned, what she had gone through, stripped away. The idea of knocking, hat in hand, on her parents' door didn't seem as horrible in comparison and she gladly welcome the chance. Her parents were cold and selfish but at least they weren't out for literal blood.

"Not exactly, Mr. Davis," Elijah sighed, "Until we know the whereabouts of Quinn and the future moves of Jude's cohorts, it would be irresponsible for us to set you out on your own."

Nora's glimpse at escape evaporated around her and she fumed, "You're still planning on using us? Humans really are just disposable tools to you, aren't we? Just like you said!"

"Miss. Goodman, please. I assure you that is not the case. Well, that is not *this* case. You were entered into a blood bond with us, and we will follow through with that. Our only intentions are to keep you safe until this mess is truly untangled. A thank you for all you have done for us, and for what you have been put through," Elijah said, putting his hand to his chest as if swearing an oath.

"It helps that the High Council chose to put you through Ascensions, too," Gabriel said with a snort. "I don't think those stink bombs would take lightly to you being tossed to the wolves with their blood still in your veins. They are such untrusting beings. Wouldn't just take our word that we keep you alive."

"What's that supposed to mean? What exactly is the Ascension thing? It seems like it's a lot more important than just healing and making us run fast," Ezra questioned.

"It is in essence a blood bond with the Fae. They have their reasons for requesting it and we are not in a place to question it, nor deny them. The fact that it gave you certain physical skills that in effect could protect you was enough for me to be glad for it to be done. Being that you did not come to us of your own choice, they believed it would be proper to hold you to a higher level of protection if we were to use you for our own personal business. Exactly why they insisted is not something I am privy to," Elijah said, straightening his ever-present silk tie as he stepped from the porch. A professional calm washed over him as if a war of supernaturals had not just taken place on the spot where he stood. The powerful, business-like demon was back, "The chaos of the day seems to have been put to bed. For now, know that we will have our eyes on you, and you will be safe." He nodded for Gabriel to join him, and they started for one of The Firm's SUVs that were parked at the curb.

"That's it?" Nora couldn't believe that they would head off into the night as if all was well. Just another day at the office. Time for Happy Hour.

"That's all for now, yes, Miss. Goodman. I would suggest heading home and trying to get some rest. You have both been through quite a lot," he advised. A man, dressed in the agents' black and white attire hopped out from the driver's seat and opened the door to the back seat for him.

"Oh, you think?" Nora exclaimed. *A lot* did not fully encapsulate the last six days of her life.

"You have my number if either of you needs anything. For now, relax, enjoy the last of the summer weather, and know that for now, you will both be physically and financially taken care of. Miss. Goodman, if you'd like to return to your apartment, this gentleman would be happy to assist you," Elijah advised, pointing to a second matching SUV parked across the street before he waved and shut the door.

Gabriel stood beside the vehicle for a moment, staring at Nora and Ezra. His eyes were narrowed, his lips pressed in a small smile. "You have my number, too. Just don't call me with any bullshit," he quipped and hopped into the passenger seat.

They drove off into the night to leave the two standing in the dim light of Ezra's lawn. She looked past him to the house. She had been wrong, there was something left to see of the evening's events. Beside his door, the hole left from the broken spindle split through the shingles to the insulation behind. Ezra turned to see what she was looking at when she shivered in the warm night air.

"Wow. Yeah, I owe you a thank you, Nora." He rubbed at the now fully healed wound above his brow, "If you hadn't...I don't even want to think about what would have happened if you didn't step in. Seriously, thank you, Nora."

She had just killed a vampire. A real vampire.

The same thing that Ezra had done to save her own life. She smiled up at him with a resigned laugh. They were just a couple of reluctant Van Helsings trying to get through to the next day.

"It's what we do, Ezra. We save each other from fucking vampires."

"I guess that's true," he said, looking at the hole in his wall. "You want to stay, or did you want to head home?"

Nora wanted nothing more than to be in her own space with Silas and she told him as much. She stepped up on the porch to retrieve Silas, who was meowing complaints from the confines of his carrier, and toted him back to Ezra. They stood staring at each other, quietly trying to process what had happened, what could have happened, and what was to come. The quiet of the street. The blood that had covered and was now gone from his face. All that was left was the two of them and a yowling cat in a cage. The calm of the moment made the last few days seem as if they had merely been a nightmare that they had finally woken from. The hole in the wall was the only reminder of the truth to be found. The idea that their new reality was being virtually trapped in a supernatural town to be protected by demons, vampires, and fairies was not something that happened in real life. That they were protecting them from the threat of being attacked by her aunt was too much to think about. There wasn't a pinch hard enough in the world that could wake her from what was now her waking nightmare. Ezra and Nora were now their very own assignment with the BITN Bureau and all they could do was wait to see what would be next. For the moment, there was a placid lull in the tsunami of menacing emergencies. It was happily taken, even though they knew it wouldn't last.

She set the cat carrier in the back seat of the waiting SVU and slid in beside him. Ezra stood on the sidewalk watching them until they turned down the next street. Thankfully she was home and inside the musty hallway of her home within minutes. The building that once belonged to the vampire that had just died at her hand. She shook her head, trying to rid herself of the thought, the smell of the embers that rose from him still in her nose.

Looking up from her bag as she dug for her keys, she saw Jenny standing in front of Nora's apartment, a small wooden bowl in one hand, the other smudging ash on her door.

"Jenny?" Nora stopped in her tracks, trying to piece together what she was seeing, "What are you doing?"

"Nora! You're okay!" Jenny cried out, closing the space between them and pulling her into her arms. Silas gave a grumpy mew in response to being jostled in the carrier. Some ash from the bowl spilled, sprinkling onto Nora's shoulder.

"Yeah, I'm alright. I'm fine. What are you doing? What is that?" Nora asked pushing Jenny back and brushing the dust from herself.

"I was so worried! There wasn't much I could do to help, so my coven has been conjuring every protection spell we knew for you and your friend," she pointed to the thumb-sized mark on the door.

"I'm sorry, your what?" Nora asked, confusion turning to surprise.

"My coven. I'm a witch, Nora."

Fucking Aumbry Valley. A town of secrets that was the gift that kept on giving.

9 781738 199136